# The Niantic Caper

### A Jack Armstrong Novel
## James Woods

moon mountain

The Niantic Caper
A Jack Armstrong Novel

© 2023 James Woods
ISBN 978-0-578-29639-5

All Rights Reserved
LCCN: 2023932680

This book is dedicated to my wife, Valerie.

"The difficult is what takes a little time;
the impossible is what takes a little longer."

Guiding phrase from Norwegian Explorer, Fridtjof Nansen

# CHAPTER ONE

"Fire in the Hole! Fire in the Hole!" he heard the cry. The customary miner's warning alerting all who heard it—just a few seconds to evacuate or find safe harbor in usual times. But this was not a "usual time." He and his colleagues were nearly two thousand feet underground in an old miner's tunnel and held at gunpoint by some Russians.

He knew that the warning was not directed at him or his companions; they had been told that if they even moved, they would be shot, and to count backward from 100!! 5,4,3,2,1, he counted in his mind. What followed was a massive explosion. He was thrown into the air and slammed onto his back. His lungs ached as the fall knocked the wind from him.

The blast was deafening. He could not hear himself think. Instantaneous with the explosion, debris began to fly; he rolled over and placed his arms to cover his head and ears, then opened his mouth wide to relieve the pressure following the blast. He hoped the others had done the same.

Small bits of needle-like rubble ricocheted off the walls and some found purchase in his back and legs, little darts. *Damn, that hurt*, he reacted. He prayed that the tunnel would not cave in, that larger rocks would not fall on him or the others. He also hoped that no one else from his group had suffered. Still, he couldn't inquire, since he could not hear or even see— the pitch-black blinded him and the dust made his breathing difficult, but not impossible.

He began to cough and soon couldn't stop coughing—he

almost choked on the dust and detritus still wavering in the chamber. In the distance, he heard the others struggling and making muffled sounds. At least some of them were alive! He then remembered: *Stay close to any sounds that make you glad you are alive*, from Hafez.

He covered his mouth with his hand and rolled onto his back. The tunnel was a shroud of black. He couldn't see anything. He lifted his hand from his mouth and raised it above his eyes: still no recognition. He began moving his extremities and they all functioned. *Thank God for that*, he thought. Nothing broken.

"Coop?" he called hoarsely. "Laura? Connor?" Though his voice was hoarse and his hearing dim, he began to make out voices attempting to respond to him. Murmurs really. He had difficulty understanding what they were saying, his hearing was only incrementally returning to normal. It reminded him of attending a Rolling Stones concert and "sitting" (really standing—no one ever sits at a Stones concert ) near the stage and being unable to hear for hours thereafter. *Sure hope my ears clear sooner this time*, he wished.

Suddenly, a slight light appeared through the dust. Then he remembered that Connor had carried a miner's light with him when they entered the tunnel. He began to assess the damage.

The walls appeared to be intact, except for the tunnel's mouth where they had entered the chamber in search of the treasure. Now that mouth, their sole way out, was blocked from floor to ceiling with rocks, sealing the exit from the chamber, and, more importantly, their exit from the mine. To be buried nearly 2,000 feet underground with no way out—

to be entombed—began to panic him. *Think*, he told himself, *Think*!

Again, he called their names: "COOP—LAURA—CONNOR—!" And again he heard some blurry noise echoing back. While searching the chamber looking for his colleagues, he noticed a figure. He could vaguely make out this person, crouched on their knees with their back to him, shaking their head and attempting to dust themself off with their hands. While he stared, the dust slowly settled; he recognized that Coop was the person kneeling. *Check one off the list*, he thought.

His eyes began to rotate around the chamber, and he noticed a body on the floor ten feet from him. The body was eerily still and showed no clear evidence of life.

His search continued, and he located his second companion—it appeared to be Connor, attempting to sit up, with his miner's light in one hand. With the other hand, Connor was attempting to dust himself off. That must mean that the body on the floor was that of Laura.

He began to crawl toward Laura, hoping that she was simply knocked unconscious. She was so valuable to the team—her knowledge of history and intuitive sense stellar. Nevertheless, he knew that she did not sign up for this much adventure. As he reached her, he noticed that she too had been thrown onto her back. He observed that her chest was moving slightly. *Thank God*, he thought, *she is alive*.

He put his hand under her head and attempted to raise her to a sitting position. She responded and opened her eyes. The liminal light made her eyes appear to glisten. A small smile brightened her face as she recognized him. He reached for a water bottle that was fastened to his belt and gently gave her a drink. Her eyes widened and she nodded, thankfully.

While he held her in a sitting position with his arm, Laura strove to speak. He looked at her and held his free hand to his ear and shook his head as if to say: "I can't hear." She nodded in understanding. Then he gestured with his free hand and made a thumbs up sign and pointed to her, as if to mime, "Are you ok?" She nodded again and she repeated the gestures pointing to him. He also nodded. Relieved by their quiet reunion, the two of them began to survey the others.

Coop was now standing and surveying the wreckage at the chamber's entrance. Connor too was upright and continuing to clean himself off. No one seemed seriously hurt, thank God. Still, those who caused the explosion had sought to either kill them instantaneously or seal them in a tomb 1,864 feet below the surface—to effect a slow death.

And it appeared that, to some degree at least, these malevolent masterminds had succeeded. Even though no one seemed seriously hurt, the future dangled precariously before them. . . How were they going to escape their underground tomb? Could they remove the many rocks blocking the chamber's entrance enough to poke a human-sized hole through which to wiggle to safety?

How deep was the rockslide, a couple of yards, or 100 yards? Did they have enough air to survive? How about water? How long would the miner's light last before they were pitched into complete darkness? Would anyone miss them or search for them? And, if they ever escaped—"Who are those guys" he mumbled to himself, recalling the film, *Butch Cassidy and the Sundance Kid*. And how did the bad guys know we were here? *Think*! Jack Armstrong told himself. *And fast.*

# CHAPTER TWO

It seemed like only yesterday that a call came while Jack was meditating. A new experiment to help him unwind after a messy divorce that had cost him dearly. Gone were half the proceeds from the start-up business he helped develop, the house he had built in the toney section of the San Francisco Peninsula and living with his much-loved son.

Not gone, however, was his beloved BMW Z-8. That beauty stayed with him. All aluminum body, 400 horsepower and retro style, modeled after the classic BMW 507. *The fit and finish—exceptional*, thought Jack. He took pleasure hand-washing the car so he could appreciate her sumptuous curves. Just touch the back side of the turn signal and feel how soft, polished, the metal lever was! Only 2500 Z-8's had been made for the U.S. over a three-year period in the early 2000s. He reminisced over how BMW had invited him and a guest to participate in a two-day driving school for Z-8 owners in Spartanburg, South Carolina. Jack had invited his brother. Two other Z-8 owners had also invited their brothers; the driving tutorial had become a Band of Brothers weekend! What an exhilarating experience to accompany a fantastic car. With the top down, he felt free as a bird gliding over the streets of San Francisco—the town in which he had been born and which enjoyed a myriad of tech booms in recent years, drawing a vibrant international crowd—Jack was now labeled one of its rare "natives."

Jack imagined one of his favorite drives along California Street and over Nob Hill. Heading East toward the Bay, he would pass The Big Four restaurant on the right, and the Mark Hopkins Hotel at the end of the block. He'd zip past the old Flood mansion, currently the PU Club, and the Fairmont on the left, and across the street is a Mason Street apartment building where *Vertigo*, the Lady in Red, and one of the Billy Bob Thornton's *Goliath* series were filmed. More important to Jack, his good friends Tom and Esty lived there. Tom and Jack shared the same birthday. As he passed these historical landmarks, there was an expansive view of The City, a term San Francisco natives employed, but never Frisco; only a tourist would say that. With the Bay Bridge directly in front of him, it was a vista to die for.

He often felt lost in the stories of this historic town, many of which were shared with him by his good friend, Tom, who knew the little-known places, interesting facts and people of San Francisco. Where did they get the name, Nob Hill? Who were The Big Four? Who was Mark Hopkins? Who built the Pacific Union Club? What effect did the Comstock Lode have on San Francisco? Jack had prided himself on knowing many of these facts as well as The City's beauty. He had a love affair with this town and he wasn't afraid to share it. On those drives, it was all in front of him.

At California and Mason, he felt he could reach out and touch the Bay Bridge just as his stomach alerted him that California Street was about to drop into the Bay. It also reminded him that the cable car crossing at California and Powell was fast approaching and a hard stop was in order. Jack mentally slammed on the brakes of the Z-8 as he exited his meditation.

The phone had rung. So much for his zen state.

"Mr. Armstrong?" a woman's voice quavered. Again, she pressed, more emphatically, "Mr. Armstrong?"

"Yes, that's me," Jack said, brushing off any remnants of his relaxed state. He reached over for the pad of paper he kept on the table next to his easy chair, ever-ready to record anything important.

"Mr. Armstrong, I have a situation. From what I understand, you might be the person to help me," the woman said somewhat breathlessly.

Not wishing to commit to anything prematurely, Jack said: "Go ahead, I'm listening."

"Is it possible for us to meet? I don't think I should . . . well, it's perhaps best to talk in person," she hesitated, "If that's ok—" She quickly added, "As soon as possible."

Jack normally didn't take on new business—even when he needed all the income he could get—without meeting a new client in person. He had learned that it is important to size people up: How truthful are they? What makes them tick? What characteristics do they possess? What unique problem was searching for a solution? Jack believed himself to be a good judge of character. And he had a bias toward affecting social justice, if at all possible. The immediacy of the request added another silver thread that intrigued him, so he said:

"Can you meet me at the Blue Fog Café, corner of Gough and Green, across from Allyne Park? Is 10 tomorrow morning soon enough?"

Her voice almost whispered, "I would rather meet this afternoon, if your schedule permits."

"Understood," said Jack wishing to wrap up the call: "I'll see you at the Blue Fog Café at two this afternoon," and he closed his phone, not waiting for a reply.

Jack used the Blue Fog Café on the edge of San Francisco's Cow Hollow—who on earth came up with that name?—as his unofficial "office" to meet with clients. It was conveniently located on the ground floor of the building where he had a second-floor apartment, plus it had good food and terrific coffee. The name of the café amused Jack. It reminded him of one of the prime reasons for which San Francisco was famous and intriguing.

A fog horn sounded in the distance. Jack loved hearing the fog horns, they were so uniquely San Francisco. Falling asleep was never a problem for Jack, but his love of a great bottle of Pinot Noir, preferably shared with a lovely companion, occasionally resulted in awakening mid-sleep, bright-eyed, mulling over whatever conundrums confronted him. The fog horns would lull him back to sleep with their steady rhythm. Some people rely on the sound of the ocean to relax them to sleep, but for Jack, the fog horn did it every time.

The fact that his resources had worn thin made a separate office out of the question. He realized he no longer needed a corner office like the one in the high rise he just left as a senior partner at his former law firm, in San Francisco's Embarcadero Center. Besides, he liked the view of the park across the street, the playful dogs and their owners, particularly the young women, who frequented the park. Jack thought he might want to get a dog one day. *Great companions and not bad for striking up conversations with the ladies,* he mulled.

Although new to meditation, it was beginning to help him find balance once again in his life. Lao Tzu's advice was a recent discovery of Jack's:

"If you are depressed, you are living in the past. If you are anxious, you are living in the future. If you are at peace, you are living in the present."

*Let's focus on the present,* he thought. *How simple is that?* Simple, indeed. And, if it is so simple, why are people depressed or anxious much of the time? We are empowered with an answer, but do not regularly employ it. Human nature, Jack concluded, gave plenty of material for therapists to sort out, starting with parents and childhood. Jack had loving parents, especially a mother who instilled confidence in him that he could and should tackle anything that came his way as well as a hard-driving work ethic. And, of course, the good nature and sage advice his father provided to him and his younger brother.

Nevertheless, recently, things had not gone the way Jack hoped. He sold his start-up tech business for a nice profit and then—whoosh!—half of it disappeared in the divorce. *Thank you, California community property laws*, Jack thought. He was weighed down with financial responsibilities for Tiffany, his former wife, who had adopted surfing with a passion. Add to that, some mortgage payments for the "family" home he didn't live in anymore, currently occupied by Tiffany and her latest boyfriend. With the divorce, it seemed things changed financially for the worse overnight. Jack rarely walked away from a commitment. Commitment, and doing the right thing, were embedded in his DNA.

He asked for the divorce after he caught Tiffany with another surfer guy. She had crossed the line; and for Jack, there was no going back. Once the trust was broken, he knew he could never love his wife again. So, it was time to start anew.

For over two decades, Jack had become one of California's top lawyers at Flexer, Steele and Page—a large, global firm with fifteen offices worldwide and fifteen hundred attorneys—one of the biggest law firms out there. He developed a National and International reputation as a high-performing partner there. Jack was the "Go-to Guy" to handle complex cases from which others shied away.

Jack recalled the very moment when he decided he would become a lawyer . . . in grade school, daydreaming in the school library, he thought it was high time he should choose a profession. He scanned over what he liked—history, writing, politics, journalism, government—and decided that those affinities made him strong lawyer material. If nothing else, little Jack was goal oriented. But, big Jack finally had his fill with Big Law after 15 years of never-ending billable hours, constant pressure to increase client billings, providing busy-work for other attorneys in his group, juggling the corporate requirements of the firm and representing some clients for whom he had little or no respect.

His success at law and the start-up company convinced him that he was creative and resourceful enough to come up with solutions to a variety of problems. Equally as important, Jack's electronic Rolodex connected him to endless varieties of people with skills that he found indispensable in problem solving. He decided to start his own investigative service which he aptly named "Jack's Solutions." As I.M. Pei once said: "Success is a collection of problems solved." Armed with his creative juices, his contacts and his new need for rent money, he was more than ready to meet his new client.

# CHAPTER THREE

Jack walked downstairs from his apartment to the Blue Fog Café at 1:50 pm. He never forgot what his former managing law partner had said: "If you're not early, you're not on time." He ordered a large black coffee and took a table overlooking Allyne Park across the street. He was wearing a muted ISAIA sports coat, custom Polo jeans and Peter Millar loafers. He might be reduced to a two-room apartment, but he hadn't lost his style. He was surveying the park when she arrived.

A stunning woman entered the café, blond, mid 30's, long legged, shapely and dressed to kill. Jack knew all the names. Chanel, Celine, Manolo. This woman knew how to wear the clothes that most women only dreamed of. He wondered how she managed to dress like that yet still needed his help. She swept the café with her deep blue eyes and proceeded directly to Jack. "Mr. Armstrong?" Not waiting for his acknowledgment, she said: "I'm Veronica Hill." She offered her hand to shake, which he accepted while she continued to survey the café.

Jack quickly stood and helped her with her chair. "Please have a seat, Mrs. Hill."

"Thank you," she responded, sans feeling.

As she sat down, he asked, "Would you care for a coffee?"

"No, thank you," she said a bit formally. Jack knew from his years of sizing up clients that she was on edge. He surmised that her quick glances around the small café meant she was searching for people who could overhear their conversation or identify her. Her trembling hand was not lost on him either.

"Mr. Armstrong," she said, "I have a little bit of an unusual situation."

Jack smiled. "Most situations that come to me are unusual, or they don't come to me," he offered. She smiled woodenly, breathed deeply and leaned forward. "How did you locate me?" he asked.

"You were recommended by a close personal friend of mine—Cathy Callaghan," she said.

Jack knew Cathy because she was one of the top litigators in the California Attorney General's office. "I see. And how do you know Cathy?" Jack asked.

"She and I attended UCLA together and shared an apartment in our junior and senior years off campus, in Westwood," she said. "We became best friends, really like sisters. I completely trust her!" Veronica declared. "Cathy said that you are very creative in your problem solving, a 'straight arrow' and know everyone who matters."

"That's generous of her to say. She's a very able attorney and a really nice person," Jack offered. "Now that I have been recommended by someone we both can trust, how can I help you?" he asked.

Lowering her voice and searching the room one more time, Veronica looked intently at Jack, as if sizing him up one last time: "I need you to swear that you will keep this a secret." Jack nodded. "I have decided to divorce my husband. He is a very difficult man. Difficult is an understatement. More of a nightmare, I have come to discover." Veronica shifted in her seat. "Yes, I know," she seemed to confess: "I married him. But you must trust me when I say this is no marital spat. I want

20

no part of living with or knowing him anymore. He can be extremely dangerous. Do you understand what I'm saying?" A small tear formed in the corner of her eye. Jack held back the urge to hold her hand and, instead, offered her a clean handkerchief from his jacket pocket.

"Mrs. Hill I must stop you. I do not handle divorces."

" No. No. This is not about my divorce per se," she said and with that she dabbed at the corner of her eye, then looked up at Jack.

*Her face looks honest,* Jack thought. *How do women like her end up with bad guys?*

"Where is he now?" asked Jack.

"He left on business for a few days. I decided it was as safe as it was ever going to be . . . for me to leave. I went to my closet to pull out some of my old boxes, you know, family mementos and things like that. This was yesterday—I wasn't sure, you see, if I would ever go back. I stumbled upon a cedar chest containing odds and ends I'd inherited from my great-great grandfather, Graham Stackhouse. . . I'd never really taken the time to sort through it before, you know, but, in combing through, suddenly one item is of particular interest. ...A story has been handed down over many years about my great-great grandfather who may have won a sizable—oh, what would you call it—'pot'—in a mid nineteenth-century San Francisco poker game. Among the items I inherited is an envelope containing a key, and a note which I had not seen until yesterday."

Veronica promptly dove into her purse and showed Jack an old key with the word "Niantic" scrawled distinctly on one side and "YB" faintly embossed on the other. The key was accompanied by a weathered old note, composed in faint fountain-penned ink, which simply said:

"This key unlocks a valuable treasure: keep it safe!" and was signed by Veronica's great-great grandfather, Graham Stackhouse, opposite the year: 1864.

Jack held the key, softly rubbing it with his fingers as if it would release magic; he turned it over and began to think to himself: *Why would someone retain a key which purportedly leads to the location of "valuable treasure," yet which the author of the note did not pursue? Did he simply neglect to discard the note and the key after finding the treasure? Did he merely keep the note as a souvenir? Why didn't Veronica's other relatives seek out this mysterious treasure? What and where is the so-called "Niantic"? What does "YB" mean? Is anyone else aware of the key and the story surrounding it? What did Stackhouse consider a "valuable treasure"? What was its nature? Would it be worth anything today?*

When Jack asked Veronica these questions exactly, she offered little by way of explanation. "Mrs. Hill, what is it that concerns you? Perhaps there is something valuable for you out there. With some uncertainty in your future, I imagine that you are anxious to find some answers?"

Veronica smiled and then added, "I am quite concerned that my husband, Max, may be aware of the key and the note."

"Why do you say that, Mrs. Hill?"

"Recently, I came home and found him snooping around in my closet and cedar chest. He is a very devious man, Mr. Armstrong. And he has ties to some very bad people," responded Veronica.

"Please tell me more," urged Jack.

"Well, I do not know all the details, but he invests large sums of money for Russian interests that may not be legal. There are several rough characters who associate with him," she added.

Coupling Veronica's last name with her husband's first, Jack questioned: "Is he the Max Hill whom authorities have been chasing for organized crime with the Russian mafia, including money laundering and tax evasion?"

"Yes," she said sheepishly. "Does that mean you won't help me, Mr. Armstrong?"

"On the contrary, Mrs. Hill. You seem to need all the help you can get," Jack said, providing her some relief. "Is he aware that you are meeting with me?" Jack asked.

"I'm not sure," Veronica said. "He's out of town, but I think someone close to him may have been following me."

"What makes you think that?" asked Jack.

"I don't know for certain. It's just a strange feeling I have lately. I can't place it exactly, but I feel it," Veronica said. Again she glanced nervously at the door to the café and the tables occupied by others.

"Do you feel in danger?"

Rather than answer him, she looked him in his eyes and directly asked, "Will you help me, Mr. Armstrong?"

Jack paused for a moment, considering the challenges of solving the historic mystery, the unanswered questions, and the danger involved with the Russian mafia, against the fact that he was not doing anything else "to pay the rent" as he liked to say. So, he nodded his assent.

Veronica sighed with relief and her eyes lit up as she beamed: "Thank you!" She then remembered to caution: "Max has drained all my bank accounts. I don't have any money to pay you." Jack slumped in his chair.

"But I am prepared to share 25% of what we find, Mr. Armstrong. Would that be acceptable to you?"

Jack raised his chin slightly while absorbing the news and quickly considered that he would have to rely on some short-term savings he had set aside to make ends meet. He also was not currently engaged with any other client, and he had to admit, the challenge and a beautiful woman in need was catnip to him. *In for a dime, in for a dollar*, he thought. "You either step forward into growth, or you will step backward into safety," as Abraham Maslow once said. He nodded to her again.

"Good then, we have an agreement," Veronica said; she offered her hand, which he took in his.

"You said that you are moving out of your home because of your husband. Do you have somewhere to stay?"

Veronica thought for a moment, then postulated: "I could stay with my best friend, Sidney."

"Fine. And where does Sidney live?"

"She lives in Stinson Beach, where she has been since her divorce. I trust her. She knows about my fears and Max."

"I suggest you call her, straight away—tell her that starting tonight you need to spend a few nights with her. If you need to go get any of your things, I can go with you. Would you like that?"

Veronica shook her head and said that she would be alright with Max out of town and could borrow a few things from her girlfriend, if necessary. "OK," said Jack. He figured if she made it to Sidney's safely, there may not be too much of a problem with the Russians. On the other hand...

"I have a few ideas to pursue and will be in touch with you. Before we part, let me take a couple of pictures of the note and the key," Jack said, taking out his iPhone.

Jack began to ruminate about Max Hill and the Russian Mafia. A bunch of tough guys. Just in case, it might not be too soon to enlist some help. That brought to mind his long-time best friend.

# CHAPTER FOUR

Whenever Jack drove over the Bay Bridge, fond memories of the classic film *The Graduate*, streamed through his mind: "Plastics my boy, Plastics," Mrs. Robinson's friend said, "The Future."

Today, he thought about how times have changed: tech, social media, genetic engineering and AI are The Future. Still he had that memory of Dustin Hoffman driving back and forth over the Bay Bridge chasing his girlfriend and humming the tune: "And here's to you Mrs. Robinson, Jesus loves you more than you will know, wo wo wo. God bless you, please, Mrs. Robinson, Heaven holds a place for those who pray, hey hey hey—Hey hey hey…" The Z-8 top was down, the wind was in his hair and the weather was warm, making it a great afternoon for a ride to Berkeley, Jack's old stomping ground.

When he considered the financial straitjacket he was in, a favored Will Rogers phrase popped into Jack's mind, "Don't let yesterday take up too much of today." He had a new and attractive client, he had an interesting and challenging case and he had a chance to make 25% of—who knows what? Life was good…and promising.

After Veronica and Jack parted, he called his former girlfriend, Laura Lovewell, and asked if she was free for dinner. She said that she was and suggested meeting him at Muracci's on Telegraph Avenue in Berkeley at 7pm.

For seven long, hard years, Jack had been a fixture at the University of California at Berkeley, attending the undergrad college with 29,000 other students, then on to the law school, formerly housed in what was known as Boalt Memorial Hall until recently, when the name was removed, acknowledging the anti-Asian views expressed by John Henry Boalt.

When Jack started at Berkeley, his grandmother had given him a picture of a young college-aged man, neatly bearded and wearing a bowler hat with a vest and suit coat. The picture bore the statement: "HARVARD? Hell no—I'm a CAL Man!!!" Jack cherished that picture and placed it in his multiple offices as he matriculated through life. Now it held pride of place in the den of his San Francisco apartment.

While in law school, Jack met Laura, an undergraduate at that time. She was bright and cute. How sweetly he remembered her deep, dreamy, big brown eyes and dynamite smile. And her tight figure ... would not stop. They dated often and made love frequently and well, as her name implied. After a few years together, Jack's eye wandered to another woman and his relationship with Laura cooled. Nevertheless, they were fond of each other and kept in contact on a friendly basis, until Jack married Tiffany.

Jack's call to Laura had surprised her; he had to first explain that he and his wife had divorced, before presenting how he wanted to discuss a case relating to her professional purview.

Laura was a Professor of History at Berkeley and had developed a national reputation for her detailed knowledge of California History. She had written several books on the subject and lectured frequently both inside and outside the classroom and the state. To solidify and expand her historical expertise, she had also earned her doctorate. Jack knew that she could shed light on the mystery of the key.

"So nice to see you, Jack!" Laura said excitedly. "How have you been? What's been going on in your life?"

"Tiffany and I have divorced," Jack repeated what he said on his phone call to her while Laura subtly smiled. "And I graduated from BigLaw to start my own investigative service: Jack's Solutions."

"That's wonderful," Laura said, then caught herself: "I mean, about your new business."

"In fact, that's why I am here. To discuss a new case that I have."

Laura's chin dropped slightly, divulging her romantic disappointment.

"Have you ever seen anything like this?" Jack asked, while showing her his iPhone pictures of the key and Graham Stackhouse's note.

Laura looked carefully at the pictures, thought for a bemused moment, then said, "No, not really."

Jack then filled her in on the background provided by Veronica. "So, we think this came from an 1860's poker game in San Francisco."

Laura thought aloud, "The 'YB' is intriguing. . ." Suddenly she blurted out: "I have an idea, Jack—what are you doing tomorrow morning?"

"Working on the case, but I have nothing scheduled for now," he replied.

"Good, I don't have a class tomorrow, so why don't you spend the night with me—there's plenty of space—I have a comfy guest bedroom in my apartment. We can catch up tonight over dinner and then you can accompany me first thing tomorrow morning."

28

"Accompany you where, Laura?" Jack wanted to keep their relationship focused on the key.

"I'll surprise you; but rest assured, it will relate to solving the mystery," Laura said invitingly.

"Ok then," he agreed. He always had a change of clothes and a few overnight essentials in the trunk of his Z-8: "just in case."

Laura's apartment, located on Blake Street, on the South Side of the Berkeley Campus, was very comfortable indeed. While in school, Jack used to live a few blocks away, at the end of Palm Court, in accommodations nowhere near this sleek—a converted attic of an old three-story Berkeley home which offered a spectacular view of the Golden Gate Bridge, a single bedroom, bath and a separate entry up an outside staircase. He used to BBQ on a Hibachi grill for which he devised a platform, just outside the sliding kitchen window. He loved watching the sunset drop between the spans of the bridge's twin art deco towers. *What a beautiful sight,* Jack thought, *and a feat of ingenious engineering too—few are aware that there are one-man elevators in each of the Bridge's towers.*

Jack enjoyed recalling San Francisco facts little known to others, many of which came to him from his father who worked for a San Francisco elevator company. His father had many behind-the-scenes stories about San Francisco and would recant them to Jack while he was growing up. Many a Saturday afternoon was spent with his father at their Cobble Hill home, watching him work on his extensive antique clock collection as he embedded his love for San Francisco history in his young son's budding consciousness. He also loved listening to *The Phantom* on the radio with his dad. "Who knows what evil lurks in the hearts of men? The Phantom knows!"

Jack's father was not much of a hugger. The most affection he had ever seen between him and Mom was Friday nights when, after dinner and the dishes were done, Dad would turn up the radio, grab Mom and they would dance to the Big Band sounds of Tommy Dorsey that he loved.

Now at Laura's, Jack wanted to make sure he didn't give her the wrong idea of his intentions. They had spent many a night at his Palm Court attic apartment, La Bohème-style, years earlier. Their love making had been satisfying to both; Laura knew exactly how to handle him, and he seemed to press the right buttons to give her great excitement and satisfaction too.

Now, so many years later, at Laura's pleasant apartment, they had a great time reminiscing about their former life together and the wilds of campus living. She and Jack remembered the Greek Theater, the Big Game bonfires, dinners at Spenger's and trips across the Bay to San Francisco. What a life!

After a few too many beers and several glasses of wine, Jack called it a night, kissed Laura on the cheek and sauntered off to her guest bedroom. He could tell that she was disappointed; she expected a late-night knock on her bedroom door by him that never came.

In the morning, Laura was up bright and early and tapped on Jack's guest room door. He rolled around, shouted, "Be there in a few." Then he found his sea legs, hopped out of bed and into the bathroom to do the necessary and tidy himself up a bit with a quick shave, shower, brush of the teeth and comb of the hair. Once presentable, Jack announced himself to Laura in the kitchen and wished her: "Good morning." She quickly reciprocated by handing him a cup of coffee. "Still like your coffee black, Jack?" she asked.

"Yes, please," Jack responded. "What do you have in store for us this morning?" Jack wondered, eyeing her and thinking how lovely she had matured. Jack thought, *Hmmm. Maybe getting to know her again ain't such a bad idea.*

"Well, Mr. Armstrong, I hope that you slept well and had sweet dreams! I certainly did," offered Laura, cheekily. "We are off on a field trip," in answer to his question. " But first, let's grab a bite to eat," she said.

She offered her hand, which he gladly took, and they headed out the door onto Blake Street, then took a right turn toward Telegraph Ave. Laura led Jack to the local bagel shop on Telegraph, noted for "20 Different Types of Bagels" as proudly proclaimed on the store window. Once inside and after a quick inspection of the menu, Jack ordered one of his favorites: the sesame bagel with lox and a schmear, while Laura ordered a cinnamon bagel with a touch of butter. They sat at a curbside outdoor table with another cup of coffee and enjoyed their bagels. "Where are we going today? Can't you at least give me a clue? You know how impatient I can get when—"

"The repository of over 600,000 items on the history of California and the North American West. It is the largest such collection in the world. If that key has a veritable relationship with San Francisco, we will find it there, in the Bancroft Library," she said.

"The Bancroft Library? Why didn't I think of that?"

"Because it is for me to know and you to find out," said Laura, sexily flexing her professorial muscles.

After their bite to eat, they walked to the Bancroft library, one of the largest and most heavily used collections of manuscripts, antique books, and rare literary materials in the United States. The thousands of books were housed in an impressive early 20th century building built in classical revival style. Jack could feel the air teeming with intellect—an "edifying" field trip, indeed!

"Let's start by checking on the 'YB' name and see what pops up." Laura typed "YB" into the Bancroft Library computer system and found the following: "'YB' refers to modern day San Francisco, formerly known as 'Yerba Buena.' Yerba Buena means 'good herb' and officially became San Francisco in 1847. 'Yerba Buena Cove' was once a shallow body of water beginning at the foot of Market Street and the shoreline extended inland to where the Transamerica Pyramid building now stands.

Laura read, "You can say that today people in The City's financial district 'walk on water.'"

She peered at Jack, whose eyes were restlessly roving the stacks of books—she knew that look all too well. She decided to release him before he became a distraction from her research: "I'll continue with my research and meet you at the Bear's Lair at noon. That will give you a chance to explore the campus, Jack."

"Okey-dokey," said Jack. *This will also give me a chance to think through the case until we meet for lunch*, he thought.

# CHAPTER FIVE

Jack figured it was time to check in with his new client. He dialed Veronica's number, and when she answered, he asked, "How are you doing, Mrs. Hill?"

"I'm fine," she replied. "I'm with Sidney, at her beautiful home in Stinson Beach overlooking the Lagoon. It even has a dock!"

"Good. I made some headway today researching the key, and I have a plan."

He shared with her that the "YB" stands for Yerba Buena, now San Francisco.

"That makes sense," Veronica said. "It fits with Graham Stackhouse's poker game in the 1860's. So, we know that the key is likely from Yerba Buena, but what does 'Niantic' mean? The only Niantic of which I am aware, Mr. Armstrong, is the American software development company based in San Francisco. Needless to say, the Niantic company did not exist when my great-great grandfather played poker in San Francisco."

"We will explore further Mrs. Hill."

"We?" asked Veronica.

"Sorry, yes, I am working with a long-time friend of mine, Laura Lovewell, a professor of history at Berkeley. She is helping me research the key, its origins and potential meaning."

"Wow, that is really fascinating. A professor of history at UC is investigating the key?!" she gushed. "I am very impressed with your network." Sidney, overhearing one side of the conversation, nodded to her, then left the room.

"Thank you, Mrs. Hill. I do have a broad, deep bench to assist me in finding solutions."

*Every successful person has someone else to thank*, thought Jack.

"Please feel free to call me Veronica; really I can't bear to have my name associated with his another minute. But, before we sign off, I feel I need to tell you something—" she intoned, slightly breathless.

"What is it?" Jack asked. "Are you alone?"

Veronica responded, "I am now. I feel uneasy. While Sidney and I were having a glass of wine and admiring the beautiful sunset over the Lagoon, we were talking. Understand, Mr. Armstrong, we share everything: clothes, recipes, man problems, stories. . . Sidney and I went to grade school together and became lifelong best friends. So, I told her about the key, Graham Stackhouse's note and that I had hired you to help me investigate it. It was just girl talk, really. Then, while we were chatting, Sidney's phone rang and it was Max."

"Max? Mr. Hill? Did he know that you were staying at Sidney's house?"

"No. No, I didn't mention this to anyone else or knowingly leave any clues as to my whereabouts. But of course, he knows that we are best friends, and I guess he concluded that I might be here."

"And Max had Sidney's phone number?"

*That's an odd coincidence*, thought Jack.

"Did Sidney tell him that you were there?"

"No way—she covered for me, said that she hadn't seen me and didn't know where I was."

"Veronica, we need to consider getting you out of there before Max catches on to where you are," Jack proposed. "I suspect that it won't be too long before Max figures it out. Do you have another place to stay?"

"Not really."

"Ok, let me make some calls, and I will call you right back. In the meantime, gather your things, say goodbye to Sidney, and tell her that you will stay in touch by phone. Tell her that you just learned that a dear friend of yours is sick and needs some attention," Jack offered.

"I understand," she answered, gravely.

Jack quickly assessed the situation. Was it truly accidental that Max called Sidney looking for Veronica, or did Max call Sidney looking to speak to Sidney privately?

*That slimeball*, thought Jack. Racking his brain, he could only think of one source of help for Veronica.

# CHAPTER SIX

Laura met Jack at the Bear's Lair, adjacent to the Berkeley Campus. They ordered some lunch: Jack, a hamburger with fries, and Laura, a Mediterranean salad. Laura began to brief him on her further research. In 1848, Laura recounted, when news of the Gold Rush began spreading, people were so desperate to get to California that they would jump in any vessel sailing in that direction. On arrival in Yerba Buena, ship captains were left with no return cargo or passengers—often even their crew bolted for the gold fields. At one time there were over 500 idle ships in San Francisco Bay. Abandoned ships sometimes found other uses, becoming warehouses, saloons, hotels, even jails!

Her research found that some ships were sunk intentionally. Most significantly, Laura had learned that, according to historic law, any land directly under a sunken ship belonged to the ship's owner! Some ships were intentionally sunk in shallow, coastal water to establish title to the underwater waterfront property. "Some ship owners even paid to have their ships towed to a proper resting place, sunk in the shallow water of Yerba Buena Cove, then sand and debris was dumped around the sunken ship until the waterfront extended around it!" Laura illumined.

"So, it was a 'land grab' strategy," Jack thought out loud, "clever, and a cheap way to 'acquire' waterfront property while easing final use out of abandoned ships. But where does this lead to our search?"

"In 1850, there were hundreds of ships in what would, a decade later, be named San Francisco Bay. Of these gold-rush ships, several have been discovered buried in the Bay under the streets which once were the waterfront. Recently, some have been discovered inland, six city blocks from today's waterfront to the foot of the Transamerica Pyramid Building and Montgomery Street—where the waterfront once existed."

"Wow. This is amazing, just from a local news standpoint—I wonder why folks don't speak of this more often." Jack couldn't hide his delight in learning new historic curiosities about the city he loved. Then he shook himself awake to the present task at hand: "You said that 'several' ships were found under the San Francisco waterfront. . . Do you know how many?"

"My research indicates that 42 ships have been discovered, buried under the waterfront."

"42? That's an incredible number of sunken ships," Jack said. "Do you know the names of these sunken ships?" he asked.

"Sure, I made a list—" Laura rifled through her copious all-purpose leather satchel and took out her iPad, "—the ships bore many names including one called the Niantic."

"The Niantic?" asked Jack. *So much for a San Francisco software company*, he thought.

"Yes," answered Laura. "I suspect that the one called the 'Niantic' and the key your client possesses are connected to the Gold Rush treasure you are hunting for."

"Good guess! And good, swift work. You're the Best, Laura!" beamed Jack.

"Thanks," said Laura, blushing.

"Next questions," posed Jack, clearing his throat a bit and stiffening his posture: "If they are connected, how are we going to find where the Niantic was sunk and whether the key is somehow connected to the sunken ship?"

"A step ahead of you," Laura presaged. "I found a map which shows the ships and where they were sunk. It looks like the Niantic is buried near the corner of Clay and Sansome Streets," said Laura.

"Clay and Sansome, that's not far from my old office," said Jack. "I'd be willing to bet the building manager of the Embarcadero Center, a friend of mine, may have some information about the discovery of sunken ships while EC One was being constructed."

"That would be a poignant piece to add to the puzzle," said Laura.

"I need another favor, Laura," he said, his shoulders softening, "Remember, I said I have a client who inherited the mystery key? Well, she is in the process of divorcing a guy— not a good guy at all. She may be in danger. She thinks he is following her and she is fearful of him hurting her. She needs a place to stay. Could she bunk with you for a few nights while we figure out where she can safely live?" asked Jack.

"Jack, you ask that I research for you, solve historical mysteries for you, and now you want me to host your client?! A woman I don't know and haven't even met, not to mention that she may be in danger? I'm a professor, you realize—not a personal assistant or Airbnb hostess—and, well I'm your former—former . . .," her voice trailed off, huffily.

"Yes, Laura, it is much too much, I know. But I don't have

anyone else upon whom to rely. You're the only one I can truly trust," Jack said soothingly.

There was a long silence while Laura fumed and contemplated what she was getting herself into. Finally, she said, "Ok, Mr. Smoothtalker, I'll do it; but only for a few nights, mind you . . . And if she even snores, she is out! And I expect you to provide me some protection. Comprende?"

"Yes , Laura, I owe you Big."

"You owe me more than Big, Jack," Laura exclaimed and pointed her slender, graceful finger at him. His eyes glistened in shades of blue-grey, just like the Yerba Buena Bay.

CHAPTER SEVEN

Gary Cooper was a former Navy Seal guy and very smart. He was retired from the military and ran his own "helpful" shop for those who needed his kind of help. Gary, like Jack, had plenty of contacts: except his were in the military and law enforcement. He never forgot that his success was attributable to being part of a team, whether it was the Navy Seal team, or another one.

Jack and Gary bonded years ago while Jack attended Berkeley and Gary was a young Berkeley cop who had just graduated top of his class at San Francisco State University with a criminology major. Gary's dad had also been a Berkeley cop during the late 60's and the People's Park Riots, where his dad was portrayed as "the peaceful Berkeley Cop" by local TV. Gary related the story of then Governor Reagan ordering the helicopter tear-gassing of the Berkeley campus and surrounding streets to break up the riots. *That's one way to do it*, thought Jack as he wondered if tear-gassing a bunch of college students from a helicopter was really necessary.

Gary had busted Jack for smoking a joint way back when it was illegal to do so. Jack was smoking during a concert and offered the guy behind him a hit, not knowing that it was Gary, a Berkeley cop, who was working undercover. Taking a rare break from his law studies, Jack had accepted a couple of tickets to see Bob Marley and the Wailers at the Greek Theater. Joints were passed up and down the rows like they were candy. Jack let himself relax into the cloud of pot smoke and waving bodies that night while Marley sang, "I Shot the Sheriff." The only wrong move was offering candy to a cop. Gary let Jack go with a warning. Not being written up by Gary, Jack thought: *Now that's a cool cop* and invited him out to dinner. Over time, they worked out together: hitting the Gym, running and biking. They found they had much in common and became fast friends. To this day they laughed out loud remembering that moment; and from then on, Jack called Gary "Coop."

Police business did not provide enough action for Coop, so he decided to join the Navy and successfully went through Seal training. One hell of an endeavor.

Jack and Coop stayed in touch, like brothers, and when Coop left the Navy, Jack helped him start his business by referring his first client to him. At. 6' 1," 180 lbs, very fit, with zero body fat, *Coop* was not to be fiddled with. He had a penetrating stare. His midnight sky black eyes said he was all business when needed, though he frequently sported an ear-to-ear grin, which invited trust from most people he met. Coop also had a passion for opera and cabernet sauvignon. His family became the first black family to own a vineyard in nearby Sonoma.

"Hi Coop, it's me," he said from his cell phone. "I need a favor. Would you mind meeting me?"

"Sure, what is it this time?"

"Let's have a drink, a bite to eat, and I will brief you." Since they both lived in The City, Jack suggested The Brazen Head, a favorite of theirs, located at Greenwich and Buchanan, a couple of blocks from where Jack lived. It also had the benefit of being quiet, tucked away, with good food in addition to a great beer and wine selection. "See you at The Brazen Head at 6."

Jack arrived a few minutes before 6 pm, spotted a table in the back of the restaurant and sat down to wait for Coop. When he entered the restaurant, Jack waved him to the table and signaled a waiter to stop by. "Hi Buddy, how are you doing?"

"I'm spectacular!" Coop's usual greeting, and he meant it. He was always in a good, if not great, mood. Nothing seemed to perturb him. Easy come, easy go, was his attitude. But when the tension rose, he had ice water in his veins and never lost his cool.

Coop reminded Jack of his favorite 49er QB, Joe Montana. Montana also pumped ice water in his veins when he played. Jack remembered the Niners Super Bowl game against Cincinnati when Montana started the final winning drive deep in Niners' territory with little time left on the clock. As Montana called signals in the huddle on the make it or break it drive, he said to the huddled players, "Hey, did you guys see John Candy over there, pointing to the stands?" That loosened everyone up and the rest was history, as Montana hit John Taylor with a pass several plays later in the Cincinnati end zone!

Jack appreciated Coop's nonchalant demeanor as well. And his casual dress: Zenga short sleeve shirt, YSL tailored jeans, Hermes slip ons and an Apple watch. "Hey, you're stylin," said Jack.

"You taught me well," responded Coop.

"How about a glass of cab and a steak?" offered Jack.

"Sounds good to me. How have you been, Jack?"

"Terrific. Mucking through my divorce with Tiffany and excited about my new business: I've called it 'Jack's Solutions'. I even have my first client, which is why I called you. I could use a hand."

"Tell me about it," said Coop.

Jack briefed Coop about his meeting with Veronica, the key and the note, and his contact with Laura and the research resulting therefrom. He also discussed Veronica's meeting with Sidney and her concerns about Max and the Russian Mafia. Jack threw in his own suspicions about Max and Sidney. Coop was familiar with Max's Russian mob reputation and money laundering activities.

"And that is where I could use a hand," Jack said. "I have arranged for Veronica to stay at Laura Lovewell's apartment for a few days and think it would be wise if you could keep a lookout for Max or any of his goons who may wish to give her a hard time. Can you do a reverse stakeout for me at Laura's Blake street apartment in Berkeley?"

"Consider it done," said Coop without hesitation. "By the way, are you and Laura cool now? She was pretty torn up when you guys split."

"No. We're cool. She's great. Don't worry," said Jack.

"Where in Berkeley is Laura living?" asked Coop.

"Blake Street, South Side."

Jack and Coop continued with their dinner and catching up. Over the years Jack had a lingering question which he now asked Coop: how he, a Black American, came to be named after a White Western dude named Gary Cooper.

"The simple answer is that my mother liked him." *High Noon* was one of her favorite films. He was always the 'good guy,'" offered Coop, "tough, smart, and honest. He was also a 'ladies man': long legged, lanky and handsome," he added. "And he was quite successful: Cooper ranked near the top among box office attractions. Only John Wayne, Clint Eastwood and Tom Cruise had better box office records."

"That's impressive," said Jack. "I wonder if your mother thinks you are living up to your name's sake?"

"I've exceeded all expectations, let's just leave it at that," Coop said, giving Jack a wink.

"What can you tell me about the Russian Mafia?" asked Jack.

"The Russians, like the Italian mafia, also engage in criminal activity: political corruption, money laundering, tax evasion and even trading uranium stolen from the Soviet nuclear program," Coop said.

"What do you think Max is up to?" asked Jack.

"He could be simply after Veronica's inheritance. It could also be more involved. Meaning that he knows something that she does not know and wants the end result," said Coop. "And it could mean that he is working with friends in high Russian places. As the old saying goes: 'Hope for the best and prepare for the worst.'"

"Agreed," said Jack as they headed to Blake street.

# CHAPTER EIGHT

While Coop took up a lookout position across the street from Laura's apartment, Jack, Laura and Veronica gathered inside. Laura invited everyone to sit in the living room while she made coffee. She couldn't help but notice that Veronica was glued to Jack's every move. While in the kitchen, Laura peered out at them. Strangely silent, Laura thought, but perhaps understandable. *The woman does seem terrified.* She arranged their coffees on a tray with a small plate of shortbread cookies she had made earlier. Research projects always over-stimulated her and she found baking a tried and true way to stay calm. Laura made her way to the living room and placed the tray on the coffee table.

Veronica and Jack accepted the coffee. Jack grabbed a cookie. *I guess this is dinner*, he thought. He was working on his second shortbread when Veronica cleared her throat.

"Mr. Armstrong and Laura—I want to thank you for your kindness in bringing me here. Please understand however, I am becoming a bit of a basket case. A text came through from Sidney earlier, asking exactly where I am."

Jack turned to the window, hoping that Coop was focused on the task at hand. He turned back to Veronica. "Did you answer her?"

"No, but I can only imagine what she might be thinking. I left so quickly!"

Jack saw Laura watching the two of them and wondered how this was playing out for her. Addressing her by her married name, Jack said, "Mrs. Hill, right now your job is to stay safe. We are trying to get that part under control."

Veronica nodded and looked up with saddened eyes. "Why is this happening? And how does the key fit into all of this?"

Jack nodded to Laura. "Let's just listen for a little bit, Mrs. Hill. Laura has a few things to tell us."

Straightening in her chair, Laura began to impart that she was able to locate the names of most of the sunken ships under and around the San Francisco waterfront and identified one ship named the Niantic. Her research also yielded that the Niantic was one of many ships that brought eager gold-seekers from around the world into the Yerba Buena (now San Francisco) Gold Rush, in 1849. According to ship records Laura was able to uncover in the Bancroft Library, the Niantic sailed in and out of Sag Harbor, Long Island, New York. It was sailed by a whaling family based in Nantucket.

Nantucket. Jack had fond memories of a vacation he once took on Nantucket with Laura back in the day. He remembered the picturesque Main Street where they met his longtime friend, Kip, living there, who had called it "the most beautiful street in the world." They had all wandered into Murray's Toggery where they almost convinced Jack to buy a pair of "Murray's Reds."

Laura, internally reminiscing too, held it together, and moved on. "After sailing around Cape Horn, the Niantic anchored in Peru and received a letter from the American consul in Panama, requesting them to carry passengers from Panama to San Francisco to 'attend' the Gold Rush."

She continued to inform Jack and Veronica that experienced

whaling in the Pacific and familiarity with its winds gave the skipper of the Niantic an advantage over other ships in the race to San Francisco and its nearby gold fields. As a result of good captaincy, the Niantic sailed West, instead of North, for days, in search of the Trade Winds that would take her North, and finally East, to Yerba Buena. Lacking patience, the passengers almost revolted in their gold-hunger to head North. The captain of the Niantic held fast, caught the Trade Winds and was one of the first ships to bring gold seekers to San Francisco.

Laura paused. "I know this is a lot of information. But you will see where I am going in a minute. Would you like another cup of coffee, or maybe a glass of wine?" Jack and Veronica shook their heads 'no'. She continued, "Upon its arrival in Yerba Buena, much of the crew headed straight away for the Gold Fields in the Sierra foothills. With little hope of returning the ship East, the ship's owners then ordered the officers to ground the ship and convert it into a waterfront warehouse store. Eventually, The Niantic joined over 40 other Gold Rush ships embedded in the San Francisco waterfront, never to sail again."

Veronica timidly raised her hand. "This is so fascinating but…"

Jack held his hand up as if stopping a bus. "Just wait."

"Unfortunately, the Niantic burned repeatedly in the fires that laid waste to the new City of San Francisco over the next several decades," said Laura. "In fact, San Francisco burned seven times before it had formed a fire brigade. After the fires, the ship was rebuilt repeatedly as the Hotel Niantic.

The Hotel was described as the 'finest hotel' in San Francisco. Then, in 1907, after a rebuilding caused by the Great Fire and Earthquake of San Francisco, in 1906, a new Niantic Building was constructed on the site where the ship sank," added Laura.

"Most recently, the Niantic was unearthed once again in the 1970's, more than 100 years after its grounding, during excavation for a modern building on the corner of Clay and Sansome streets, near the Embarcadero Center and the Transamerica Pyramid building," reported Laura. "Construction was stopped for a brief period for preservation and study by archeologists."

Jack sat quietly before he spoke. "So, what's the chance that the Niantic's archaeological finds relate to Veronica's key and note?"

"Bingo," said Laura. "Many of the artifacts removed from these ships were often related to the passengers and their 'feverish' desire to get to the gold mine camps. Some were desperate and small fortunes were risked in poker games in order to 'hit it big.' We should find a clue to the key in the archaeological memorabilia."

Entranced, Veronica and Jack sat, absorbing the history and wondering where this would all lead.

# CHAPTER NINE

Across the street, as Laura related the story of the Niantic, Coop noticed a man peeking in her first floor apartment window which was partially open. The man was tall, muscular, with a thick wrestler's neck and a bulky build. Rather than confront the man and disclose to him that he was being watched, Coop decided to give his old friend Captain Thomas Murphy, "Murph" as he was known at Berkeley Police Department (the BPD), a quick call.

"Hi Murph, Coop here." Coop was glad to have maintained his friendship with his old friend, the two met on 9/11, when they both watched in horror the collapse of the twin towers in NYC. Murph was one of BPD's best. He liked working the "Third" shift: nights between 4pm and midnight. That was the shift where the action occurred, and action passed time quickly. The "Dog Watch" (midnight to 8 am) had some action, but was generally quiet and wearing because one had to be up all night, every night one worked. The "Day Watch" was normal and had some action too, but it was the Third that Murph liked the most.

"Hey Coop, how are you doing?"

"Doing great Murph; but listen, I wonder if you might give me a hand. I'm on a private watch and have spotted a peeper looking into the apartment of UC Professor Lovewell, at Blake Street. Do you think you can send a car or two over and check the guy out?"

"Will do Coop; I'll send cars 40 and 30 over right away."

"Preferably Code 2, Murph." Code 2 was flashing rear lights with no siren. It was easier to sneak up on a culprit. "And Murph, let cars 40 and 30 know of my presence, please."

"Will do, Coop! They should creep by in 3 to 5."

"Thanks, Murph! You're the best," Coop offered.

Coop waited and watched. The peeper kept his gaze and ear focused on Laura's open window as Car 40 quietly rolled down the street heading West and stopped opposite Laura's apartment. The officer reached up and switched off his patrol car's ceiling light and quietly opened the door. Simultaneously, Car 30 quietly arrived heading up Blake and parked in front of Car 40. Both cars parked nose to nose. Officers quietly exited their vehicles and approached the peeper who had his back to the street and continued to focus on the window.

"Can we help you, Sir?" the officer from car 40 asked.

The man was startled, turned around and took a quick step as if to run, but stopped when he saw the two officers opposite and flanking him.

"I was lost," he said in a thick Eastern European accent.

"Perhaps we can help. Please show us your ID."

"I don't have one," he said.

"Well, what are you looking for?"

"I was looking for a friend of mine who lives somewhere around here, Officer."

One of the patrolmen then said, "Sir, you will have to move along and stop looking into people's apartments. We suggest that you go home and check where your friend lives. In the meantime, I'll take a quick picture of you with my phone, in case we have to consult you in connection with any complaints we receive."

The peeper said: "Hey, what are you doing? You can't do that! You can't take my picture. I object."

"Oh yes we can, Sir," Car 40 said. "If you don't like it, file a complaint. Now get out of here before we run you in!" If he filed a complaint against them snapping his picture the officers knew that they had him on their constantly rolling videos which they wore from their shoulder mounts. The video would provide the evidence they needed. Besides, and more importantly, their questions and interest in him would telegraph what they wanted: he would be remembered and better not try anything questionable on this beat tonight or in the near future. The last thing a perp wants is to be IDed in the crime area.

Coop watched all this from across the street and could hear the dialogue clearly including the peeper's accent. He thought about what he had witnessed and knew that Jack's instinct was right—they had a problem. Max was onto them.

Coop waited until the peeper had left, then walked across the street to Laura's apartment. He knocked on the door and Jack opened it and invited him in. "Laura, you remember Coop," said Jack.

"Yes, I certainly do," acknowledged Laura, with a bright smile.

"Hi Laura," Coop waved and responded.

And Coop, this is our client, Mrs. Hill. Coop gazed admiringly at Veronica, then proceeded to cross the room and softly shake her hand. "I am very pleased to meet you, Mrs. Hill. Jack has briefed me about your situation. We are delighted to be of service to you."

Veronica nodded bashfully while Jack smiled at their reaction to each other.

"How nice," Jack responded. "If the peeper is one of Max's goons, it is likely Max will know where Veronica is now. We should give some thought tonight and decide in the morning where she will be safe." *And how did Max track Veronica to Laura's apartment?* thought Jack.

# CHAPTER TEN

Max Hill was briefed by the Russian who listened at Laura's Blake Street apartment. Max asked, "Are you sure you have it right: that the key is connected to a sunken ship? Shit, I don't want to go on a wild crazy ride for nothing."

The Russian also added that the police were likely onto him and he needed to be less visible.

"Stay on it. We need to know where they go and what they are up to," commanded Max. "And damn it—be careful. We don't need you stirring up trouble with law enforcement." Max's goon was not the sharpest knife in the drawer, but did what he was told, for the most part. Max decided to say no more.

Max sat back and composed himself. Veronica had been a pleasant woman, but Max knew he had outgrown her. She was so easy to manipulate and so were her friends.

The next morning, Jack gazed out the bay window of his second floor apartment overlooking Allyne Park. The fog was creeping through the Golden Gate and parting itself around Alcatraz Island. Jack marveled at how the fog acted as San Francisco's natural "air conditioner," cooling the Bay Area when the California central valley heated up and sucked the fog in from the nearby ocean. It was a convenient and inexpensive way to cool the Bay. There were those who were not prepared to experience "summer" in San Francisco: tourists hopping off the Cable Cars in their Bermuda shorts and shivering. What is it that Mark Twain was alleged to have said? "The coldest winter I ever spent was a summer in San Francisco."

Nevertheless, Jack liked the moderate temperatures and the lack of snow, heat and humidity offered in Baghdad by the Bay, as the old San Francisco columnist, Herb Caen, called The City. Indeed, he remembered only one time as a kid when snow fell in San Francisco. How amazing it was—to see the number of sleds that suddenly appeared on the hills of The City, which enjoyed a Mediterranean climate year round and yielded about 22 inches of rain annually. *Very comfortable,* Jack thought.

As he thought about the fog, he also noticed a woman and her dog heading into the ground floor entrance to his building. No doubt she had just finished the morning walk with her pooch in the park across the street and was headed back to her apartment. Jack had not noticed the woman before and grew interested as he gazed at her from his window and took in her beauty: long legged, very shapely, a brunette and casually dressed, but chic. *Probably in her late twenties or early thirties*, he thought.

A few minutes later, Jack heard her unlock the door to her apartment on his floor and decided to open his door and introduce himself. "Hi, I'm your neighbor, Jack." The woman was initially startled, but recovered quickly, turned and looked at him.

"Hi, I'm Sara," she said.

"I just moved in. It looks like we share the same floor," said Jack. "Nice dog you have. What's the name?"

"Miss Charlotte," Sara announced.

"What kind of dog is it? Jack inquired.

"A labradoodle."

"Interesting—a lab and poodle mix. Bet she's smart," offered Jack

"Definitely," agreed Sara, "and she has a killer personality to boot." That intrigued Jack.

"Hi, Miss Charlotte," he said while emitting a soft whistle to attract the dog. The dog's ears perked up and Miss Charlotte turned her head to the left, as if to inquire: "Hi there, can I help you?"

"She likes people," Sara confirmed.

"Do you mind if I pet her?" Jack reached down toward the pup.

"No, go right ahead." Sara said, as she led Miss Charlotte toward Jack. Jack knelt down and looked the dog in the eyes, then began scratching Miss Charlotte behind her ears. The dog started to wag her tail and whole rear end vigorously, in a Rumba-like manner. Charlotte was uniquely marked for a labradoodle: white, not brown, with brown spots on her ears, eyes and tail.

"That's a good sign," said Sara, "when she likes someone, she shows her love by wiggling her rear end back and forth. You have scored points with her!"

"Well, I am glad I scored points with Miss Charlotte, Sara." Jack did not see a wedding ring on her hand.

"If you haven't yet had it, the coffee is darned good downstairs. I am usually there by 8 am. Stop by if you get a chance."

"Sure, that would be nice," Sara responded as she turned toward her door and disappeared.

*Very interesting*, thought Jack. Immediately he began to envision Sara and Miss Charlotte at his place as he grilled salmon while jazz tunes warmed things up. *She is just the kind of gal I like*, he mused.

# CHAPTER ELEVEN

Coop called Captain Murphy and asked if he'd had a chance to run the picture of the peeper at Laura's apartment taken by Cars 40 and 30 the previous night. "The pics came back as a positive identification of a known Russian mafia operative: Boris Bettinoff," said Murph. Now, Coop knew that they had to be careful and wondered how much Boris had heard outside Laura's apartment.

"Jack, I confirmed our thick-necked voyeur from last night." Coop explained what he had learned from BPD. Jack had to assume that Boris had heard the story about the key and note and had reported the same to Max Hill. So now it was a race to find the connection between the key and the Niantic. Jack thought a good first step was to visit the building in which his old law firm was located. He asked Coop to join him.

As they walked into the building manager's office at One Embarcadero Center, Jack recalled that the Center was the inspiration of city planner Justin Herman to create a "city within a city." The concept won him acclaim—a plaza at the Embarcadero Center, was created and named in his honor.

Jack thought that the office towers reminded him of ice cube trays balancing on their ends. The towers resembled modern day versions of Rockefeller Center in New York City. Portman, the architect, was aware that corner offices sell; so on each floor he created multiple "corner" offices at each end of the floor given the angular shape of the buildings. As Jack used to like to say to clients and friends, "and I have a corner office!"

The building manager Jack knew was a fellow by the name of Mac McBride, from his days in the Embarcadero Center. Jack explained to Mac that he and Coop were interested in the construction of buildings in and around Embarcadero Center. Mac had been with the Embarcadero Center for years and was familiar with all construction and excavation in the area. "What do you need to know, Jack?"

"Mac, what do you remember during construction near Clay and Sansome? Was there a possible link to a sunken ship?"

Mac paused. "I remember it vividly, because construction was stopped so archaeologists could examine the ship's remnants and arrange for preservation of what they could save. That cost the builders a bundle," Mac said. "What a pain in the neck!"

"Do you recall the name of the ship that was uncovered?"

"Nope, I don't."

"Do you know if the remnants were removed and preserved?"

"Let me think," Mac said, gazing out at the Bay Bridge from the upper floor window of his office. "I think the salvageable remnants were taken to some sort of maritime museum in The City."

"Please excuse me for a second while I make a call," said Jack.

Jack turned his back on Mac and dialed.

"Who are you calling?," asked Coop.

Holding his finger in the air to Coop as if to say "Hold on," Jack said, "Hi, is Laura available? Please tell her Jack is calling."

"Hi Laura. Are you aware of a San Francisco maritime museum where some sunken ship remnants from the Embarcadero Center construction may have been taken?"

"Yes, they likely are housed at the Maritime Museum, located near Aquatic Park," she responded.

Jack repeated her answer aloud for the benefit of Coop and Mac to which Mac replied:

"That sounds right, Jack."

Jack pocketed his phone and turned to Mac. "Thanks, Mac!" Jack beamed, "You've been a big help."

As Jack and Coop left the building, Coop looked at the corner of Clay and Sansome and ruminated, "Do you realize that we are walking on top of the very site of a sunken ship that may hold the answer to the case on which we are working?"

Jack cast a glance at the street below and nodded his head as the two best friends walked across the street to the Alcoa Building where their car was parked. "Heck, I bet if you asked ten people in The City, nine of them would have no idea what is buried beneath the streets of San Francisco," replied Jack.

As they neared Coop's SUV, a BMW X3 M Competition, they noticed a note on the windshield. It read:

BACK OFF IF YOU KNOW WHAT'S GOOD FOR YOU AND YOUR FRIENDS...STOP NOSING AROUND AND GO LIVE YOUR LIFE WHILE YOU STILL HAVE ONE

Coop looked at the note and smiled. "Game on."

# CHAPTER TWELVE

While Coop had shown an interest in Veronica, Jack decided to try his luck with Sara. He stopped by her apartment and asked her if she would like to have a cup of coffee with him downstairs at the Blue Fog.

They met at the sidewalk tables outside the Café across the street from Allyne Park. It was a pleasant afternoon with blue skies and not a wisp of wind, the temperature in the high 60s, just right for San Francisco in late summer. Jack was dressed casually with fitted Polo jeans, Sid Mashburn slip ons and an Untuckit shirt. Sara appeared like a mirage, gliding gracefully to the table: her slim, curvaceous silhouette had Jack slack-jawed.

"Hello Sara. Am I glad to see you! Have a seat and I'll hustle up some coffee from the Café. How do you like yours?"

"How about a small nonfat latte?" she said.

"Coming right up." Jack went inside the coffee shop to place the order. He returned with the latte and a large cup of black coffee for himself. He unwrapped a paper bag with two biscottis to share.

"So, tell me about yourself. What brought you to this little corner of the world?"

"I'm a playwright. Currently I'm working on a script for the Magic Theater at Fort Mason."

"Playwright—theater. Interesting. What's the subject?"

"My mother was a therapist and worked from home. The play is about the characters she encountered and issues she had to deal with and how she handled them. I've called it,

*Thirty One Flavors*. Did you know that today more people use therapists than ever before?"

"No, I didn't. I tend to be a 'do it yourself' type of guy who tries to solve his own problems without outside help. So far it has worked well for me," Jack replied.

"Well, someday you may be in need of a second opinion," offered Sara. "Hearing from a professional about personal matters can be very beneficial."

Trying to avoid further discussion about the need for therapy, Jack asked, "Would you like to take your latte and go for a walk in the park?"

"Sure, let's do it!" Sara stood eagerly and grabbed her drink.

They strolled through the park. Sara began to hum with conversation. "I love it here. It's so close to the park which is convenient for Charlotte and me, and safe. Don't you love how Cow Hollow takes you right onto Lombard Street, then Crissy Field and the Golden Gate Bridge? And there is the Broadway Tunnel and Downtown. So accessible!" Sara blushed, "I feel like I'm babbling on. Too much?"

Jack shook his head. "No. Please go on."

"I love great restaurants." she added, "Fillmore Street has some terrific ones. And who can beat this weather? We are so sheltered from the wind and the fog which is off shore in the Bay, but entertaining. Maybe that's why they call this area 'Cow Hollow', at least for the Hollow part of the name," she mused.

Jack looked intently at Sara's big brown eyes, which sparkled with her radiance. "I'm a huge fan of The City too," said Jack. "And it's becoming more interesting by the minute."

"What do you do, Jack?"

"I'm a lawyer, but I stopped practicing law earlier this year and took up private investigating. So, I guess you can call me a PI."

"An interesting choice. Why did you switch?" she asked.

"After a while, I just became stifled by the constant push for billable hours and the never ending administrative oversight. I'm not a guy who likes having to take 20 steps when I can do the same thing in 5. I also founded a tech startup that had some success. I have to say, I developed quite a large network of connections over the years between the legal practice and Silicon Valley. I can and do call on them when needed. It works. After a few clients sought me outside of the law firm to solve their problems, I realized I could be more effective starting, 'Jack's Solutions'—the name of my company."

"That's fascinating, Jack," said Sara. "But why be a PI? Why not create another startup?"

"One path satisfies corporate interests and the other satisfies human connection. I like dabbling in social justice: making sure the 'good guy' wins. I figure one does not preclude the other; and the skills for both have some connection—determination, creativity and problem solving."

"I saw you being dropped off earlier today by someone. I'm not one to pry, but is he one of your 'contacts'?"

Jack decided she was too adorable to be a spy. "Coop? Yes, he is probably my best friend. I met him in law school while at Berkeley. He was a police officer and once busted me for smoking grass in the old days, but he cut me some slack. We ended up being great buddies. After we met, he went off to go through Navy Seal training, while I finished law school and started practicing law. Fast forward, he started his own firm to provide people with physical services of the type he specialized in: dark ops and stuff."

Sara stopped and looked at him. "That sounds a little scary. Don't you guys worry about being involved in some of that stuff?"

"Nah, it's not that big of a deal. I have referred several cases to him and, I guess, I became a good 'client' of his. In fact, we are working on a case together now."

"Can you tell me a little bit about it?"

Jack kept all clients' privacy under lock and key. Without mentioning names, he said that it involved an inheritance, a key and some missing treasure. Sara was impressed by his background and the current case he was investigating. She smiled thinking that he was easy on the eyes and easy to talk to. She also respected his rule for confidentiality.

"Besides writing, what other likes do you have?" asked Jack.

"I am a total nut for classic films."

Jack smiled. "I was thinking of going to the Presidio Theater tomorrow night to see the *African Queen* with Bogart and Hepburn. Would you like to join me?"

"Only if I can buy the popcorn. That film is one of my favorites. Didn't Bogart receive an Oscar for his performance?"

"If he didn't, he should have," Jack replied. "Call me old fashioned but I don't mind a little heroism and chivalry." Jack wondered if perhaps he ought to have kept this to himself. Some of the young women he'd met often took the sentiments far differently than his innocuous intention.

Sara smiled warmly at him as a cool breeze off the Bay swirled around them. He instinctively wanted to give her his jacket but held back. *Don't move too fast, fella*, Jack thought to himself. They walked back to the apartment building and set their date for 6:30 pm the next night.

*Mission accomplished*, he thought. *What a lovely woman to get to know.*

## CHAPTER THIRTEEN

Early the next morning, he called Laura. "Do you happen to know the curator of the San Francisco National Maritime Museum?"

Laura replied, "Yes, I do. Would you like an introduction?"

Jack wondered if she was starting to cool on the project. "If it's no bother, I'd really appreciate it. I'd like you to join us, if you can. We can explore what he might know regarding the key and the note. So, maybe tomorrow morning? Then you and I can get some lunch with Coop and go over what we learn." Laura agreed and said she would get back to him soon about meeting with the curator.

About an hour later, Laura called Jack and said: "We're on. The curator, Dr. Richard Altmeir will see us at 10 am tomorrow. I mentioned that we wished to discuss remnants of some sunken ships and memorabilia, which may have been preserved, and his knowledge of Maritime Law and Gold Rush history. He is delighted to help. I have known Richard for over a decade, and we have worked together on a variety of projects. I'll see you at Aquatic Park at 10 am," Laura signed off.

Jack then called Coop. "Hey Buddy. Any news on our peeper, the Russian Mafia, and the note left on your car?"

"Yes, I checked back with Murph. He did a search and confirmed the Russian Mafia link to the peeper, Boris Bettinoff. He said that he has been busted for money laundering and has a record for strong arm stuff."

"Could you tell whether the money laundering or strong arming stuff involved Max Hill?" asked Jack.

"Still working on that, but the chances are good. Boris comes from Brighton Beach, New York."

"Brighton Beach? Ok, tell me more," Jack implored.

"Brighton Beach is the principle home of the Russian mafia. Russians coming from there are the real deal. Do we know if Max is from there?" asked Coop.

"Good question. I'll check with Veronica. If so, we will have to be especially careful," said Jack. Then he asked: "Did you mention the windshield note to Murph?"

"Yes, even though it is not within his jurisdiction, he said he would run the note through the State CII, the California Bureau of Criminal Investigation and Identification and see what pops out."

"Great," Jack said with optimism. He then briefed Coop on his visit to the San Francisco National Maritime Museum scheduled for tomorrow morning and what he hoped to achieve. "If your schedule permits, please meet Laura and me at McCormick & Kuletos at 1 pm. And, Coop, please keep an eye out for our Russian friends. I don't want to give them any more information about our treasure hunt than they may already have, and I certainly don't want to expose Veronica or Laura to them."

"My eyes are everywhere," assured Coop.

# CHAPTER FOURTEEN

Jack decided to go for a bike ride. He used his bike to stay fit and to cogitate. He remembered a saying from G.K Chesterton: "One sees great things from the valley; only small things from the peak."

Many a mystery or complex problem had been solved during one of his bike rides. There were some questions that needed to be answered. He pulled his Ibis carbon fiber mountain bike out of his apartment and headed toward the Bay. He liked riding a mountain bike in San Francisco because the wider wheels helped him navigate the potholes, ruts and rough streets he often encountered. The sturdy shocks helped soften the ride. The gearing on a mountain bike made hill climbing manageable in San Francisco. All in all, a great bike for The City.

He breathed in deeply as he rode past Fort Mason and the Marina Green which connected him to Crissy Field, once a landing strip for postal air, now a trail leading to Fort Point's breathtaking views from under the Golden Gate Bridge. Then, he would double back and make his way up the Golden Gate Bridge approach and proceed across the bridge with Alcatraz on the right and the Farallon Islands 30 miles away on his left. He would become mesmerized watching the fog creep steadily in from the Pacific ocean under the Golden Gate and parting eerily around Alcatraz, an unusual but regular occurrence, particularly in the summer. Just down the hill from the Golden Gate lay Sausalito, the quintessential Mediterranean town clinging to the side of a hill and touching the Bay. All thoughts of sinister doings tended to slip away while riding through this picturesque town.

On his return home, before crossing the Golden Gate, Jack remembered his early dating days when he would head up the hill in his car toward the Marin headlands. He had fond memories of being "on top of the world" as he used to say when he took a date to the top of the Marin Headlands overlooking the Golden Gate and The City.

During his 20 mile ride, Jack thought about Veronica's case. *How did Max know where we would be when a note was left on Coop's car after our meeting in the Embarcadero? Someone must have told him about our plan to search for the Niantic. Who could that be? Or, someone was watching me and Coop very closely.* Jack doubted that Max knew where the key led even if he knew about the key. Still he seemed to be in step with their search. *Something isn't adding up*, Jack thought, as he rode along.

As he exited the bike path off the Bridge, suddenly a car came so close as to force him off the road and down an embankment. Jack went head first and landed on his back in the brush. He lay there for a couple of minutes mentally checking himself over to make sure nothing was broken. Thank God for his bike helmet. He wiggled his toes and fingers and began moving his arms and legs. All seemed to be in order so he sat up and began dusting himself off. He turned around, saw his bike behind him and walked over to check it out. His bike was not damaged except for a bent handle bar which he quickly righted by straddling the front wheel and straightening it. *Lucky*, he thought to himself.

Jack carried his bike back up the small hill, mounted it and began the ride to his apartment. Was the close encounter with the car an accident, or did someone intend for him to receive a message in addition to the one left on Coop's car? *The signs are starting to point to danger,* thought Jack. *Not good.*

## CHAPTER FIFTEEN

He met Sara at The Vogue theater in Presidio Heights just before the 7 pm movie, *African Queen*. Amazing how one remembers classic movies: the acting, the dialogue, the plot and the cinematography. *All good stuff,* thought Jack. *And how enduring it has been. A 70 year old movie which is still captivating. Why can't the new ones hold our long term interest?*

True to her word, Sara bought the popcorn, and Jack escorted her into the theater. They chose a row midway toward the big screen and took the two seats nearest the aisle. As they sat down, the movie began and Sara offered Jack some popcorn. He took a small handful and began to munch. Sara held the bag gingerly with both hands over her legs, crossed, and he did his best not to stare. Gorgeous legs, beautiful face and sweet. He lightly placed his right hand on her left knee and gave it a squeeze. She didn't remove it and seemed to lean in to him. *This was going well,* he thought.

And what a movie. Bogart and Hepburn in one of the old-time greats movies. It had everything: romance, adventure, Victoria Falls, leeches, German patrol boats and fabulous acting. "We will have to search for another one like this," said Jack as they left the theater.

"Great thought," Sara warmly agreed.

Afterward they walked back down the hill to their apartments in Cow Hollow and held hands. *She's very bright and engaging,* Jack thought. And she had a killer smile: lit up from ear to ear. They discussed the movie, how it was created, its history and why it has been so popular for so long.

The conversation was easy—quiet moments coming and going without the typical date panic of trying to fill every moment with something witty. Sara began to feel for this man who had come out of nowhere. *Keep your eye on the ball, Missy*, she thought to herself. *Disappointments come from out of nowhere too.*

They arrived at Sara's apartment and decided to take Miss Charlotte out for her nightly walk in the park. Miss Charlotte was showing her excitement at their homecoming by wagging her tail vigorously. She was like one of those old "Slinky" toys on overdrive. They both laughed. Sara looked up at Jack. "You've scored more points with Miss Charlotte. Way to go!"

*What did Mom used to say? The way to a woman's heart is through her dog*, thought Jack. *Mom will never meet Sara.* Jack contemplated and was surprised that he began wondering if his mother would have liked her. Mom had passed away a few years back and Jack still missed her wisdom and loving ways.

As they returned to Sara's apartment, they paused at her door. Sara leaned forward and gave Jack a soft kiss on his cheek. Jack searched her eyes, reached for her, scooped her to him and kissed her meaningfully on the lips. She did not resist. What separated them was squirming Charlotte who kept jumping up on each of them. They laughed and Jack said, "Let's touch base tomorrow. I had a great night with you, Sara." Sara smiled bright as she entered her apartment and closed the door behind her.

# CHAPTER SIXTEEN

Jack had a restless night. Sara occupied every waking thought that night; there were many. Could he actually begin a new relationship so close on the heels of the failed marriage he still had to pay for? He knew what his friends would tell him. "Jack, don't get so involved with this gal. You don't even know her!" But true to type as a neverending optimist, he asked Sara later that morning if she had any desire to see one of his favorite spots in San Francisco. Sara had woken late after a similar night of wondering thoughts.

"Good morning to you. I'd love to."

It was one of those beautiful autumn days in San Francisco. The walk there was mostly downhill and as they arrived at the Fisherman's Wharf area and approached the Buena Vista Café, Jack realized that they were actually the first customers to enter that day. He was slightly embarrassed. But, confidence was his best attribute and that was the card he would play. A Sunday morning, sunny and sublime in San Francisco. What could go wrong?

Neither seemed in a rush to talk. It was the comfortable silence between two people who felt just right as they shared a comforting cup of Irish coffee at the Buena Vista. Jack mentioned that the Buena Vista was established in the early 1900s when the first floor of a boarding house was converted into a saloon, and Irish Coffee was introduced in the early 50's. "The Irish coffee here is the best anywhere," Jack proclaimed. The server stood by and asked if they would like another round. Jack looked at Sara. She shook her head "no." Jack asked for the check and said, "I have a better idea. Would you be up for seeing another unique part of The City?"

She nodded and said, "Why not?"

Jack said, "Follow me." Out the door they went across the street to catch the Hyde Street Cable Car. Sara loved the adventure. She held the outside Cable Car poll and leaned back as the Cable Car took the steep Hyde Street hill. The gripman and conductor were entertaining, rhythmically ringing the Cable Car bell, acting as Ambassadors to The City. Noting that Sara was enjoying the ride and performance of the gripman, Jack commented that annually there is a Cable Car bell ringing contest in San Francisco.

About a mile later, they got off on California Street and took the California line downtown for several blocks to Powell Street while taking in the fabulous view of The City and the Bay. Jack pulled Sara close and guided her as they hopped off at Powell Street and waited to transfer onto the Powell street line to take them three more blocks toward the Bay. As the Car stopped, Jack announced "Here we are."

Sara said "Where's here?"

Jack pointed to the building across the street and said, "At the Cable Car Barn and Museum!" As they entered the Museum, they noticed the loud clatter of active machinery. Jack pointed out the "sheaves" that turn the cables that pull the cars up and down the hills of San Francisco. Jack explained that San Francisco is the last city in the world with an operational cable car system. "It all started in the late 1800's," he explained, "when Mr. Hallidie saw a group of horses dragged to their death down a slippery cobblestone slope. Hallidie then envisioned the cable car system, in part due to his love of animals, since he was a founder of the ASPCA, and in part because he owned a wire rope company."

"This is fantastic," Sara said. "I had no idea. What a unique experience, Jack. I hope we can share more adventures!"

Jack then leaned forward and kissed Sara on the cheek. She reciprocated by turning her head and kissing him on the mouth. They held hands and left the Museum. Jack escorted Sara back to her apartment. They embraced, both looking forward to seeing each other again soon.

At 10 am, the next day, Jack and Laura arrived at the Museum office of Dr. Altmeir. His office was near the waterfront. Laura breezily proclaimed: "Hi Richard, we appreciate you meeting with us on short notice. We are attempting to learn more about a key we have in our possession and where it might lead. We are told that it was the subject of a poker game in the 1860s in San Francisco." Jack showed him a pic of the key from his iPhone.

"Niantic and YB," Dr. Altmeir read aloud. "Before The City was named San Francisco, it was called Yerba Buena, which is what 'YB' probably means. And the Niantic is likely a ship which was in Yerba Buena cove at that time. Most likely the Niantic was involved in transporting passengers to the Gold Rush."

"Yes," agreed Laura, "We have traced the Niantic to be a whaler from Nantucket which became a Gold Rush passenger ship when it rounded the Horn and left Peru for San Francisco around 1848 or 1849." Nantucket reminded Dr. Altmeir of the book: *Heart of the Sea* which caused him to tell the group about a famous whaling ship, the Essex, that struck out from Nantucket, had bad luck whaling in the Pacific, then was sunk by a whale that rammed the ship.

"The tale even involved alleged cannibalism! The book was a precursor to Herman Melville writing *Moby Dick*. *Heart of the Sea* is required reading for anyone visiting Nantucket," Dr. Altmeir explained.

Laura smiled at the Doctor's historical recollections and remembered that he had taught Maritime Law at Stanford before becoming the Museum's curator. She continued with the information she had found. "We think that it was sunk at what is now Clay and Sansome streets near One Embarcadero Center. Jack and Coop spoke with Mac McBride, the Center's manager, and he confirmed that remnants were discovered when a nearby building was constructed in the early 1970s. He told us that those remnants were likely moved for storage to the Museum."

"My guess is that we have them here," offered Dr. Altmeir.

"The Gold Rush put San Francisco on the map: The City grew from a population of 850 in 1848, to 5,000 in 1849, when Gold was discovered, and 25,000 by 1850. Thereafter, the City more than doubled by 1860 and reached 150,000 by 1870. A 600% increase in 20 years! Way before California's agricultural and tech revolutions, the Gold Rush of 1849 started California on the path toward becoming the World's 4th largest economy," said Dr. Altmeir.

"And now we have the Genetic Revolution as described in Walter Isaacson's book *Codebreaker*, helping us cope with pandemics and genetic engineering," added Laura.

"Back to the issue at hand, do you think, Doctor, that there is a remnant or an archaeological find to which the key relates?" asked Jack.

"There may be," said Dr. Altmeir. "In our Maritime Research Center we have nearly 50,000 historical artifacts."

Jack whistled. "How do you think we should tackle this?'

"Why don't you bring the key in and I will assign one of my top staffers to help look for a connection in our archives."

"That would be great," Jack commented. "I will suggest that the owner of the key, Veronica Hill, together with Laura, arrange a visit with the staff person you designate, Professor. Is that ok with you, Laura?"

"I would like to do some hands-on investigation of the fit for the key, Jack, so—yes—I'm in," replied Laura.

"I think Victoria, my chief assistant, would welcome such a visit, as well," offered Dr. Altmeir.

"Doctor," warned Jack, "please handle this discreetly and instruct your staff to do so as well. We have reason to believe some individuals who do not intend us well may be seeking the key and its meaning."

Jack called Veronica and explained the plan, then he and Laura walked to Ghirardelli Square to have lunch and brief Coop.

# CHAPTER SEVENTEEN

Coop was waiting at the restaurant when Jack and Laura walked in. "What took you so long"? he asked.

"We may have found the Mother Lode when it comes to sunken ships and paraphernalia," Jack commented. "The Museum has thousands of artifacts and could lead us to a fit for Veronica's key." Then Jack explained the plan to have Veronica visit the Museum with her key and work with the curator's chief assistant to try and find a fit.

Coop nodded in agreement. "Sounds like a plan. How long do you think it will take?"

Jack said, "I have no idea. Laura, do you have a handle on the time it may take to see if we have a winner?"

"Unfortunately, no. It all depends ..."

Coop interrupted and switched subjects, "What are we going to do about Veronica's living situation?" Laura's ears perked up. "Max is onto her living with Laura because Boris no doubt reported the same to him when he eavesdropped at Laura's place."

"I think we will have to move her again," said Jack. " Let's wait until she meets with Victoria at the Museum. Laura, have you seen any suspicious people around your apartment or following you on campus?"

"No, I haven't. Thank heavens."

"Keep alert," Jack recommended. "Let us know if anyone appears to be suspicious."

"I think we need to get Veronica out of the Bay Area, Somewhere Max would not connect to her," said Coop.

"Any ideas, Coop?" asked Jack.

Coop thought for a few minutes, then said, "How about if I arrange to have her stay with my parents on their vineyard in Sonoma? They have a guest cottage on their property which is pretty cool. As you may recall, when Dad retired from BPD, he moved to Sonoma with Mom and took up wine making as a hobby. That was years ago when property was relatively inexpensive—today, forget it!"

"Great idea, Coop. I'll discuss it with Veronica. And Laura, you can have your apartment back! In the meantime Coop, I would appreciate it if you could keep an eye on Veronica while she works with the curator's staff."

When Jack mentioned to Veronica a relocation to Sonoma, she was delighted to give it a try. "Sure. Why not?" she said. "I don't think Max has any connections there, so he won't think of me living there. Besides, I wouldn't mind a glass or two of wine!"

The next day, Veronica, Laura and Victoria looked for a fit for her key among the Museum's artifacts. The group struck out. Laura mentioned the same to Jack and after asking her several questions about the approach that she, Veronica and Victoria had taken, he concluded that it was back to the drawing board. "But, before we come up with Plan B, let's get you moved into Sonoma."

As they prepared to depart the Museum, Coop, as a lookout, noticed two guys in a pick up truck parked a block away from them with apparently clean sight lines to the front door of the Museum. He called Laura and asked her to delay their departure for a few minutes while he took care of something.

"Sure, Coop," replied Laura.

Coop ran around the block, away from the Museum and through a back alley parallel to the street upon which the suspicious characters were parked. He came up to the truck and was careful to avoid being seen in their rear view mirrors. This required him to approach the truck from behind and low. As he reached the rear of the truck, he deployed from his sleeve an object like an ice pick with a surgically sharpened point. He reached under the tailgate and quickly punctured the inside side wall of the right rear tire and immediately did the same to the inside left. He thought that should keep them busy for a while.

After he retreated away from the truck and around the corner, he called Laura and told her that they could leave now, and he would meet the two ladies at the front of the museum. Laura could head back to her Berkeley apartment in her car while Coop drove Veronica to Sonoma.

As they drove down the street, Coop watched in his rear view mirror with amusement, the false start of the pick up truck and the reaction of its two occupants. Veronica asked, "What's so funny?" Coop described to her the truckers' predicament, their quizzical looks at each other when the truck wouldn't move with any speed and one pointing a finger at the other, then the other calling someone and yelling in frustration. They had lost Veronica's trail.

"This is what makes my day," Coop said to Veronica. He could only imagine the "conversation" that the two truckers were having with their boss. Imagining it probably went something like this: "What do you mean, you had two flat tires? Idiots!"

Coop couldn't stop laughing as he began heading to the Golden Gate Bridge with Veronica; it made for a light heart during their 45 minute drive from the bridge to Sonoma.

# CHAPTER EIGHTEEN

Veronica stared out the window as they left the bridge behind and headed up 101 toward the Highway 37 turnoff to Sonoma. The drive to Sonoma was relaxing. Turning left off Highway 37 past Sears Point Raceway onto Highway 121, Coop decided to break the silence. "If you haven't been up here before, this section is pretty much what I think of as the gateway to God's country." The meandering highway, passing cows and vineyards were peaceful and normally kept Coop's mind from dwelling on some of the rough characters he encountered with his work, but today he had Veronica to think about. To protect. He wondered if she was worried, which was ridiculous—of course, she was. After a few miles along Highway 121, the road became Arnold Drive parallel to Highway 12. The view was golden, gorgeous.

Veronica sighed. "I can see why you love it here. Max and I took a trip to Napa a few years ago. Funny how a travel companion can affect whether you want to return to a place. Driving with you here, it's quite lovely."

Coop stayed focused on the road as he tried to keep Veronica's mind off her worries and his mind off of her! "The two main highways run 30 miles, pretty much the length of the Valley. I like how they flow: so relaxed and with the gently sloping mountains acting as bookends on each side divided by verdant vineyards. Do you know Sonoma Valley winemaking produces over $1 Billion in annual revenue?" Coop glanced over at Veronica who seemed to be leaning towards the passenger side window with a developing interest in her surroundings.

"Thank God better thinking prevailed years ago and the proposal to create two four lane highways with interchanges was defeated."

Coop decided playing tour guide might be doing the trick with her. "There is likely no more beautiful place on earth. Sometimes I close my eyes and imagine I am in Tuscany. I sometimes call Sonoma, 'Tuscany West.'"

Veronica turned to Coop. "What else could you want? Bucolic landscape everywhere you turn."

He continued, "If you are lucky, my parents will insist on taking you to one of their favorite spots, Jack London State Park. Besides Sonoma's drop dead natural beauty, it has been called the 'Valley of the Moon' by Jack London. What a prolific writer: 50 novels, in the short 40 years he lived."

"Wow. I wasn't aware. Please tell me more about him, Coop," Veronica implored.

Coop continued to explain that Jack London's lifestyle and political philosophy was intriguing; born into poverty in 1876 and later, living like "lord of the manor" with 1400 acres on Sonoma Mountain. He and his wife began building a three story, 26-room, 9-fireplace mansion with a reflecting pool, named Wolf House. Meanwhile, he lectured on the benefits of socialism throughout the country because he felt the U.S. system prevented the poor from bettering themselves and earning a decent living. Not only that, he was a true adventurer who sailed and traveled the world, an inventive farmer who applied restoration and conservation methods that he observed in Japan and Korea to his Beauty Ranch on Sonoma Mountain. "Quite a guy, if you ask me."

*It takes one to know one*, Veronica thought. How different Coop was from the difficult man she had been with over the past six years. She had been sizing Coop up ever since they had met at Laura's apartment. Coop was thoughtful and strong at the same time. He cared about things like the beauty of Sonoma Valley. Something she was just learning about. She could see herself with someone like him. Audibly breathing out a sigh, she kept her eyes on the road ahead

Coop, all the while acting as docent for the day, couldn't stop himself from glancing at Veronica's shapely legs, crossed in a feminine manner. Her light cotton cropped pants had embroidery at the pockets and hem—just the right length to expose her exquisite ankles. He saw that she had on a pair of Chanel flats. He was always amused that folks rarely imagined he knew about these things. His good buddy, Jack, had fostered his interest in stylish clothes back when he left the Berkeley P.D. "Coop, never show up late or under dressed," Jack had jested back then. But Coop knew there was truth to it, and he made it his mission to always keep 'em guessing, whether it was an operative he was hunting down or a lovely lady sitting next to him on a meandering drive.

Coop turned the car from Arnold Drive onto a long dusty lane which led up to a gate with an arched sign and the words, "Casa Bella Vineyards." As he leaned out the window to push the code buttons to open the gate, he laughed and said, "I always give my folks a buzz from the gate. You never know what they might be up to." Veronica smiled and immediately was excited to meet his parents.

They were welcomed by a handsome couple, Jake and Angela Cooper, into the Craftsman home, built in the 20's with a wide open front porch, intentionally exposed beams, brackets and rafters, and a stunning bay window. The home was solidly built and perfectly maintained.

Inside, Veronica found a cozy, unpretentious and sunny home. Distinct living and dining spaces centered around a large kitchen with a farm style dining table. With its carefully crafted woodwork everywhere, Veronica loved the rustic warmth.

"Thank you for inviting me to stay with you, Mr. and Mrs. Cooper," she said.

"Please call me Jake and my wife, Angela," Jake suggested. "We have heard much about you from our son."

"We are pleased to help," added Angela. "Let's have a cold drink and get to know each other," she suggested. Veronica joined the Coopers on the porch where Angela served some iced tea and the group sat in comfortable adirondack chairs with a view of the vineyards and surrounding mountains. "We understand that you have been through a tough time, Veronica," said Angela.

"Yes, I have, I suppose. I appreciate your generosity," Veronica replied.

After 30 minutes of getting to know each other, Angela said: "Why don't we get you comfortable?" Then she showed Veronica to the guest cottage. The cottage, a mini version of the Cooper Craftsman home, was complete with a view of the vineyards and Moon Mountain. As Veronica placed her sweater in the bureau drawer, she heard Coop outside the door. "How are you settling in?" he asked.

"I'm doing fine, thanks. What a beautiful place your parents have," Veronica said.

Having Coop's father as a former BPD police officer on the property also gave Veronica comfort and the feeling of security. Coop told Veronica that once she was settled in, his parents would show her their town.

As if on cue, Jake appears and suggested that they drive to The Plaza, formerly El Pueblo de Sonoma, which was surrounded by significant historic buildings. As he drove, he began to offer a brief history of the town.

"There is the Mission San Francisco Solano, founded in the early 1800s by Father Jose Altimira after which a local school was named." Jake explained, "The Mission was the last one built in Alta California after Mexico gained its independence from Spain. Ten years later, Mexico decided to close all the Missions, so General Vallejo was directed by Governor Figueroa to administer the closing of the Mission."

Angela pointed out a statue of General Vallejo which amused townspeople by being seated on a bench located on the Spain Street side of the Plaza facing a group of historic buildings and the nearby mountains. The artist had created the unique pose that allowed visitors to sit next to the statue and pretend that they were chatting with him while he maintained his finger in his book *Recuerdos* to mark his place.

Veronica watched Jake as he spoke and thought, *So that's who Coop will look like when he's older*. Jake was tall and muscular, like his son, and shared with him a fondness for Sonoma Valley.

Jake continued to recount a brief history of the area. "Many don't realize that Governor Figueroa had additionally received instructions to protect the area north of San Francisco from foreigners who had been seeking to establish their presence while hunting, fishing and farming much of what is today's Northern California. The Russians built Fort Ross on the coast near Mendocino and trapped south of there in Bodega Bay."

Upon hearing this, Veronica shared the thought that this might be a long held goal of Russia and could be part of the reason Max with his Russian connections had such interest in the history of the area and any historical treasure it bears.

"Some think the Russians still own Fort Ross," offered Coop. "A deal to sell the Fort may have never been finalized. The Russian sale of the fort was intended to be made to John Sutter upon whose property gold was found, igniting the Gold Rush. Apparently, Sutter failed to pay the full price for the property. In effect, he short-changed the Russians. If that is true, Fort Ross may still be Russian, and I am sure there is Russian interest in other land and historical artifacts in California that also may be mythically Russian. The Pomo tribe refutes this, saying that the land was only leased to the Russians. Do you think Max's interest in your key and the treasure you seek is related to the Russian obsession with California, Veronica?" asked Coop.

"Max kept me in the dark on any business matters. But, I wouldn't be surprised," she replied.

Jake continued with his historical tutorial: "To protect the area North of Sonoma, Governor Figueroa ordered Vallejo to fortify Sonoma by building a Barracks opposite The Plaza," which Angela pointed out to Veronica.

Governor Figueroa also instructed Vallejo to establish a Pueblo around the old Mission," Angela continued.

"At dawn on June 14, 1846," Jake told the story: "33 American rough riders, in rebellion against the Alta California government, arrived in Sonoma, and took down the Mexican flag from the flagpole across from the Barracks in the Plaza. In its place they raised the California Republic Bear Flag, with the word 'Republic' misspelled and the Bear looking more like a Pig with their crude artwork."

"The flag, in part, was made from a woman's petticoat," Angela added. "Thereafter, the rough riders visited Commandante Vallejo in his residence about a mile away and after having drinks, arrested him."

"The Bear Flag Revolt took place right here and is celebrated on June 14th each year," Coop said, pointing to the flagpole in the Plaza across from the Barracks.

Jake continued the tale: "Upon learning of the Bear Flag Revolt, Captain John C. Fremont traveled from his ranch near Sacramento with about a hundred men to Sonoma and, on July 5, 1846, convinced the Rough Riders to join him. The Bear Flag Revolt and the 'California Republic' ceased to exist less than a month after the Bear flag had been exchanged for the US Flag in front of the Sonoma Barracks.

A block from the Bear flag pole and across from the Presidio Barracks is the yet to-be-restored Blue Wing Inn, built in Sonoma in the 1850's and the only hotel North of San Francisco in those days. The Inn attracted some characters such as Kit Carson and Joaquin Murrieta."

"You certainly know your history," said Veronica. "Your son seems to have inherited your affinity for California history. Hopefully, if he has some time, he can show me the land that Jack London owned. It sounds fascinating."

"Gary, will you stay another day? We can make you and Veronica a picnic to take with you up on Sonoma Mountain," Jake searched his son's face for any clue as to what he was thinking.

Coop restrained himself. After all, he was "working." "I may be leaving tonight. Don't know."

After dinner that evening, Veronica helped Angela dry dishes, but kept her thoughts silent. Angela sensed that something was going on. "Let me finish all of this. Why don't you go out on the porch? The moon rises so beautifully at this time of night."

Veronica thanked her and headed out to the covered porch only to find Coop sitting alone. He looked up as she approached, and a soft smile crossed his face. "Thanks for helping Mom out."

Veronica sat next to him on the porch swing. "Coop, it's so beautiful here. I actually can't imagine a more perfect place to 'hide out'. Am I really using that word? Hideout… my mother would be nodding her head right now, if she were alive. She warned me not to marry Max. I can't help but wonder how much danger I may be in." She suddenly leaned her head on his shoulder.

Coop allowed her head to rest there. He wished he had an answer for her but he was not the Answer Man. Jack was, and

Coop suddenly hoped Jack would get his hide up here and soon. The Russians were clever and a little detour to Sonoma and a couple of flat tires were only a temporary fix. Still, for now at least, her head was on his shoulder.

## CHAPTER NINETEEN

Coop walked Veronica back to the guest house. He stood a safe distance from the front door. Veronica knew they had some chemistry, but it was late. She was tired and somewhat grateful he didn't want to come in. Just as she was shutting the door, slow wheels on the driveway beyond alarmed her. She was constantly at battle with her fear of Max or his cohorts finding her. A few moments later, she relaxed and remembered Jack was due soon. She'd see him in the morning, hopefully.

Veronica fell into a fitful sleep. Her dreams were sporadic and edgy and she woke and slept in stops and starts. She dreamt she was with Coop, holding his hand and walking through a vast forested area. Old stones paved their way as they continued toward a mysterious destination. At times feeling lost, at times afraid, Veronica didn't let go of Coop's hand. Suddenly he placed his finger to his lips to be quiet and pushed her into a small glade. He was gone and soon she felt cold and in imminent danger. She began to run through the pathways, a maze which kept leading her to dead ends filled with cobwebs and decaying animals. She smelled smoke giving her hope that Coop might be ahead, building them a fire for the night. As she approached, she saw him standing atop large stone columns with fire all around him. He was reaching out to her and she climbed higher toward the columns when he suddenly fell into the fire, screaming, "Veronica!" She sat up in bed, shaking. Realizing her whereabouts, she glanced at the clock—5 am She arose from the bed and decided to take a shower and get ready for the day to shake off her night terror.

That morning, Coop and Jack met Veronica privately on the front porch and reviewed where they were with the mystery of the key: the name on the key led them to a sunken Gold Rush ship named the Niantic buried near Embarcadero Center One and the Transamerica Pyramid Building. The remnants of the ship were collected and deposited in the San Francisco Maritime Historical Museum. Discussions with the curator of the Museum and a careful search of its inventory yielded no clues to the treasure that the key and note promised.

"Where do we go from here?' asked Coop.

"Could something have been missed? We could go through the artifacts in the Museum again, maybe with a different team," suggested Jack but he was not convinced a rerun of the Museum would be fruitful. "Veronica, are you convinced that your Great Great Grandfather intended for his children, grandchildren and great grandchildren to inherit something of significance? It seems a stretch that the object of the inheritance would survive for generations."

"All my life I have heard about Graham Stackhouse. My mother and grandmother always spoke highly of him and told me that he was an industrious, self-made man. A person of his word, Jack. I have to believe he meant what he said in his note: 'This key unlocks a valuable treasure: keep it safe.' And, the key did lead us to a sunken ship which existed near the time he was involved in the poker game. Isn't that a lot of coincidence?"

Jack looked at Veronica. "So, those who preceded you simply may not have had the interest in hunting for Gold Rush treasure. Where would they begin and, even if they had the knowledge we possess, they may have given up when they discovered the Niantic was sunk under the streets of San Francisco. And, thinking whatever the key led to is now gone, or unreachable, or forgotten and they just gave up. It's a stretch, but I think there is something there. I can feel it in my bones. We have to be creative and keep digging. Who has a bright idea?" asked Jack.

"One thing Stackhouse did not have was the Russians breathing down his neck," said Coop.

"That's true," said Jack, unless the Fort Ross sale is evidence of their interest in all things California."

"I don't think so," said Coop. "The Russians wanted to hunt and fish as well as keep the land upon which to do so. They didn't seem interested in gold or other commodities."

"They certainly seem motivated for something other than hunting and fishing now," said Veronica.

"I keep noodling on something you said several days ago, Jack," said Coop.

"What?"

"Didn't you, or Laura, say that the owner of the sunken ship also owns the land under the ship when it is sunk?"

"Yes, so…"

Coop continued. "What if ownership of the land under the Niantic provided some modern day value or clue which can somehow be tied to the key and the note?"

"You may be onto something, Coop," Jack opined.

"We need to figure out who has the title to the land under the Niantic," commented Coop.

Veronica asked, "What good would that do?"

Coop answered, "I'm not sure, but it's worth investigating as we have nowhere else to turn."

Jack said he had represented a large group of title companies and personally knew the chief legal officer. He could give him a call in an effort to investigate the Niantic title issue further.

"Good idea," nodded Coop.

# CHAPTER TWENTY

On his return to the City, Jack and Coop crossed the Golden Gate and headed toward Crissy Field and then to Lombard Street. He took a right on Gough. "Where did that guy come from?" asked Jack as Coop drove his BMW.

"I saw him start to tail us along Lombard Street," said Coop, referring to a black Range Rover with four guys in it. "Let's have some fun!" Jack grimaced; he rarely enjoyed Coop's wild chases.

Coop swiftly drove up Gough street, took a left onto Broadway and headed across Van Ness into the Broadway tunnel toward Chinatown. The tunnel was clear and Coop gunned the car, doing well over 60 in no time at all. He took a hard right on Powell Street with the tires squealing and raced up to California. He had to be careful of not hitting pedestrians as they were on the edge of Chinatown and there was lots of foot traffic on the cramped streets.

The car tailing them was beginning to drop further behind in traffic and missed a light. Coop took a quick right on California, dodged some people waiting for the cable car, then caught part of a Cable Car track and began to fishtail as he climbed Nob hill to Mason. He corrected the car and in a couple of seconds topped California Street and then took a right turn. He was off to the races: telling Jack to "Hold on!" Coop blasted between the Fairmont Hotel on the right and the PU Club on the left. The car became airborne in front of Tom and Esty's apartment building where Mason Street dropped precipitously toward the Bay and Coop said calmly, "Remember *Bullet* with Steve McQueen? Yahoo!" Jack held tight to the grab handle next to his head. Coop hit Union Street, turned hard left and made another left on Gough and pulled into Jack's apartment garage at Green and Gough. The Range Rover was nowhere to be found as the garage door closed and Jack let out a deep sigh.

Breathless, Jack whispered , "That was quite a ride, Partner. Where did you learn to drive like that?"

Coop laughed. "Instincts, Buddy, instincts."

# CHAPTER TWENTY ONE

"Peter, it's Jack Armstrong," Jack said on the phone.
"Hi, Jack, how have you been?"
"Terrific. You?"

Peter Windsor was the Chief Legal Officer for Universal Financial, the country's largest group of title companies and a former client of Jack's. Jack wanted to learn if Peter could help him by tracing titles to the owner of the ground underneath the Niantic. Hopefully, this would provide a lead to where Veronica's treasure was hidden. "Peter, I need a favor."

"So what else is new?" Peter asked sarcastically.

"Hopefully this will not be too much of a lift. Can you tell me if land title records in California go back to the 1850's?"

Peter thought for a moment, then said, "Yes, I think they do. In fact, that is just about the time that land title records began to be recognized in California as I recall."

"Good, let's get together, and I can brief you. And, hopefully you can fill me in on some California land title history," suggested Jack. "How about lunch at Tadich's Grill at 11:30am tomorrow? Lunch, of course, is on me." Jack knew that if you weren't early for lunch at the popular San Francisco restaurant, you didn't get a seat until after 1:30 pm. Also, he knew one of the waiters and could arrange for a booth with curtains to give them some privacy.

Jack spent the next morning doing research on California land title history. Since he didn't have to be at the restaurant until 11:30 am, he decided to walk the two miles from his

96

apartment in Cow Hollow to Tadich Grill, which would give him plenty of time to think about the case. He liked the route along Green Street over Russian Hill to Columbus Avenue. As he hiked over Russian Hill he recalled its founding in honor of Russian sailors who died while working the Gold Rush and were buried in a small cemetery there, long since removed. The walk also gave Jack a chance to glance left toward Lombard Street, the crookedest street in the world, as some say, with eight sharp turns in one block. And, of course, the views of the Bay were truly spectacular. With its blue water and crystal clear sky, he felt that he could reach out and touch the Bay.

He brought his mind back to focus on the case and was hopeful that tracing title to the land under the Niantic would help lead to Veronica's treasure, but he also needed time to process Max's involvement in the matter. Max seemed to be taking the treasure hunt much more seriously than the nebulous target (an unidentified treasure) called for: having one of his men follow Veronica to Laura's apartment in Berkeley, warning Jack to stay away from the case with the note on the windshield of Coop's car, possibly knocking him off his bike on a ride near the Golden Gate and having four of Max's goons chase him and Coop through the streets of San Francisco. By now, Max had to know that Jack was not backing off. What was his next play? Jack appreciated having Coop as his partner. His cleverness in IDing the peeper at Laura's apartment, "hiding" Veronica at his parent's home in Sonoma, tying the treasure to the land under the sunken Niantic, and his skill at dodging the Russian goons chasing them, was masterful! If this thing ever paid off, he would have to remember a nice bonus for him.

# CHAPTER TWENTY TWO

Jack checked in with the head server, Sam. "Sam, how are you? It's been a while. Doing well?"

Sam, easily past retirement age but still fall of spark, patted Jack on the shoulder. "Great to see you, Jack. The usual spot?"

Jack nodded and smiled. "You always treat me well, Sam."

Jack mentioned he was waiting for one more. Sam assured him that he would be seated even though his guest had not arrived, a violation of the House Rules, and something that rarely happened at Tadich. It was one of San Francisco's longest continually running restaurants, having opened around 1850 as a coffee house. Specializing in fresh seafood, the cooks started cooking on a mesquite broiler in the 1920s and offered a little of everything for everyone, even ham and eggs. Its Art Deco interior design and casual feel gave the restaurant an authentic look that Jack liked. Sam led Jack to one of eight private booths, showed him in and closed the curtain over the doorway. Jack had a moment to check his iPhone for messages and seeing nothing important, closed the phone and placed it on the table, face down. Peter Windsor walked in.

"Hi Peter," said Jack.

"Great to see you," responded Peter as they shook hands. Peter and Jack had met in law school at Berkeley. They were in the same class. After law school, Peter went in-house corporate while Jack went private. They both were successful in their chosen professions as attorneys. Peter had climbed the corporate ladder and became Chief Legal Officer of a Fortune

500 company which was listed on the NYSE. If there was an issue regarding land title, Peter was the person with whom to consult. And, he hired Jack when he needed extra assistance with a unique legal problem.

While Peter loved living in San Francisco with his wife and kids, his dream was to retire eventually and buy a home on the hills overlooking the Santa Barbara Channel. He was also a fabulous violinist and his father had been the concertmaster of a European orchestra. Jack would put the two music lovers together: Peter and Coop, except he knew that they would clash. Peter would say opera, Coop's passion, was nice but for the "singing that got in the way of the music."

Jack ordered his favorite, Petrale Sole meunière, and Peter ordered a grilled salmon. They decided to share some steamed spinach and a few french fries as part of a "well balanced" diet. Jack stuck to an iced tea and Peter had a diet coke. Before they were served their entrees, Sam brought some of San Francisco's famous sourdough bread and butter. They each helped themselves to a couple of pieces. Jack was pleased that he had walked from his apartment and worked up a bit of an appetite.

"So, what's up," Peter asked. Jack related the story about the ownership of land under the ships found near the Financial District. He gave Peter the coordinates for the Niantic and asked if there was a way to trace the title to the land under the ship.

Peter had done some research after Jack's call that morning and was able to share that California adopted a recording system for land titles in 1850. As well intentioned as the recording system was envisioned, it was overwhelmed by the crush of people and conveyances surrounding the Gold Rush. The average person in San Francisco at that time was uneducated in the elements of common law conveyances and could not make use of the San Francisco Recorder's Office. Thus, a cottage industry evolved with conveyancers, abstractors, real estate attorneys and land use experts who would furnish "certificates of title" and in time, companies that insured land titles.

Peter showed Jack several advertisements for real estate conveyance and title services from the early 1850's that the California Land Title Association had accumulated. These services often relied on "abstractors" to assemble title information that was used by real estate attorneys in their written opinions upon which the conveyance or transfer of title was made. Often the abstractors had their own libraries of title information on large blocks of real estate from which they would create an abstract of title for a particular property. The abstracts of title, explained Peter, were the histories of title for a property. The abstracts of title which served as the basis for a title search and a certificate of title were often voluminous: for example, an abstract of title for the City of San Jose was contained in 37 large volumes.

"Whoa!" exclaimed Jack. "Are you telling me there may be multiple volumes describing the transfer and conveyance of title and title related information contained in abstracts of title for the San Francisco waterfront?"

"Yes," said Peter. "In fact, knowing your general interest, I ordered from the Universal Financial Records Department an abstract of title beginning in 1850 for the San Francisco Waterfront. That should include the Niantic land and any conveyance of the title thereof. I should have the volumes related to the Niantic abstract by tomorrow afternoon. You can stop by my office and we can examine what is reported."

"That would be terrific, Peter. Thanks. Hopefully, this will lead to something concrete in our search.. If it's OK with you, I will stop by your office tomorrow afternoon and take a look."

Armed with this new information and hope for a substantive clue, Jack enjoyed the walk back to his apartment.

Coop slowly followed behind Jack in his BMW, making sure he returned home safely. These Russians were beginning to worry him.

# CHAPTER TWENTY THREE

Upon returning to his apartment, Jack decided he would say "hi" to Sara if she was in, and knocked on the door to her apartment. She opened and smiled broadly when she saw him. He returned the smile and invited her for a cup of coffee and a chance to catch up since their recent date. Charlotte was wagging her tail madly and hopped on the sofa when Sara told her to stay and closed the door.

They took their usual table at the Blue Fog Café, and Jack ordered a latte for Sara and a black coffee for himself, the usual. Sara asked how the case was proceeding and Jack told her there were some recent developments which looked promising but did not elaborate out of respect for client confidentiality. Sara said she understood.

"Jack, do you like to travel?"

"Sure, I've traveled extensively throughout the country and internationally."

"What's your favorite city?"

"Other than San Francisco, it would have to be New York and London, Paris, or Rome. New York is so vibrant," explained Jack. "The restaurants, museums, Broadway, Wall Street: the action in that city explodes! London's a totally different scene with its history, people, arts, theater and literature and who doesn't love the Pomp and Circumstance!"

And Jack related the time he was in Rome at the Piazza de Ricci where he had lunch al fresco and, at the table next to his, was the president of Ferrari with his family.

"How cool is that?" asked Jack rhetorically. "Incidentally," he added, "The Ferrari president and his family when finished with their mid-afternoon lunch departed on bicycles! "

"Wow, you *have* been around."

"What about you? Any special places you like?"

"I've been in Paris with my sister once and would love to return. London was so fun. I was a student there for a year. Locally, I lived in Westwood while I was attending UCLA. After school I moved to a spot in Santa Monica. I had a one bedroom apartment overlooking the Santa Monica Canyon and Will Rogers' State Beach on Ocean Avenue Extension. I was told F. Scott Fitzgerald lived next door to my apartment from 1937 to 1940. I used to imagine his ghost as I attempted to write my first play."

"What made you leave?"

"I just thought a change was needed. So I moved here."

Jack wondered if there was something else. "Has the move been worth it, Sara?"

"It's working just fine. I like The City: sights, weather, people, restaurants and vibe. I'm enjoying our new friendship," she said shyly with a sudden rosy cheek.

"Ditto," Jack said as he squeezed her hand.

Jack suggested they continue their conversation over dinner that evening and Sara agreed.

# CHAPTER TWENTY FOUR

"Three volumes, Peter?" Jack asked when Peter presented him with the title record volumes in his office, located in the fashionable Salesforce Tower.

"We have three volumes of Abstracts of Title for San Francisco Waterfront beginning in 1850." Peter showed Jack to a nearby conference room where he could quietly and privately review the title books.

"Let's take a look," Jack said to himself.

He began thumbing through a thousand pages of title records and noted how detailed the descriptions of title transfer were. This seemed unusual. Not only did the records disclose the address of the property, or the approximate address if a formal address had not been established, but the record also included a detailed description of the way title was transferred. Approximate addresses included mention of how many feet and in what direction the property was located from another parcel which bore an exact address. For example, 157 feet from the Western boundary of the property located at 343 Sansome Street, thereafter extending 200 feet South so as to complete a rectangle.

Jack drew on his former legal expertise and was able to follow the history of a property from its current location through years of prior ownership and conveyances. He started with the buildings on Clay and Sansome streets and followed building conveyances back in time until he noticed a reference to "the ground under a ship named Niantic." Jack thought he had hit gold. The reference directed him to an Appendix

104

for further information. There he traced the reference noted and was astonished to find a detailed description of how the ground under the Niantic was transferred.

Abstract of Title, Volume 49, San Francisco Waterfront, Appendix, page 337:

The Niantic ground was established in 1850 when the ship Niantic had run aground and land was filled around her. The vessel was converted from a ship into a warehouse and saloon. In 1857 the grounded ship was transformed into a hotel which some said was the finest hotel in San Francisco.

In 1864, the Niantic hotel and the ground upon which it sat, became the subject of a poker game which resulted in its conveyance. The poker game was attended by someone calling himself a member of The Associates together with individuals named: James Flood, Samuel Clements, Samuel Brannan, John Sutter, Graham Stackhouse and a Civil War General.

Jack's heart skipped a beat upon reading the name Graham Stackhouse. He was there, and he had a connection to the Niantic!! Jack had tracked him down and began to breathe a sigh of relief. So this was the famed poker game where the treasure was presumably created. *What was the treasure and who were "The Associates?"* Jack wondered. Was this Flood and Brannan from the San Francisco history books? How was Sutter involved? Is Samuel Clemens, THE Samuel Clemens/ Mark Twain and, if so, what was he doing there? Who is the Civil War General? How does this poker game lead to Veronica's treasure? Jack had to meet with Laura right away.

"Peter, the information you provided is very important and helpful. Can I trouble you for a copy?" asked Jack as he headed to Berkeley and a meeting over coffee with Laura.

"Laura, how are you? Everything ok?" Jack said while ordering a cup of coffee for Laura and himself.

"What now, Jack?" Laura sounded a bit irritated.

"Ok, sorry I haven't been in touch. But, you won't believe this as he began to brief her. "Picture the 1860s in San Francisco. Is it possible that Mark Twain visited?"

"I thought you knew your San Francisco history," Laura retorted. "Mark Twain, aka Samuel Clements, visited San Francisco several times during the 1850's and 1860's. He also lived and worked in Virginia City, while he was employed by the Territorial Enterprise as the paper's City Editor. *Roughing It* chronicles his adventures in the West. "

"Ok, fair enough. It's been a little while since I took California history in grade school. How about James Flood?"

"Flood was one of the Silver Kings who struck it rich, discovering the Silver Bonanza 1200 feet deep in the Consolidated Virginia Silver Mine, a part of the Comstock Lode under the streets of Virginia City," explained Laura. "Some estimate the value of the Bonanza to be over $300,000,000 in 1870 dollars and likely worth over $500 Billion in today's dollars. Flood was joined by his San Francisco stock brokerage partner, William O'Brien, and two other men: John MacKay and James Fair. MacKay was a miner through and through, hard work and fair play. One might say he was 'a man for all seasons', and he became one of the richest men in the world at that time. Fair was a very pleasant man whose daughters built a hotel atop Nob Hill in his name: The Fairmont Hotel. To this day it has breathtaking views of San Francisco and The Bay, as you well know.

"The four were known as the Silver Kings and very wealthy, even by today's standards. The Flood building, on Market Street, was built as a tribute to the life of James Flood by his son after the turn of the century, and the PU Club on Nob Hill was once his residence."

"And who were The Associates?"

Laura continued with pleasant confidence. "They called themselves 'The Associates' and together were publicly recognized as The Big Four: Leland Stanford, Collis P. Huntington, Charles Crocker and Mark Hopkins. They built the Transcontinental Railroad. From Sacramento to Omaha, Nebraska, the railroad was built in fewer than eight years and completed in 1869 by driving the Golden Spike at Promontory Point, Utah.

"As you know, Huntington and Hopkins have hotels on Nob Hill named after them and Crocker was known for a well recognized bank. CP Huntington was also known for his poker games, one of which resulted in General Patton's father winning the Patton estate in San Marino, near the Huntington Library, Art Museum and Botanical Garden."

Jack paused, letting Laura's extensive commentary sink in. He also asked if she wished for more coffee or a bite to eat.

"No thanks." She continued: "The Big Four's completion of the Transcontinental Railroad enabled travelers to reach San Francisco in eight days, not months, by covered wagon or by ship around The Horn or through the Isthmus of Panama.

To gain some perspective, Jack, the attraction of gold and the means to reach San Francisco in a few days created an economic explosion for the state which has never stopped."

"Bear with me a bit more. How about a fellow by the name of Samuel Brannan?"

"Samuel Brannan, after whom a street in San Francisco is named," Laura offered, "was a prominent businessman who made his money during the Gold Rush selling products and provisions to the Gold Rush miners rather than mining for gold himself. He owned one of the first hardware stores between San Francisco and the gold fields. His shrewd business dealings in San Francisco and Sacramento caused him to become California's first millionaire without mining an ounce of the yellow metal."

"Laura, my word, how do you know all this?" asked Jack.

"I'm a Professor of California history at UC Berkeley: enough said!"

"Point taken! And John Sutter. What can be said about him?"

"Sutter's remembered most," she said, "because of the discovery of gold at his mill in Coloma in 1848 which kicked off the Gold Rush. He was also noted for building a fort in New Helvetia, now known as Sacramento, trading with the Russians over the purchase of Fort Ross."

"Now I may have a real riddle for you ... Can you guess who the unnamed Civil War General was?"

"Give me a minute to think, Jack. The only Civil War General who had connections to San Francisco was none other than Ulysses S. Grant. He was ordered to California at the time of the Gold Rush to help with law and order. The Civil War broke out in 1861 and ended with Grant defeating Lee in 1865."

"I'm trying to figure out what these people and Veronica's inheritance have in common," said Jack, confounded. "Still, it amazes me how all of these historically prominent persons, including Mark Twain, could have been in San Francisco at the same time and participated in an 1860's poker game."

"Each of them was in San Francisco at about the time of the poker game. Remember, Jack, the Gold Rush was the most significant financial event in U.S. history at that time. It attracted many prominent people as you are discovering. Perhaps it is not their presence at the same meeting but what transpired at that poker game which will be significant," Laura speculated.

Jack returned to the copy of the Abstract Appendix from which he had been reading. After mentioning the participants at the poker game, the Abstract noted Graham Stackhouse won a very large "pot" containing various railroad and silver mine shares and bonds together with stocks and bonds of related entities and, of course, a sizable amount of gold coin.

*All together, the Stackhouse winnings had to be worth millions even in 1860-dollars,* Jack thought. *Was this the object of Veronica's inheritance and the Russians' interest?*

*Wouldn't it be interesting to be a fly on the wall at that poker game?*

# CHAPTER TWENTY FIVE

With Veronica safely housed in Sonoma at Coop's parents home, Jack wanted to investigate a gnawing feeling he had: something wasn't right about Sidney. Immediately after Veronica's departure from Sidney's Stinson Beach home, Max and his Russian goons were all over him and Coop. They even seemed to be one step ahead of their moves. What role did Sidney play? Jack had to find out.

He stood outside the grand entrance of Sidney's home in Stinson Beach which was easy to find based on Veronica's description. *A classy joint,* thought Jack. *Let's see if its owner matches the house.*

Jack rang the bell and peered through the window. No movement. Maybe she was out. He decided to walk around the side of the house and peer over the fence. He saw a woman in a bathing suit, lying topless on a chaise lounge and talking on a cell phone. He strained to hear, but no luck.

He moved into her sightline. He knew he was crossing a line and that she had no obligation to speak with him, but he decided to give it a shot.

"Excuse me, sorry to bother you."

The woman looked over at him, said something into the phone, then laid it down. She pulled a light robe over her shoulders and walked toward the fence.

"Should I call the cops?" she drawled sardonically. "Or, perhaps you are the cops. Either way, unless you have a piece of paper proving you need to be here, I'm busy." She turned

110

and walked back to the chaise lounge. Her figure was tight and she allowed her sumptuous breasts to be visible with her robe pulled only slightly in at the waist. Her eyes were a striking blue which stood out with her copper colored locks.

*That was quite a show,* Jack thought. *I wonder if she did that on purpose? Carefully styled and curated. It takes money to keep that up.*

He was surprised this was Veronica's supposed "best friend."

"I'm sorry to stop by unannounced. Jack Armstrong, a friend of Veronica's. I was hoping I could ask you a couple of questions."

Sidney walked back to the fence and unlocked a gate. "Come on in. Veronica never mentioned you'd be here and some people tend to peek into the property as if it's a tourist destination. But, please come in. Nice to finally meet you. Veronica's said great things about you and how much you're helping her. May I offer you a drink?"

"Some water would be great," he said with a slight smile.

"Give me a minute, I'll be right back. Sidney slipped inside the house and returned wearing a light cotton mini dress, her tanned legs exposed including a tattoo on her inner thigh with a word he couldn't decipher. She handed him a beautiful etched crystal glass filled with water.

"How can I help you? Anything for my lovely Veronica."

Jack spoke slowly and to the point. "I was just wondering if you had any thoughts on what's been happening to Veronica of late. She must have spoken to you, of course."

"Poor dear. She's been having a rough time, to say the least,"

Sidney stood facing the lagoon. "Isn't the sun gorgeous this time of day? Scintillating sun sparkling over the water before it heads down to the horizon. That is my absolute favorite hour… And, you've arrived just in time to see it. The best way to watch is with a cocktail in hand. I make the absolute best Greyhound; Titos and sparkling grapefruit juice over ice with a squeeze of fresh grapefruit. May I fix you one?"

"Thanks, that sounds great, but only a quick one. I have a dinner appointment to get to."

Sidney slipped back inside. He took in the beautiful view of the lagoon, the dock and surrounding hills, which the floor-to-ceiling windows featured. As the home faced East with a view across the lagoon, he imagined the sunrise was spectacular, rising slowly over the mountains and flooding the lagoon and Sidney's home with fresh morning sunlight.

Sidney was back with his drink and one for herself. "Tell me how I can help you."

Jack would have to be careful here. "You've known Veronica and her husband, Max, for some years, right?"

Sidney nodded and looked at Jack.

"What do you make of her problem?"

Sidney responded "Problem?"

"Yes," said Jack.

"Do you mean her divorce from Max, or her inheritance?" she asked.

"I guess both. Veronica seems worried about things. Do you think she has anything to worry about?"

"A divorce is never anything to take lightly. Goodness, most of us have been through one. It's not fun, but there's almost always light at the end of the tunnel. And Max is not really a bad guy'... it's complicated."

"Yours and Veronica's impression of Max seems to differ, Sidney. Why do you think he is not so bad.?"

"I just tend to not let things throw me like she does. He seemed to care for her and was concerned when she went missing. He called here looking for her," she offered.

"He seems to have some questionable alliances, wouldn't you say?" asked Jack.

"I think that was long ago. From what I can see, he's just a determined businessman." Sidney stood up. "It's getting chilly. Do you mind if we move into the house?"

Inside, Jack looked around. *The home was a bit over the top for a beach house,* Jack thought. Some high end sofas resembling what he had pre-divorce.

"You have a gorgeous home. You're an accomplished decorator. Great style," commented Jack.

"Thank you," Sidney responded proudly.

"May I borrow your restroom?" Jack asked as Sidney sat down on the sofa.

"Of course, it's right down the hall."

Jack walked down the hall towards the bathroom and quickly peered into Sidney's bedroom. He noticed on the nightstand next to the bed some photos in addition to books. One caught his eye. It was a photo of Sidney, maybe a few years back, on the beach with a man next to her. He'd seen a picture of Max from some online photos soon after Veronica first came to see him. Was this Max Hill? They were holding hands.

Jack quickly returned to the living room. "Why don't you

113

sit for a minute while I get us a refill?" Sidney asked with a melodic tone.

*Tempting*, Jack thought. "I'm good with one for now."

Sidney smiled. "I'll be right back. I never like just one of these concoctions." She moved into the kitchen and grabbed her phone and began texting Max. "Armstrong is here nosing around."

Within an instant, Max responded. "Get rid of him!"

She walked back to Jack who was sitting on the sofa.

He looked up at Sidney. She sure was a knockout. "What do you understand about her inheritance? Can you shed some light on the mystery?"

"You mean the key and the note?"

"Exactly," said Jack.

"I expect there may be a significant treasure to be discovered, Jack."

"What makes you think that?"

"Why wouldn't a key connected to a gold rush ship in San Francisco Bay not bear the possibility of significant treasure? At least, I hope so for sweet Veronica's sake."

*I hope so too*, thought Jack. "Please excuse me, I have another appointment I have to get to. It's been nice meeting you, and thank you for your hospitality."

"Before you leave, where is my Veronica and when will I see her again?"

"She's staying with some friends across the Bay. I expect you'll see her soon," replied Jack.

As Jack drove away from Stinson Beach, he thought about the meeting with Sidney. He picked up his phone and dialed

Veronica. He was pleased she picked up on the first ring. He asked her what she had told Sidney about the key, the note, and the treasure.

"Nothing really."

"Nothing? She just told me you were pursuing significant treasure involving a key and a gold rush ship in San Francisco Bay. She must have learned it from someone."

"I guess I did share with her a little bit about the gold rush ship and the key," Veronica explained. "It was so interesting. But on the other hand, I find it odd you would go to see her. You could have warned me. She's my friend and I don't like the idea."

"My job is to get your problem solved, Veronica. She didn't seem alarmed at all. In fact, she was quite calm. An interesting friend for you to have, by the way." Jack paused to allow Veronica a moment. There was silence on the other end. "Please keep what we discuss confidential, even with a supposed trusted friend. It would be unfortunate if she accidentally mentioned any details to other parties, if you know what I mean."

"You mean Max, don't you?" Veronica's voice sounded strained.

"Yes, we're trying to keep your inheritance safe for you, not anyone else. If Max and his Russian friends were involved, it could sabotage any progress we might be making. You mentioned Max had been in contact with her. And we have had a few incidents that are coincidental with Russians."

"You're right, Jack. Sorry," she responded.

"Also, I found it curious to see a picture at her beach house showing someone who may be Max with Sidney, holding hands."

"What?" said a startled Veronica. "This is outlandish—she's my best friend and you're suggesting Sidney may be involved with Max?"

"I saw the photo. Max is on to us. Either Sidney gained information about our treasure hunt from Max or from you, or both of you. In either case, it's not good," stressed Jack.

"Furthermore," Jack continued, "Coop and I have had to dodge some of Max's Russian cohorts on several occasions. I'm not trying to scare you, but you need to know this is getting dicey. It's probably best we keep information between ourselves from now on. If they do have something between them, it's best you don't let on. I know your ego may be bruised and you may feel betrayed, but you're finished with that guy. He's a bad apple, Veronica, and you're better off without him. And, maybe Sidney isn't all she's cracked up to be. But keep up the appearance of friendship for now. Just keep in mind whatever you tell Sidney's likely to get to Max and his Russian friends."

Shaken, Veronica agreed.

Jack proceeded to describe what he had found in the abstract of the title involving the Niantic, the sizable winnings at the poker game and the need to investigate further what transpired at that game. He asked Veronica if she could provide him with more information. She said through the years there had been mention of the poker game, and reference had been made to some "celebrity" attendees at the time: people of character, wealth and uniqueness. She could not recall the names of the attendees other than Graham Stackhouse.

She'd speculated that relatives had not pursued the key

and it's implications due to their lack of resources. Given their progress made and effort expended, who would disagree?

Jack asked if any of the following names registered in her mind: James Flood, CP Huntington, Samuel Brannan, John Sutter, General Grant, or Samuel Clemens, aka Mark Twain?

Veronica thought quietly for several moments and responded:

"I do remember Mark Twain, as I am sure many do. He was a great author. I'm told Graham Stackhouse had once met him. The other names are unfamiliar to me, Jack, except perhaps General Grant. Wasn't he a Civil War General?"

Then she interrupted herself and exclaimed:

"Wait a minute! There exists a description of that very poker game in an old newspaper clipping that Graham Stackhouse left behind. I saw it with some of the items I inherited. Would that be helpful?"

"You bet," Jack exclaimed. "Send a copy to me."

"Consider it done," she responded.

Jack headed back to The City.

# CHAPTER TWENTY SIX

Returning from Stinson Beach, as he crossed the Golden Gate Bridge, he gave Sara a call.

"I would love it, Jack," said Sara in response to his request for dinner. "Where should we go?"

"How about my place 8 pm? I'll fix dinner for you!"

"That would be special."

Jack had to hurry and do some shopping for dinner. He went to the Marina Safeway (the popular singles grocery store), to pick out a couple of halibut fillets, capers, lemons, butter, parsley, potatoes, sour cream, bacon bits, lettuce, caesar dressing, croutons, several chocolate chip cookies and some Frank Family California Chardonnay. He had in mind a New York Times recipe he'd seen and saved.

Shopping done, he rushed back to his apartment to tidy things up, set the table, take a quick shower, cook dinner and light the candles: just in time for the doorbell to ring.

"Hi, Sara," he welcomed her.

"Hi Stranger," she responded while stepping inside and giving him a nice kiss on the lips. "Long time, no see," she said.

"I know. Unfortunately, I've been traveling throughout the state and this case has consumed me."

"You making progress?"

"Yes," he answered and proceeded to give her a brief overview of the progress that'd been made since they last met.

"What are the next steps, Jack? Do you think you're getting close to solving the treasure mystery?"

"I do, but this happened so long ago with plenty of time for events to intercede, that there is no assurance it will ultimately be worthwhile. And it's possible there is more to the story that meets the eye."

"What do you mean?"

"Not sure, but we've had some interference and it's a bit perplexing."

"If anyone can figure it out, I think that guy is called Jack."

Let's have a glass of wine and some dinner." Jack put on some Chris Botti music to accompany them while they had a drink.

The next morning, as Jack rolled away from Sara and exited bed, he checked his email.

Veronica had sent the information containing the news clipping about the poker game. He made some coffee in the kitchen and began reading. His excitement grew as he immediately saw it would be very helpful in identifying, and hopefully even locating, the treasure.

The piece was entitled,

### EUREKA! THE POKER GAME
by Mark Twain (*Territorial Enterprise*, 1864)

Does one ever imagine how Archimedes, the famous Greek mathematician, physicist, engineer, investor and astronomer, felt when he shouted 'Eureka!' before Christ was even yet born? And what was it that gave way to this spontaneous exclamation? My gentle readers, the mere discovery of a test for gold based on its buoyancy. If that was a Eureka moment and, admittedly, the first ever recorded, did Archimedes think there would be other Eureka moments? How about the discovery of gold at Sutter's mill, or discovery of silver in the Comstock Lode, or the striking of the Golden Spike at Promontory Point, Utah? Surely, these must have been Eureka moments. Since all occurred during a short span of my life time, I set out to capture the Eureka of these Eureka moments and any others, the what-fors and whys as well, and perhaps the who contributing to their moment.

A poker game can be exciting or boring depending on one's perspective: will I win a lot, or lose a lot? Why don't the cards favor me this time? Talk to me cards, one might say, encouragingly. If I just keep playing, luck *will* surely return!

But it's the people at the table who attract me most, I have to admit. Who are they? What have they done with their lives? Why are they here? What do they hope to accomplish? What impact will they have on this world, country, state or city? And did they experience Eureka moments like Archimedes thousands of years ago?

I've roughed it across this country and written about it: riding with Mormons to the Great Salt Lake. Visiting that glorious city called Virginia City, Nevada. Mining the Comstock and exploring miles of tunnels beneath the Virginia City streets, all while pretending to be the City Editor of the Territorial Enterprise. Don't tell my friend Dan DeQuille though, who apparently felt he needed to rename himself so he could write. Additionally, I experimented with figuring how a frog jumped in Calaveras County (was it noise, the sudden startle, or a pin pokin' its rear that caused that frog to jump the farthest: to think like a frog is to act like a frog...).

What better way to learn about those who unearth things than to participate in a good ole fashioned San Francisco poker game, where the movers and shakers of our world attend.

The game transpired at a saloon called the Auction Lunch, owned by the honorable James Flood and the impeccable Charles O'Brien, located at 509 Washington Street in San Francisco, a few doors West of Sansome. It was advantageously located next the Washington Market, the city's most popular produce market and near the newly established San Francisco Mining and Stock Exchange.

Besides the fabulous and minted new location right on one of the city's busiest blocks, it was situated for the very convenience of those exchanging in the mines, or at least shares of their stock.

(Jack thought for a moment and recognized the Auction Lunch address as being near where today's Transamerica Pyramid Building is located.)

The Auction Lunch Saloon provided customers with food along with their two bit drink. Nothing like a free lunch counter to entice the hungry and the thirsty. A slice of roast beef, corned beef, ham— always well received I might add. And why not: it was free (additional purchase of drink the prerequisite, of course).

A senior Chinese, Wong Lee, mastered the slicing knife with expertise and even entertainment, while O'Brien acted as host to incoming patrons; Flood established himself behind the bar to pour appropriate amounts of alcohol on to the masses. (Uniquely, Mr.

Flood was noted for wearing a traditional gray business suit, of impeccable material and natural fit, even for one who worked behind the bar.)

Around the table sat John Sutter, Samuel Brannan, CP Huntington, James Flood, Graham Stackhouse and me, your trusty journalist: the one who learns by inconspicuous observation. Also buzzing around the poker room was the ever present barfly: a true source of distraction and sometimes irritation. Further, and more to the point, I suppose, is to observe whose head the fly will land upon and dispense its "bad luck": for it is the fly who knows and the journalist who is well advised to heed the insect's progress round the room!

"Who are these characters?" I asked myself. Usually I'm a good judge, I do believe, but in this case, not as easy as some. Simply put, they included : the man upon whose property the Gold Rush started; California's first millionaire who found wealth by selling provisions to miners, not mining himself mind you; the leader of the Transcontinental Railroad and one of the Big Four; a partner in several Comstock mines and of the Silver Kings; a professional gambler, and moi, City Editor of the largely unread, *Virginia City Territorial Enterprise.* (By the way, thank you, dear reader...)

What an odd lot. Well, I thought: there are many paths to the top of the mountain! And, as I have said: The two most important days in your life are the day you are born and the day you find out why. Let's find out why these gentlemen were born shall we?

To be a bit more precise and with respect to each of the culprits, I mean players, there was John Sutter, a man of many countries. Born in Germany, claiming to be Swiss (and even labeling himself improperly Captain of the Swiss Guard), a Mexican citizen allowed him by the Mexican Governor, Juan Batista Alvarado, nearly 50,000 acres of land in the center of California astride the Sacramento River, enabling him to build New Helvetia, or, New Switzerland. A Francophile, Sutter threatened to raise the French flag over California and place New Helvetia under French protection. During the Mexican-American war, Sutter supported establishment of an independent California Republic, but when General Fremont seized control of his fort, he did not resist.

Some classify CP Huntington (and his Big Four) as a Robber Baron. Did they rob anyone? Just because they arranged millions of dollars in state grants for the construction of the Transcontinental Railroad during a period when their President, Leland Stanford, was also Governor of California, did that make them Robbers? Be honest now,: tell me the truth!

Or, was anyone hurt simply because they cleverly formed the Pacific Association and used their combined assets to bribe Congressmen to obtain nine million acres and a $24 million loan financed by Federal bonds?

As to the Barons, part of the allegation was that they were anointed as if Royals by family name? If not a Robber Baron, then what were they?

One could say the Big Four were men who got their way. And one could say each was a 'nabob'. A person of prominence and wealth who lived on Nob Hill.

(*Is that where the name originated*? thought Jack.)

The big four consisted of: Hopkins (of hotel fame) Crocker (of banking fame) Huntington (of railroad fame) and Sanford (of Governor standing).

(Jack mentally added to Stanford's attributes the fact that later in life he was the founder of the Cal Bears rival: Leland Stanford "Junior" University, which was named after Stanford's son.)

Another of the Nob Hill gang was one James Flood. Flood, of the Silver or Bonanza Kings of the Virginia City Comstock Lode, investor in several mines. After graduating from saloon keeper with his partner William O'Brien, the two joined James Fair and John Mackay to capture silver mining treasure in Virginia City. Since they had the vision of establishing their San Francisco saloon near the Mining and Stock Exchange, why wouldn't they possess the foresight to find silver buried in a mine under the streets of Virginia City?

As we like to say: "There are many paths to the top of the mountain," even when one is "down a mineshaft!"

Samuel Brannan, on the other hand, sailed into Yerba Buena with a sizable group of Mormons who quickly outnumbered others residing in the small society of San Francisco. Promptly, off he went to Sutter's Fort in Sacramento, excuse me: New Helvetia, and opened a hardware store. He would buy any and all picks, shovels and pans in San Francisco for 20 cents and sell them for $15 a-piece at Sutter's Fort. In nine weeks, he made $35,000!

As the meagerly paid servant of the *Territorial Enterprise*, $35,000 a week sounds rather nice, I might add. Yes, yes indeed.

Lastly, this odd fellow named Graham Stackhouse. This professional gambler 'earned a living' at San Francisco's poker tables. Little is known about him but he was truthful, contributed titles to the land and holdings atop the land occupied by the Niantic, which included a fashionable hotel (the Best in San Francisco) which he'd won in, you guessed it, a poker game!

Strangely enough, none of the three prominent business men (Huntington, Brannan, Flood) made any money mining gold! Nor did Stackhouse. And the one who did (Sutter): went broke. So much for wealth through the Gold Rush.

So it was that the six of us, as sadly described, sat to play a friendly game of poker. Why do people insist poker is a friendly game? Losing is never friendly and too often too many are losers and only one ends up a winner.

As Brannan began to deal the cards, a loud banging at the door sounded. The waiter attended to the rude knocking and opened the door. In walked a sizable man complete with military uniform. He announced: Room for one more?

Brannan told him to take a seat. Then he asked the intruder to introduce himself. "I'm United States General Ulysses S. Grant, delighted to participate in this game of chance accompanied by a drink or two."

"General, your money's welcome and your service to the Union Army and our great nation is invaluable. Indeed, we have no idea how you have managed, with your important schedule during a civil war, to be in San Francisco. Perhaps you can enlighten us," inquired CP Huntington.

"As you may know," the General announced, "I have a great fondness for San Francisco, having been ordered here during the inception of the Gold Rush to keep a bit of law and order. My return prompted two needs: (1) some R & R as we are on the cusp of defeating the

Confederate rascals, (I thought a short break would benefit me before the final push against the mighty General Lee); and (2) more personally important, I bivouacked my wife and our new baby here and yearn for a quick visit with them."

"Well deserved, General," said CP Huntington, an authoritative and direct businessman, "We wish you everything for which you had hoped. Now, let's play poker, Mr. Brannan."

"Before dealing, Mr. Brannan, I wish to express my heartfelt gratitude to Mr. Flood and his colleagues for their contributions to the Union cause. Without their financial help, we would not have been able to press for victory against those Confederate rascals!"

"Here, here," offered Mr. Sutter to which all hoisted their glass in tribute to General Grant.

"Brannan dealt the cards. After everyone had a chance to examine theirs and mentally establish their value, Brannan opened bidding by offering $5,000 in gold coins. With some optimism, Sutter saw him and upped the ante another $1,000 in gold. Brannan commented, "I see that you are doing quite well, Mr. Sutter."

To which Sutter replied he was "fine, but nothing was the same after the discovery of gold by Marshall at his Mill in Coloma."

"*I can only imagine*, thought Brannan, knowing that he created a mini Gold Rush in San Francisco single-handedly while he ran through the streets yelling "Gold, Gold" at the top of his lungs, waiving a 12 ounce bottle of gold dust.

Those watching and reacting to Brannan's exclamations did not realize Brannan was spiking the need for supplies miners would require and which would make him California's first millionaire! As Brannan said: "Why get one's hands dirty mining when one can get them dirty handling miners' money?"

"So we are off to a roaring start," I exclaimed. (I, of course, a lowly newspaper reporter, simply watched the proceedings and recorded the event, regularly folding my cards after the ante, but reliably cheering the others on.)

"You in, CP?" I asked.

"Yes, of course," Huntington curtly replied glaring at me as if to say 'How dare you question my wealth, intelligence, or courage' and offered six shares of Transcontinental Railroad stock, stating, "I prefer to pay in stock rather than cash, if no one seeks to object," looking at each of us directly with his dark, penetrating stare. Needless to say, no one objected.

"Are you sure those shares are worth $1,000 a piece?" asked Sutter.

"They're worth a lot more than that," said CP. "In a few more years the Transcontinental Railroad will be complete and people will be able to travel coast to coast in eight days, across the country, rather than months, around the horn, or across the Isthmus of Panama. Thousands of travelers will avail themselves of this new convenience. And the effort made to construct one of the world's great wonders, will finally be recognized."

"How is the construction coming along?" asked Stackhouse.

"As you know, the Union Pacific has the longer, but flatter route to take. We in the Central Pacific must bore through Sierra granite, sometimes only making progress of a foot a day. Thankfully, we have thousands of Chinese laborers who work round the clock and risk their lives. So the going is tough, but we have been able to obtain generous government support for our bonds, land grants and the project in general. Mr. Lincoln wants to see this project completed! And fast!" added Huntington.

"I'm in too," said James Flood, offering shares of some mining stock.

"Can you let us know how you value those shares," asked Graham.

"Well, we're currently selling shares at thousands of dollars per foot of mine," responded Flood.

"And how are the market conditions for Comstock Lode stock, Mr. Flood?" asked Mr. Sutter.

"We have our ups and downs in the mining industry," responded Mr. Flood. "I have faith the wealth created by the Comstock Lode will continue for many years to come, Mr. Sutter. So, in my opinion, these shares are equal to $6,000, unless anyone objects."

Each player looked the other in the eye and nodded his head in agreement during this most very friendly game.

Hearing no objection and recognizing everyone had put in the requisite amount, Stackhouse called: showing his full house.

No one came close!

As the game progressed that fly managed to stop on nearly everyone's head except the one possessed and conveniently attached to Graham Stackhouse, as he continued to win!"

Jack noted Twain in his article described the winner's pot as follows:

Thus, in addition to the offered gold, the professional gambler won an untold number of  shares of the Transcontinental Railroad and assorted Comstock Lode mining stock. Winnings of Mr. Stackhouse included: the Virginia & Gold Hill Water Company (which supplied water to Virginia City mills);  the Pacific Mill and Mining Company (which owned and operated the mills that reduced the bonanza ore); and shares in Pacific Wood, Lumber and Flume Company (which held vast holdings of timberland in the Sierra, together with sawmills and flumes to convey wood products down to Carson Valley).

*All together the Stackhouse winnings had to be worth millions, even in dollars of his day, and many times that in today's dollars,* thought Jack.

"As the winner of the pot," Graham asked Flood, the saloon keeper as well as Silver Mine speculator, for a lockable box in which to place his winnings. With little prompting, Flood left the room, then returned an hour later with a strong box he had secured from the nearby Niantic Hotel, together with a key bearing the same name.

Stackhouse thanked Flood for the strongbox, "How fitting," he said, "as I am staying at the Niantic Hotel!" He also thanked the gentlemen for their contributions to his winnings which he gently placed into the strongbox, closing the lid and locking it.

"What will you do with all of it?" I, your reporter, asked.

"I don't know. I sure as hell don't need shares in all these companies. I'm a simple man. Just give me the basics, some meat and potatoes and a nearby poker game," he said.

Stackhouse announced he was headed out of town and asked Sutter and Brannan if he might accompany them while they returned to New Helvetia, to which they agreed. Simultaneously, as City Editor of the *Territorial Enterprise*, I asked whether anyone minded if I tagged along on the way to Virginia City, thinking perhaps to gain more fodder for a subsequent story. Hearing no objection, the group proceeded to gather their belongings and leave San Francisco."

To Be Continued /S/ Mark Twain, August,1864

*Wow*, thought Jack. *What a revelation and how cleverly written by Mark Twain to provide real insight into the rich and powerful of the time.*

# CHAPTER TWENTY SEVEN

"So we know that Graham Stackhouse left the San Francisco poker game with sizable winnings, including shares of some potentially valuable mines and some gold. All was placed in a strongbox labeled Niantic and locked presumably with the key that Veronica possesses. He expressed little interest in spending the winnings and headed off to New Helvetia with Sutter, Brannan and Mark Twain," Jack summarized for Coop's benefit.

"Perhaps we should saddle up," said Coop "and head to Sacramento, or should I say, New Helvetia."

"I agree. Let's ask Laura to join us: she can act as a tour and history guide—we will no doubt need her historical assistance in locating the strongbox. Why don't you slide by in your well equipped BMW and pick me up at my apartment. Then we can head over the bridge to Berkeley and pick up Laura?"

"Good idea," Coop agreed as he called Veronica and promised her he would return and that she would be safe at his parent's home in his absence. She expressed her agreement and, not visible to Coop, she shed a tear envisioning their departure.

The ride East along Interstate 80 toward Sacramento was easy, traversing part of California's Central Valley rich in farm land. About 30 miles from Sutter's Fort, Laura noted the University of California at Davis, which geographically is the largest of the University's campuses, noted for its veterinary and viticulture schools. As if proving the latter point, Laura noted the Mondavi Center near Interstate 80 on the UCD campus which is famous for the Mondavi wines of Napa.

As Coop drove, Jack mentioned they had picked up a tail by a motorcycle.

"Are you sure, Jack?"

"Yeah, let's see if we can shake him on the Yolo Causeway. Laura, tighten that seatbelt."

Laura nodded nervously. Coop gunned the car to 100 mph. The motorcycle kept pace while weaving through traffic. Once on the Causeway, the motorcycle began closing the gap.

Jack asked Coop if he had a plan in mind. "Of course," he responded. "This guy will expect us to stay on 80 but I have another idea."

Just as the motorcyclist pulled up along the left side of the car, Coop exited 80 to the right onto Highway 275 at 110 mph! At that speed, the motorcyclist had already committed to heading straight along 80 and couldn't recover in time. Off he went, flying up 80 while Coop waved goodbye.

"Nice work, partner," laughed Jack.

"Now we can thread through the Capital and get over to Sutter's Fort between K and L on 28th," commented Coop. "Incidentally, we should keep our eye out for the motorcyclist—he may be gone, but shouldn't be forgotten."

"Laura, can you give us some background of the Fort so we can think where Stackhouse may have hid the strongbox?"

"Are you guys kidding? After that crazy ride, you need a history lesson??"

Jack smiled and said "Sorry, Laura. Are you ok? Laura took a deep breath and said, "I think so."

A minute later, Laura had recovered and explained that Sutter's Fort was established by John Sutter as a trading post a few years before gold was discovered. In fact, gold was discovered not at Sutter's Fort but at Sutter's Mill, located 40 miles away on the South Fork of the American River near Coloma.

"The Main Building at the Fort is a two-story structure. It was here that James Marshall met privately with Sutter in order to show him the gold Marshall had found during the construction of Sutter's sawmill."

"Thanks for the tutorial, Laura," Jack said. "Let's take a look at the Main Building and try to figure where Stackhouse may have hid the strongbox."

Off went Jack and Coop, exploring the Fort and its Main Building while Laura preoccupied the Fort's curator. The Main Building had walls 2.5 feet thick and 15 to 18 feet high. Jack and Coop searched the first floor and discovered nothing that interested them.

They proceeded to the second floor and located John Sutter's personal office. The office where they'd been told John Marshall first disclosed the discovery of gold to Sutter. While examining the office, Coop was attracted to a built-in bookcase embedded in the wall of Sutter's office. He carefully traced the woodwork around it. His pushing and pulling yielded a gentle rocking of the bookcase. As he continued to rock it, he noticed there were scratches on the floor below the bookcase which suggested it was movable. He pursued his pushing and pulling more aggressively and finally the bookcase gave way and opened left to right on an axis to some darkness beyond.

"Jack, look at this," Coop summoned.

Jack produced a pocket flashlight he always carried with him and which produced 200 lumens, enough to light up a room behind the bookcase.

"Interesting," said Jack. "Let's check it out." They entered the room. It was small, about 12 by 12, and contained a seating area composed of two sofas and a coffee table between them.

Coop said, "Sutter must have used this as a private meeting room."

"That's what it looks like," said Jack. "Maybe this is where Marshall showed the gold samples he'd discovered at the Mill."

There was a barrister, commonly found in England, which had two shelves and rotated for ease of use by someone who needed frequent access to books for their professional work, like a lawyer. The barrister contained a few volumes of early California history. Coop thumbed through the books looking for clues, but found none.

On the walls were a painting and several lithographs. The lithographs depicted some Native Americans at work. Laura said Sutter employed Native Americans in constructing the Fort, working in and around it and at his Mill. The painting illustrated a pastoral scene with a Mill and raceway, presumably representing the location where gold was discovered. The painting was labeled: "Where It All Began."

Jack and Coop continued their search of Sutter's hidden office for another 30 minutes and found nothing exceptional that would lead them to the Stackhouse strongbox.

As they were leaving, Coop said: "Just a second." He returned to the painting.

"Jack, come here a second. Do you find anything odd about this painting?"

He looked carefully at the painting and thought for a moment. "Yes," he said, "the raceway is pointed in the wrong direction: away from the river! Shouldn't it be running toward the river?"

"You got it," said Coop.

"I wonder why?"

"Instead of pointing to the river, maybe the raceway is intended as an arrow pointing to something away from the river." offered Coop. "The painting's labeled 'Where it all began.' Perhaps that's a clue to where the trail leads to the strongbox," surmised Coop.

Jack nodded his head. "Coop, I think that's a long shot, but worth a look. Let's find Laura, saddle up and head to Coloma."

As the men left Sutter's Fort, they didn't notice a man watching them from across the street. It was the same man who'd previously been following them on the motorcycle before being cut off on the freeway.

Coop saw the man out of the corner of his eye, unsure whether he presented immediate danger, or was merely following them. He told Jack and Laura to get in the car and start driving to Coloma without him. While they did, he knelt down behind an adjacent car and waited for the mystery man to ride past on his motorcycle.

The motorcyclist had to stop at the nearby stop sign before continuing to follow. At the stop, Coop jumped from behind the car and hopped on the back of the motorcycle.

"Pull over so we can have a chat," yelled Coop, wrapping

one arm around the cyclist's waist. The cyclist thought he only had one chance to escape and quickly popped the clutch, did a wheelie and attempted to throw Coop off the back of the cycle.

Expecting as much, Coop maneuvered and quickly grabbed the cyclists' coat collar with his free hand and yanked him off the bike with him.

Now the cyclist lay on his back on the ground with Coop kneeling on the stranger's chest with a gun pointed in his face.

"Now as I was saying, let's have that chat."

# CHAPTER TWENTY EIGHT

Jack and Laura were barely out of Sutter's Fort when Jack's phone rang. The voice at the other end spoke with a neat clip.

"Jack, it's Coop."

"What the heck are you doing, partner?"

Coop continued, "I bagged us a bad guy."

"The one following us?"

"He's the guy," responded Coop.

"Did you do a catch and release?" asked Jack.

Coop smiled. "Yep, but not before learning what he was up to. Why don't I fill you in when I catch up to you, said Coop.

"How are you going to do that with no wheels?" Jack asked.

"Oh, I have wheels. They just aren't mine: I borrowed them from a "friend", see you soon in Coloma," declared Coop.


At Coloma, Coop jumped into the back seat behind Laura surprising her. "How you doing? You must be getting a little tired of Jack and me playing war games."

Laura managed a small laugh. "Guys, this isn't exactly what I signed up for. Should I stay around? I do want to make it out alive and back to my students at some point!"

Jack looked over at Laura. "I'm sorry, Laura. I know this has been a little crazy. Would you like to go back? We can try to make sense of some of the history along the way without you."

Laura paused for a moment. "You and Coop are two of the most capable men I know. I said I would do this and… well, it's great to be with you two again. I think I can handle a little more excitement. Let's keep going."

Jack placed his hand softly on Laura's arm. "You just let me know if it gets to be too much. You have been invaluable to our effort."

Coop returned to his account of the interaction with the motorcycle goon. "After some persuasion he said that he had been instructed by one Max Hill to follow and report back on our whereabouts. Perhaps it's time we gave Mr. Hill a visit."

Jack thought for a moment, then said: "I have a better idea. Remember the time you helped the son of Sean O'Shea, the Irish chieftain?"

"Of course, I saved the kid's life."

"And O'Shea said he was forever indebted to you?"

"He did say that, but I never took him up on it."

"Maybe it's time to do just that, partner."

Coop sighed. "And I'm sure you have a plan."

Jack laughed. "Rather than have us return to The City and confront Max, I think O'Shea or one of his representatives could pay Mr. Hill a visit and chat with him; making it clear we should be left alone."

"The Irish never did like the Russians," added Coop. "Consider it done," he said, "I'll give Sean a call."

"This looks like a ghost town," Jack said, eyeing the town of Coloma.

"It sure does. Some people still live here," observed Laura, "but the civic buildings, like the jail, have been abandoned and left to decay, so no wonder it looks so creepy. The town's hay days were in the mid 1800s when Marshall's discovery of gold in early 1848 was announced at Sutter's."

"Let's do some wandering," Jack said. They walked down Coloma's main street and they noticed the post office, painted white, and Robert Bell's red brick store, together with other old buildings. They even walked by James Marshall's wooden cabin with its covered entry, peaked roof, and large windows adjoining each side of the front door.

They asked a local where they could find Sutter's Mill and were pointed in the right direction.

"Why the heck did Sutter construct a mill 40 miles from his Fort," asked Coop.

"It was near a sizable, flowing river, actually the South Fork of the American River, near trees." Laura said. "Lumber could be floated down the river or carted by wagon over the rough roads to New Helvetia."

As they approached the Mill, they saw the raceway. The reconstructed raceway at the Mill was properly tilted toward the river, not away from it as depicted in the painting they had seen at Sutter's Fort.

"Rumor has it," Laura explained, "gold was discovered by the Indians working under John Marshall's supervision at the Mill. While they were adjusting the raceway to properly expel water from the Mill, the Indians and Marshall noticed gold specs and small nuggets appearing."

"The story goes that Marshall collected a sample of the gold he and the Indians had discovered, took it to Sutter at his office in his Fort in New Helvetia.

"Although Marshall tried to keep the discovery of gold a secret, word leaked and soon San Francisco had 300,000 people seeking their fair share of gold having arrived by hundreds of ships then left stranded in the Bay.

Indeed, Brannan incited gold fever by parading up and down the streets of San Francisco, saying 'Gold's been discovered, Gold's been discovered.' Of course, Brannan wanted gold fever to spike the sale of equipment he'd purchased at a fraction of the price and was selling to expectant miners. This made him a very wealthy Californian."

As Laura spoke, Coop and Jack examined the raceway and in particular the area near and under the portion that adjoined the Mill, the area to which the raceway pointed in the painting, *away* from the river.

There was nothing remarkable about the landscape or old wood raceway, until Jack said: "Coop and Laura, take a look at this," he pointed to two trestles holding the end of the raceway furthest from the river. Very faintly there appeared the letters "TE/VC" on one side of the trestle and "SB 1864" on the other trestle.

"What do you guys make of that?"

Laura said: "TE/VC is meaningless to me. However, if we break it apart, TE could stand for Territorial Enterprise and VC must mean Virginia City. SB 1864 clearly refers to the poker winnings contained in the Strongbox during the year 1864."

Coop asked: "Why would anyone leaving clues to the treasure make such an obscure reference to where it was located, or at least where the next clue could be found."

Jack began to speculate. "This is what we know from the poker game: First, the treasure's significant in value and was important to hide as Stackhouse had little interest in realizing its immediate value, Secondly, perhaps the wrong people would lose interest or be misdirected with such obscure information. And finally, remember Stackhouse was traveling with Mark Twain of Territorial Enterprise and Virginia City fame."

"Sounds logical to me," said Coop. "Stackhouse wanted to squirrel away his winnings either for later use by him or someone else. Besides, he was probably looking for the next poker game in Virginia City."

"I agree," Laura confirmed.

Just then a shot rang out and splintered the raceway post they had been examining. Jack yelled for them to "take cover." They ran behind the adjacent Mill and Jack quickly guided Laura under a small set of stairs leading to the mill. The shots came from a nearby forest which lay behind the Mill. It appeared there were two shooters.

Coop pulled a weapon, a Glock 19 Mariner, his weapon of choice and returned fire to keep the bad guys alert to the fact that Jack and his gang were not defenseless.

More shots rang out but none hit Jack and his colleagues.

"I thought that you said you delivered a message to the follower."

"I did. I think this must be a different but associated group."

"Kinda like the Seven Headed Hydra in Greek mythology," said Jack. "We wack one head off and another appears."

"Let's decapitate the whole freaking bunch," said Coop. He then told Jack that he had a plan and gave Jack his Glock. He said that he was going to use the Mill for protection and run to the river and head downstream, then circle around the bad guys and either head to his car for some heavier armament or do something else.

"Give me 15 minutes to work my magic!"

"Ok, I'll hold them here," said Jack. "Go for it."

Coop reached the water shielded by Sutter's Mill from the attackers, while Jack provided some return gun fire, to keep them honest. Once in the water, Coop quickly floated and swam downstream reminding him of his old Seal days. After a hundred yards he exited the water carefully and with a telescopic monocle he had in his pocket searched the surrounding area. He saw no one and quickly jumped out of the water and ran to the tree line keeping low. Once there, he stopped and listened. Other than the occasional gun shot from where he'd come, he heard nothing.

Coop realized Jack had his weapon. The Glock had a 17 round magazine for which the pistol was fitted. Jack could soon be out of ammunition so he hurried through the woods and after 50 yards decided to turn in the direction of the earlier gun fire. As he crept closer, he noticed two men who were behind a log opposite the raceway and Mill. He didn't want to be too close and accidentally take a shot from Jack, but he had a thought.

He reached for his phone and set the alarm for 5 minutes. Then he crawled silently toward them as close as he could and placed the phone on the ground. Next, he retreated from behind the shooters on his belly and when sufficiently clear, crouched and moved laterally to the left until he was in line with them on their left side and hid behind some brush.

Slowly Coop began to move toward the bad guys as Jack continued to provide them with something else to think about.

Suddenly, Coop's phone alarm rang, both intruders turned to their right, guns in hand in search of the noise. They pointed guns toward the ringing and opened fire. As they began to turn, Coop ran toward them knowing that they would be looking away kind of like blindsiding the quarterback in football. He grabbed the gun hand of the shooter nearest him with both hands.

The gunman's partner turned to shoot Coop, but hit his partner in the right shoulder when Coop used him as a shield. Coop used the gun he'd grabbed to shoot the man opposite him in his right shoulder. Down he went, his injured shoulder forcing him to drop his weapon.

Coop punched the gunman he held in the throat with his left hand. The guy began gasping for air and quickly released his gun he'd been holding allowing Coop to take it. He was clutching his throat and the windpipe, while his partner was howling in pain from the gunshot wound.

"Hey Jack," Coop yelled. "Stop firing! I have them. It's safe. Come on over and give me a hand." He kept the firearm pointed to the two men on the ground.

When Jack arrived with Laura, he shook his head. "Nice job. How did you do it?"

"It is all a matter of tendencies."

"Sure, tendency to shoot you."

Coop explained what he was thinking: If someone turns to investigate a noise or something behind them, they'll likely turn in the direction of their natural hand, to the right if they're right handed. The hand in which they hold their weapon. Otherwise, if they turned to the left, they would have a weapon out of position to address the presumed danger.

I noticed both of these guys were right handed and thought they would turn right to investigate the alarm I'd set with my iPhone. That gave one the advantage of disarming the man nearest me and using him as a shield from his partner's gunfire. From there it was easy to use his weapon on his partner. My only real concern was that you were going to shoot me with one of your wild shots from my own gun!"

Jack smiled. "Thanks for the vote of confidence, buddy."

They searched the two men and found no identification. The man with the injured windpipe was unable to speak, so Jack called his friend, Murph, at BPD and explained what had happened. Murph said he would coordinate with local law enforcement and instructed Jack and his team to wait until they arrived.

Thirty minutes later, two police cruisers and an EMT pulled up. While two officers met with Jack, Coop and Laura and took their statements, the EMTs treated the injured gunmen and loaded them into the ambulance and took off.

After interviewing the three of them, the officers said they were free to leave, but to be available if they needed to contact them.

Coop said, "Nice to have friends in high places! What's next, kemo sabe?"

"We have to get to Virginia City. I have a hunch that VC is the end of the rainbow for the Niantic Strongbox and for us. Let's bunk at Lake Tahoe on the way to Virginia City. It's only an hour and a half away. I have a friend who keeps a hide-a-key for me at his vacation home, if I happen to roll through."

"I'm on board," said Laura.

"Same," said Coop.

# CHAPTER TWENTY NINE

Max answered his phone, "Yep."

The voice responded, "You had instructions from Brighton Beach. What happened?"

"Who's this?" Max demanded.

"Mr. Hill, this is Sergi Adamoff."

"Sergi Adamoff?" asked Max. "Who the heck are you?"

"I'm the Minister of Mining and Energy for Russia, Mr. Hill."

Max was taken aback by that pronouncement . He had not expected a high ranking Russian government official to be questioning him let alone speaking to him. The Minister of Mining and Energy. Wow, thought Max. After absorbing the situation, he composed himself and said, "How can I help you, Mr. Adamoff."

"You may start by doing what you have been instructed to do by Brighton Beach," said Adamoff.

"Regarding what?" asked Max.

"Regarding Jack Armstrong," replied Adamoff.

Why would Adamoff be concerned about Armstrong? thought Max. He must have heard of our failure to pick him off at the Mill and run him off the road near the Golden Gate Bridge.

"We're tracking him and know precisely where he is, " Max said proudly.

"I don't care that you are tracking him, Mr. Hill. He must be deterred from exploring Virginia City and its mines. If that's not possible, I want him eliminated. Do you understand me?"

"I understand you. I'll take care of it," assured Max.

"You had better, Mr. Hill," Adamoff warned.

So now Max had the Brighton Beach gang and a high level Russian Government official breathing down his neck. All because he alerted them to Veronica's inheritance and some news clips describing the poker game? Go figure. Why would the Russian Government be so hard up for an 1860s treasure? Or, were they...?

While Max was concluding his call with Adamoff, Jack drove into Tahoe and marveled at the beauty of the area. He and his former wife and son had spent many summers on the lake and he wondered who owned the home he had to sell in the divorce.

To Laura and Coop he announced: "'My friend's home is on the Northshore overlooking Carnelian Bay. Let's head in that direction. And when we leave the Lake we can take Highway 431 over Mount Rose and head down the hill into the Carson Valley and up Mount Davidson to Virginia City which is about an hour and a half from here."

Laura mentioned that Tahoe was a favorite of Mark Twain's. Especially the North Shore where they would be staying. "He used to pop over the hill from Virginia City and camp around the Lake," said Laura. "And in *Roughing It*, he offered this description of the Lake:

We plodded on, two or three hours longer, and at last the Lake burst upon us—a noble sheet of blue water lifted six thousand feet above the level of the sea, and walled in by a rim of snow-clad mountain peaks that towered aloft a full three thousand feet higher still! It was a vast oval, and one would have to use up eighty or a hundred good miles in traveling around it. As it lay there with the shadows of the  mountains brilliantly photographed upon its still surface I thought it must surely be the fairest picture the whole earth affords.'"

Coop turned and looked at Laura. "Wow, you are quite the Twain aficionado."

Laura smiled and continued: "I taught a semester on Twain and his influence during the Gold Rush. It's somewhat sad that those rushing to the gold fields in the 1850s never had a chance to enjoy the Lake and environs. When the flow of traffic reversed to accommodate those rushing to the silver mines in Virginia City ten years later, again the Lake was merely a stop over on their route. Still, it provided precious timber, water and ice to the silver mines of Virginia City."

Jack realized he was falling into using the Lake as a roadside rest stop Laura had just described, instead of appreciating its world class  breadth and beauty. Normally, he would have sat back and immersed himself in the Lake's mesmerizing effect, but today he couldn't stop thinking about Veronica's case.

He considered what he and his colleagues had found and who was trying to deter them. The clues found in Sutter's secret office and, more significantly, those found etched on the tail raceway at Sutter's Mill, seemed to point them in one direction: Virginia City and the Territorial Enterprise.

What continued to baffle Jack was the effort to deter him and his team from pursuing the treasure. And now the elevation of the deterrence to a threat of death. Who were the shooters? Who sent them? What did they wish to accomplish with the ambush? None of the answers were any good.

Jack wondered if Coop might learn more from his law enforcement connections and the interrogation of the injured shooters once they were medically treated. In the meantime, Coop thought he heard one address the other as "comrade" when he was secretly approaching them. If so, it was further proof that the Russians were involved. And Russian involvement had to mean Max Hill involvement.

Jack didn't have enough evidence to swear out a criminal complaint against Max. But he knew instinctively that Max was involved. What mystified Jack was how a lost 1860s strongbox could motivate someone to attempt to murder him and his colleagues. There was no doubt in Jack's mind the efforts of the gunmen were meant to kill, not simply scare them away. Apparently Jack not getting "the hint" and his persistence called for stronger measures.

*There must be more to the treasure than meets the eye*, he thought. *What can be so valuable?*

Coop's Beemer slowly rolled into the driveway of a two story wood clad home with pronounced decks on the side facing the lake. It was beginning to get dark and Jack was tired. They pulled their belongings from the car and found a covered walkway leading to the front door. The walkway had a peaked roof for snow protection and was completed in fine wood. If one were ambitious, an artist could paint the inside of the peaked roof with telling pictures like those Jack had witnessed on similar covered walkways in China. He made a mental note to suggest the same to his friend, Stan, the Man.

Beside the front door stood a 5 foot tall carving of a black bear. Below it hung a sign with the name "Oski" carved into it.

"Everyone, meet Oski the Bear," Jack announced. He knew Stan was a Cal grad and a big Bear fan: "Go Bears!" yelled Laura. Jack reached behind Oski and found the hid-a-key Stan had left for him.

"Stan is normally in Mexico fishing this time of year. Luckily, the key's still here," Jack said as he opened the front door and entered the alarm code. They all entered the house and immediately walked straight through the Great Room to the back deck with its sweeping view of the Lake.

"Magnificent," commented Laura breathlessly.

Coop also opined, "Holy Moley what a view! It's as if the entire Lake is at your feet. How big is the Lake, Jack?"

"It is 1600 feet deep and if some great force were to tilt it on its side and empty it, the Lake would cover the entire State of California with water to a depth of 4 feet. It's one of the largest and deepest lakes in the world, 70 miles around and 13 miles across. If one views the Lake from one side, the circumference of the earth prevents a look at the water's edge on the other side.

"I once did a training ride around the Lake's 70 miles and nearly died. Given the 6600 foot altitude and hills to climb along the way, I simply ran out of gas three quarters of the way and had to catch a ride on a bus. Problem was the bus only went two miles before telling me it was the end of the line! After resting a bit, I managed to stagger across the finish line at my Northshore home, many hours after my start. A few months later, I trained and came back prepared and had no trouble making it round the Lake in a few hours.

"There are also great mountain bike rides in the backcountry," said Jack, spreading his arms and motioning behind the house. "Once, when I had to work out some stress, I decided to go for a ride late in the Fall afternoon beginning at my home near here on the Northshore. Up over the hill and down the slopes of some logging trails in the National Forest. The sun was setting, and it was definitely getting dark. I had no lights on the bike and began to pedal fast over the 20 mile trail to get back before I lost all light.

"Then, at the bottom of a several mile long hill as I began turning toward home, still 5 miles away in the backcountry, I encountered a controlled burn Cal Fire personnel had left for the night while the burn continued. It was quite exciting riding through a burning forest.

"After a mile or two, I exited the burn and passed a meadow, looked to my left and spotted a big black bear sitting and watching me ride by. Although I considered stopping and taking a pic with my iPhone, I decided the better part of valor was to pedal as fast as possible and put some distance between me and the bear.

"Made it home as the night settled in and I was enveloped in blackness. Needless to say, the stress I had left with no longer existed."

"I bet you went out the next day and purchased a light for your bike," said Coop.

"You got that right," commented Jack. Then there was my annual August birthday mountain bike ride, up the backside of Mount Pluto, 8600 feet high and the end of the chair lift for the Northstar ski resort. After walking around at the top and checking out the vacant buildings, I decided to have a seat on a ledge overlooking the ski run below and eat a sandwich I'd brought. Soon I heard a couple of voices and glanced back to see two couples who were interested in the view atop the ski run. Without even saying a word to the couples, I finished my sandwich and departed seeking the solitude of the mountain.

"Fast forward a couple of days later and I was on a plane landing at JFK. I asked the guy seated next to me whether he was coming or going. He responded that he was coming and had just finished a vacation. I asked him where and he said 'Tahoe.' Oh, I was in Tahoe too, I said, 'Where were you?' He said, 'Northstar'. I said, 'What an odd coincidence, I too had been to the top of Mount Pluto at the end of the Northstar ski run. He said he and some friends had been there too. I then asked, 'Did you see a guy seated at the top of the ski run eating a sandwich?' He said 'yes'. 'That was me!' What are the odds...'.

"You live a charmed life, Jack," said Laura.

"No doubt about that," said Jack. "Let's go inside, have a beer and focus on what next needs to be done," He moved into the Great room.

"Laura, Coop. Have a seat. We need to make a decision. In view of the danger which persists in connection with the attempted recovery of Veronica's treasure, danger which now is life threatening, I ask you: should we proceed? As of the moment, no one has been hurt and our expenses except for our time and creativity have been reasonably minimal. If we proceed, it's clear to me our personal safety will be jeopardized. So, again, I ask: should we proceed?"

Laura thought for a moment, then replied: "I haven't had

this much fun and excitement my entire life. And to apply my years of experience and knowledge to the process in a valuable way makes it all worthwhile. Even though there *is* recognizable danger, which you correctly describe, what's the purpose of all this experience and knowledge if it can't be applied to find what we would set out to find? I say let's go for it!"

"Coop?" asked Jack.

Coop stood up and smoothed the fabric of his pants along his thighs. He looked at them. "There's no way we're turning back now. I can sense we're close and good instincts will lead us to what we're looking for. They will help protect us from harm. I, too, am in favor of going for it! As Winston Churchill said: 'Wars are not won by evacuation.'"

"Thanks to both of you. That makes the three of us in agreement. I'll check in with Veronica and make sure she has no objection to proceeding."

# CHAPTER THIRTY

The next morning Jack met with Coop in the kitchen for a cup of coffee and a few biscuits they found in the pantry.

"Good night's sleep last night,?" Coop inquired.

"The best," said Jack. "Slept like a rock. How about you?"

"Very peacefully," said Coop. "Damned quiet up here."

"Have you spoken with Sean yet?" asked Jack.

"I have. He met with Max already and laid down the law. Max didn't take it lightly. Sean said we might expect more trouble, but Sean will be with us all the way. He's a stand up guy. Did you have a chance to speak with Veronica?"

"I did, she's in, so we can proceed unanimously. Did you find out from Sean why Max is so interested in our efforts?"

"He said he was aware of the note and key Veronica has and suspects there may be a payoff at a location of some interest to him. He would like to be present when it occurs so he can take his fair share."

"'Helluva guy, that Max!" Jack scoffed. "What's fair about taking what is the rightful inheritance of his wife and marital separate property?"

"Something tells me he's not too interested in legal niceties, Jack. He doesn't play by the rules and wants what is hers, period!"

"And what does he mean about a location that may be of some interest to him?"

"Beats me," said Coop.

"Speaking of Veronica, how did she sound when you spoke

with her?" Jack realized at that moment Coop and Veronica had something between them, something Coop had not shared with him yet.

"She sounded fine to me, Coop. However, I'm concerned that her safety may soon be impossible to guarantee with the way things are trending. Do you get the feeling there's more of a pot at the end of the rainbow than what we currently think? Why else would Max employ deadly force?"

"I get your drift. As they say, 'something is rotten in Denmark, and it's not the cheese.' Anyway, this guy, Max, is like a dog with a bone. It's as if he doesn't want us to go near the treasure."

"Could Sean figure out how Max is keeping abreast of our moves?" asked Jack

"No, but he thinks someone's alerting him."

"I think Sidney is a turncoat and has a thing for Max. I suspect she's our leak and unfortunately Veronica has fed her info unsuspectingly. I've alerted her to be careful in what she tells Sidney."

Coop sighed. "Ok, so we need to be careful what we reveal to Veronica. But we also need to keep her safe."

"Agreed," said Jack. "Unless we want to plant some wrong information with Sidney via Veronica for Max's benefit."

# CHAPTER THIRTY ONE

"Laura, what can you tell us about Virginia City and the Territorial Enterprise?" asked Jack as Coop drove along the North end of the Lake toward Highway 431 and Mount Rose.

Laura opened a notebook and began to read from her class notes: "Virginia City, Nevada, expanded significantly when the Comstock Lode was discovered in 1859, 10 years after the Gold Rush began. The town increased to 25,000 residents in the mid 1870s then receded when the silver deposits began to decline. 2010 Census lists Virginia City as having a population of only 855."

"Wow, from 25,000 to less than a thousand. That's quite a nose dive," echoed Coop.

"In its hay day," Laura continued reading from her notes, "seven million tons of silver ore were mined, valued at well over $500 billion dollars today. More importantly the wealth from these mines financed the building of a modern San Francisco and financed the Union in the Civil War. Without these resources, there may not be a United States as we know it today! There are over 400 mines and many miles of tunnels beneath the streets of Virginia City," she added.

"From under the streets of San Francisco to under the streets of Virginia City," thought Jack aloud.

"We are becoming The Under the Street Gang!" said Coop.

"This may be a lost cause, but I guess we can try," offered Jack.

Laura continued. "I would start with the Territorial Enterprise.. It was founded in 1858 and Mark Twain became its City Editor while he tried his hand at mining and did a poor job of it," explained Laura.

"Does the paper exist today?" asked Coop.

"Let me see," said Laura, consulting her notes, "After the Territorial Enterprise changed hands several times, it ceased to exist in the 1960s."

"That is over 100 years from its Founding," said Jack.

"There is a Mark Twain Museum at the Territorial Enterprise Building which may have some useful background. I suggest we start there," Laura recommended.

"What cover story shall we use so as not to disclose our real mission?" asked Coop.

Jack responded, "How about searching for Mark Twain memorabilia buried in Virginia City mines?"

Laura agreed: "That's plausible."

Once inside, they discovered impressive artifacts including the original desk of Mark Twain when he was the City Editor, an early Linotype machine, and composing tables upon which Mark Twain "used to take a nap" as indicated by museum signage. But there were no useful clues as to where the strongbox might be located.

Laura searched out the curator of the Museum, a woman named Maryanne, probably in her early sixties and began chatting with her. She explained they were searching for Mark Twain memorabilia which may have been buried in one of Virginia City's mines.

Laura asked, "Is it possible Mark Twain left a clue in one of the Territorial Enterprise articles he published?"

Maryanne looked baffled. "It is possible, but most of the older newspapers have been destroyed by The Great Fire of 1875 in Virginia City."

"If you are sure, then I suppose we've hit a bit of a dead end?" thought Laura aloud.

Maryanne perked up. "I have an idea. Before the Great Fire, some artifacts including a couple of copies of a Territorial Enterprise had been secreted in a time capsule which was recently recovered. The remnants of the time capsule were kept in one of the Museum's storerooms. If you want, I will see if I can find them."

"How kind of you," said Laura.

While they waited, the group continued to examine the various museum showcases.

Suddenly, Maryanne emerged from the storeroom, her straightlaced expression somewhat tilted. "You are in luck. Normally, this would be a needle in a haystack that might take months. I believe I have what you require here," gently placing the aged publication on a glass top table and handing Laura a large magnifying glass. "Please treat the pages carefully. I will be nearby should you need any assistance."

They examined the newspaper copies and located the Mark Twain story entitled "The Poker Game," at the end of which the column read "To Be Continued in next week's edition."

"Do you have the following edition?" Laura asked Maryanne.

Maryanne nodded. "I do. It too was buried in the time capsule," thrusting it into Laura's hands. Maryanne then returned to her work elsewhere.

Jack and Laura peered through the magnifying lens scanning for the second Twain installment. Jack and Laura read the story silently together with goosebumps forming in their bodies:

A STRONGBOX AND ITS JOURNEY

Once upon a time there was a strongbox, not any old strongbox, but a special one! This strongbox, Graham Stackhouse's Strongbox and dated 1864 originated from the great ship, Niantic, was an excellent traveler together with its colleagues: Stackhouse, Sutter, Brannan and Twain of gold rush poker fame. From San Francisco whence they came with winnings to satisfy the most curious, to a barge in San Francisco Bay, the strongbox traveled without delay.

Up the Bay, it made its way: first North of The City, then East to Benicia, the town named after General Vallejo's wife and an early capital of California. Onward as Christian Soldiers, Marching on to War with the Cross of Jesus Going on Before, the strongbox rode.

"Then, saluting the town of Rio Vista passing by its side, the box slid into New Helvetia, where Sutter and Brannan did reside. Now safe with Stackhouse and Twain by its side, the strongbox continued its ride on the American River to Coloma where Sutter's Mill yielded a clue yet to be untied.

Off put the box by handlers with heavy glove and onto a wagon destined for the mountains above. But not before inspecting Sutter's raceway and etching "TE/ VC" on one end thereof and "SB 1864" on the other so as to provide guidance to future hunters of the treasure hereof.

After several day's wagon travel, the box neared the Lake and its journey's end. But first through the Carson Valley then up Mount Davidson to a Mecca known as Virginia City! Its Goal, of course, was to find a safe place in one of the many mines until an heir of Graham's discovered it and its contents, only to disturb its rest.

Should assistance be needed in directions to that safe hiding place among Virginia City's many mines and tunnels, one need only visit my favorite "C" street saloon and look for BoB."

"Well, that does it," said Jack. "We are clearly on the right track! Now for the Easter Egg hunt! We need to find Mark Twain's favorite 'C' street saloon and his friend named BoB."

While Jack and Laura were busy with their historical research, Coop decided to wander about the town. As he exited the Mark Twain Museum, he looked carefully for the presence of anyone who may have followed them. He had an experienced, careful eye as if his head was on a swivel. He proceeded along "C" Street and as he walked, he looked for reflections from the windows he passed. He decided to head for the Bucket of Blood Saloon. The saloon, Coop read from the plaque on the side of the building, was constructed after the Great Fire of 1875 and sat on the remnants of the old Boston Saloon. He ducked inside for a beer and a chat with the bartender. Bartenders and taxi drivers were some of the most knowledgeable people with whom to consult on local issues, Coop had experienced. He asked the bartender where he would look for Mark Twain memorabilia that might be buried nearby?

"Well, to state the obvious," the bartender said, "it could have been hidden anywhere. Who would have hidden the memorabilia?"

"A guy by the name of Graham Stackhouse," said Coop.

"Stackhouse. Hum. I've been here for over 20 years and heard many stories, but none mentioned Graham Stackhouse."

"How about Mark Twain?" asked Coop.

"Twain, as you know," said the bartender, "was a prominent figure in the history of Virginia City. Indeed, he mined a bit while here before taking on the Territorial Enterprise as its City Editor. Twain reportedly was a crappy miner. By the time he began mining "he was finding quartz, not silver ore," the bartender said in a condescending tone.

That caused Coop to notice the sign over the bar:

I learned then, once and for all, that gold in its native state is but dull, ornamental stuff, and that only low-born metals excite the administration of the ignorant with an ostentatious glitter. However, like the rest of the world, I still go on underrating men of gold and glorifying men of mica. Commonplace human nature cannot rise above that.

MARK TWAIN, *ROUGHING IT.*

"Do you happen to know where Twain liked to drink?" asked Coop.

"Try the Union Brewery and Saloon on "C" Street," responded the bartender.

"Thanks," said Coop. After downing his beer and leaving a generous tip, he took a peek out the door. Coop didn't see anything unusual but had a bad feeling. And when Coop has a bad feeling, he minds it. He returned to the bartender and asked if there was a back way out of the bar. The bartender pointed to a hall labeled "restrooms" and told Coop to follow the hall to its end and exit through the last door.

As Coop exited the Bucket of Blood, he noticed a stairway leading up to a landing near the top of the building. He took the stairs two at a time and once on the landing, he walked around an outside balcony to the front of the building. From there he could look up and down "C" street and check out any unusual activity. Convinced there was an unwanted encounter due any minute, he took off his backpack and reached inside and took out a device he kept for just these occasions.

It was a small, very hi-tech, CIA drone he'd helped create and then named "Tinker Bell." She was so small some confused her for a dragonfly. Controlled by his phone, Coop launched her from the deck over the Bucket of Blood and off she went 30 feet into the air. Coop checked the picture transmitted on his iPhone and confirmed it was working and crystal clear. He then maneuvered Tinker Bell over C street and proceeded to direct her down the street from whence he came. He lowered her and saw two shady looking characters hiding in a doorway two buildings away from the Bucket of Blood. "Ah Ha " Coop said to himself. "Got you, you bastards! Just as I thought."

Coop realized the shady characters were operatives, based on their skillful moves and ability to stay under the radar. As they continued peeking around the doorway in the direction of the Bucket of Blood, Coop decided to double back (an old bear tracking trick) in the direction of the suspects, but a floor above. When he got to the edge of the balcony he hopped over the rail and hurtled himself to the next building which conveniently had a balcony of the same height. He was in a groove, stealthily racing along the second balcony to its end. He checked Tinker Bell once more and noticed that the jerks were now below him: one more balcony to leap over and connect with the nearly adjoining balcony and he would be behind them.

He did so, following the second story balcony to the back of the building, then taking the stairs down to the alley behind the building. He sent out a command to bring Tinker Bell home and raced back to the museum to brief Jack and Laura.

Meanwhile the operatives who had been trailing Coop, realized they lost him. "We'd better locate him and the others soon so we can avoid reporting our failure to Max," the taller one said.

His partner nodded and responded, "I'm more concerned about who Max reports to than Max."

"We should be worried about everyone in the higher chain of command, Podrooga" the tall Russian counseled, slipping back into his native language. "Did you ever figure out why following Armstrong and his group is so damned important? This is getting me tired and I'm hungry. And that one, the dark skinned man? He's a pain in my head!"

"English, speak English, ok? I live in America and am planning to marry one gorgeous U.S. girl and have multiple babies, so try to speak the language, 'friend'. I only know what you know and that is that we need to deter them from finding what they're looking for. We should use any and all force to persuade them to, shall we say—go home, or disappear."

# CHAPTER THIRTY TWO

Coop found Jack and Laura at the Mark Twain Museum and told them about the tail and his discussions with the bartender. Jack thought they must be getting close to the strongbox given the more obvious attempt to follow them.

"Let's go out the back of the Museum and head to the Union Brewery, " said Jack.

They proceeded down a back alley paralleling "C" street and after passing six buildings, they cut through a sandwich shop and darted across the street through a Laundromat into another back alley. That alley led a few hundred feet to a back door sign that said "Union Brewery." Coop gave a quick look up and down the alley and seeing no followers, slipped inside the saloon with Jack and Laura.

Coop surveyed the saloon and did not notice any unusual characters. Jack motioned them to the bar and summoned the bartender.

"What will you have?" he asked.

"Three Sierra Nevada's and some information," Jack requested, placing a $50 bill on the counter.

"What information?" the bartender asked, pocketing the money.

"We heard Mark Twain frequented this saloon."

"Yes, that is what I understand," said the bartender.

"Did he have a friend named Bob?" asked Jack.

"Bob? How would I know?" The bartender scratched his beard, thinking for a minute. "I know the story goes that he had a writing partner, William Wright, at the Territorial Enterprise who used a pen name… yes, he used the name Dan deQuille and Wright's pen name inspired Samuel Clemens to adopt the pen name Mark Twain. But I'm not aware of any 'Bob' in Twain's life."

Jack began to think this could be a needle in a haystack but decided to persist. "We're pursuing Mark Twain memorabilia that could be the result of some San Francisco poker winnings."

"What did the TE article say about 'Bob', Laura?"

"Hold on, I copied it with a pic from my iPhone." she said. She read it aloud:

"Should assistance be needed in directions to that safe hiding place among Virginia City's many mines, one need only visit my favorite "C" street saloon and look for BoB."

"Let me see that," said the bartender. As he looked carefully at the language, he began to smile. "I never seen a guy named 'Bob' spell his name like that," he said. "Notice how it's spelled: initial capital "B," lower case "o" and another initial "B." I think you got some kind of an abbreviation maybe?"

"He could be right," mused Laura. "More like an anagram."

Coop began laughing: "It is staring us in the face! Look at that, he pointed." Coop was pointing at a large, framed mining map hanging at the "Back of Bar."

"That's it," exclaimed Jack. 'BoB' stands for Back of Bar! How clever is that?" asked Jack. "Twain wanted treasure hunters to find clues to the treasure in his newspaper articles and put some distance between those who were aware of the poker game with its sizable pot and the likely heirs to the strongbox. Also, one would have to know how to find Mark

Twain's favorite watering hole and unravel the misdirection of the name and abbreviation BoB."

"Clever indeed," remarked Coop. "Now we need to locate where the treasure was buried in one of Virginia City's 400 plus mines."

"Do you mind if we take a closer look at the map behind the bar?" asked Laura.

"Not at all," said the Bartender, inviting them behind the bar.

"It is a map of the Comstock Mines and Sutro Tunnel," commented Laura.

"Comstock Mines and Sutro Tunnel?" asked Jack rhetorically.

Laura consulted her note book again and replied: "The first significant mine discovered was the Ophir Mine in 1859. The various mines that followed under the streets of Virginia City comprised the Comstock Lode, the first major silver deposit discovery in the United States. By 1876, Nevada produced over half of all the precious metals in the United States.

"Mining operations were hindered by extreme temperatures in the mines caused by natural hot springs. Miners often could only work in 15 minute shifts and had to be cooled down with water or ice. Adolph Sutro built the Sutro Tunnel over many years to drain the hot spring waters from the mines to the valley below, over 20,000 feet, nearly four miles, and create ventilation."

"Look at this," said Coop, whispering to his colleagues, "the arm of one of the mines seems to bottom out at 1864 feet. Isn't that the year in which the poker game was played? Also, it's the year the strongbox was transported to Virginia City, and it is the year stamped on the Sutter's Mill tailrace."

"A trifecta!," said Coop.

"I don't see any other mine terminating at that level," said Jack. "All the other mines stop well short of that depth, or proceed well beyond it. I bet the mine's depth and the year in question are a coincidence intended to be noticed."

At that moment, Laura found a notation at the bottom right corner of the mining map that said, "Niantic SB 1864."

"That does it for me," said Jack, "Niantic Strongbox 1864." "Laura, can you take a pic of the map with your iPhone? We need it to help guide us."

"Let's head to the beginning of the Ophir Mine and start our descent there," directed Coop.

"Wait a minute Big Guy," Jack said to Coop. "Hold your horses." As they began leaving the saloon, Jack tipped the bartender another $20 and told him to keep quiet about what they'd found. He explained several rough characters of Russian descent were tailing them.

The bartender said he didn't like Russians, period. "This is America! Land of the Free and Home of the Brave, and no Russian was going to do harm to it or our people! Incidentally, you likely will need some help finding your way among the miles of tunnels below the Virginia City streets. If so, you can't go wrong with my brother: he knows these mines like the back of his hand and better than anyone. If you're really serious about finding Mark Twain's treasure, you should engage him to join you," the bartender said.

"What's his name?" asked Jack.

"Connor, um, Connor Corroon," said the bartender.

"And what is yours?" asked Jack.

"Dillon. I mean, Dillon Corroon," said the bartender, extending his hand, which Jack accepted.

Jack smiled. "I never met an Irish man who didn't love his brother. Ask your brother to meet us here at 8am tomorrow morning: we have a job for him."

Jack thought back on the 'Irish Employment Agency' he'd heard of in New York City. When an Irishman was 'off the boat' and looking for work, he would turn to the 'Irish Employment Agency', the local Irish bar. After a quick chat with the Irish bartender, he would be instructed to return the next day and would be given a job in his given profession: carpenter, electrician, plumber, or otherwise. Quick, neat and efficient, thought Jack!

# CHAPTER THIRTY THREE

The next morning Jack and Coop met at the Union Brewery for some breakfast and to meet Connor. He ordered a couple of eggs over easy with bacon, an English muffin and some fruit, not potatoes. Coop had a breakfast burrito. Both ordered black coffee.

"Where's Laura?" asked Coop.

"She'll be along in a few," responded Jack.

As they were enjoying their breakfast, a sizable man walked in with a determined look on his face. Without hesitation, he headed directly to the table occupied by Jack and Coop.

"Anyone sitting here?" he asked, pointing to the seat next to them.

"No," said Jack.

"Which one of you is Jack?" Connor asked.

"I am," Jack replied with some amazement. The guy sure was self assured, thought Jack.

"I'm Connor," he said curtly.

"And, I'm Coop."

"Pleased to meet you," Connor said, reaching out to grasp Coop's hand.

Jack liked what he saw in Connor, not the least was his size at 6'3," 220 lbs and built like a rock. He also had big "miners" hands which produced a powerful hand shake. "Something by which to measure a man," Jack remembered what his father had taught him, while Coop reciprocated with a strong handshake.

Jack briefed Connor on their mission including Russian

involvement, offered him $500 a day for his help and asked if he were "in." Connor nodded and extended his meathook-like hand to consummate their agreement. He also added that "he ate Russians for breakfast." Slightly amused by the two brothers' seemingly passionate dislike for Russians, Jack then asked Connor what he thought about their conclusion that the treasure was likely buried at the 1864 foot level of the Comstock Mines.

"It's a sound theory," Connor said. "The only mine with a depth of 1864 feet; and, the comments by Twain all add up to a possible location at which the treasure of memorabilia is buried."

Coop waited for a pause before speaking. "From what I can see, perhaps we start at the Ophir Mine?"

"You are correct," said Connor. "The Ophir leads to the Consolidated Virginia and we can also take the Sutro Tunnel part of the way to shorten the route to, shall we say, Mine Shaft 1864?"

Jack looked at Coop and nodded as if to say: "This is our guy."

Just then Laura arrived and took the empty seat. Jack introduced her to Connor, and they exchanged agreeable nods acknowledging each other from across the table. Jack then turned to Laura. "May I see the picture you took of BoB with your phone?"

Laura showed him the picture of the Comstock Lode Mines and Sutro Tunnel Map. Jack offered it to Connor who studied it carefully and nodded as if in approval. He then pulled from his pocket an 8 x 10 inch paper map, unfolded it and looked up at the group. "Just thought I would bring this along when my brother told me what you are interested in."

"Any things we should be mindful of?" asked Coop.

"Of course," Connor said. "There are cave-ins, rock slides, darkness, lack of ventilation, poisonous gas and heat. There are lift dangers whereby some fall 1,000 feet, the possibility of getting lost, and occasionally, bats and other varmints."

"Are you sure you want to go down there?" Laura asked Jack and Coop.

"This is not out of the ordinary for me," Connor said, "but Laura, please don't feel you must do this, right Jack?"

"We have to be honest though," said Coop. "It's the only way we're going to find the treasure at this point." Coop turned to Jack for confirmation.

Jack nodded in agreement.

"This was not in your job description, Laura. We can get you to a safe spot and come back..."

Before Jack could finish, Laura looked each member of the group in the eye, pondering the latest turn of events and said, "Guys, it's been a heck of a ride. Considering the Russians following us everywhere, I don't know if I would be safe anywhere. I feel safer with you than anyplace...so I'll take my chances."

Jack patted her on the shoulder in acknowledgment of her courage and commitment, then looked at her. She really was an amazing woman. What the hell was he doing taking her on this crazy journey. And where would they be without her? But there was no turning around now and things would have to be what they would be. He gave her a little hug.

"We are going to be as safe as we possibly can. He looked at the group he had assembled and raised his voice another octave. "Come on everyone. Let's hustle up and get to the mine!"

"Excuse me. I'm wondering…" said Laura. "First: is there special equipment we need to take with us?"

Connor listed the equipment that they should have with them: miner's hats, a shovel or two, a couple of pick axes, flash lights with 400 lumens, layered clothing and a first aid kit and some bottled water. Also, radios with limited telecommunication capabilities in the mines and a couple of candles and matches.

"And where might we find those?" asked Laura.

"In my locker at the mine head," declared Connor.

"You're too much," commented Jack.

Connor looked at Laura and said, "What was your second question?

"Have you seen any Russians hanging around Virginia City recently?"

"Yea, glad you mention it. I have. A little buzz about it in town and with the locals," said Connor.

"What were they up to?" asked Laura.

"I'm not sure. They asked a lot of questions about the mines. They also expressed an interest in purchasing some of them."

"Purchasing a mine?" asked Coop.

"Correct," said Connor. "It's odd because, as you may know, the production days of these mines ended over 100 years ago."

"What value could they see in a 100 year old abandoned mine?" asked Jack.

"Beats me," speculated Connor. "Unless they're looking for the same treasure you are."

"How would they know about that?" asked Laura.

"I wonder if Veronica, our client, was a little too open with her best friend Sidney during one of her Stinson Beach stays," thought Jack aloud. "And her friend Sidney spilled the beans to her boyfriend, Max." Jack looked at Coop wondering if he had heard anything in his communication with Veronica. If they were communicating. He had no idea.

"Perhaps Max read the same Territorial Enterprise article that Veronica produced from her inheritance possessions," offered Coop.

"That would help explain the existence of the strongbox, its contents, Mark Twain and the other players including the connection to Graham Stackhouse," concluded Jack. "But it still doesn't nail the location of the strongbox."

"Even so," said Coop, "How do they seem to know where we are going at the same time we do?"

Just then, Coop turned to Laura and asked her if after Boris was caught eavesdropping on her apartment, she noticed anything suspicious or disturbed.

Laura thought for a moment. Then said, "As a matter of fact, I did notice a few of my things somewhat out of order. A hair brush was placed on the left, not right side of its tray; a closet door was slightly ajar, when I make it a habit to close them; and several of my dresses and coats were separated where I had not left them. If there was an intruder, what do you think he was looking for?'

Coop said, "He wasn't necessarily looking for anything. But he may have planted a bug on you. Come over here please."

She approached Coop and he asked her to hand him her shoes which he examined carefully then handed them back. He also checked her belt and found nothing. Same with a close inspection of her coat. Next, he examined Laura's purse and its contents. Mystified, Coop asked Laura what she usually took with her when she traveled with us. Her coat, shoes, belt, purse were interchangeable as was the rest of her clothing. He thought quietly for a moment, when Laura's phone rang.

She answered the ring, responded briefly, and closed the phone. "It was one of my teaching assistants asking when I would return."

"Let me see your phone, Laura," Coop requested.

She handed Coop her phone. He asked her for her password and entered it. He flipped through her iPhone apps until he found one labeled "find my phone." He clicked on it and found that the tab: Share My Location had been turned on and no doubt our Russian friends had tracked their movements by following Laura's phone.

"I don't recall anyone taking my phone, or missing it. How could they have enabled the Share My Location without my knowledge?"

"Do you ever leave your phone in your apartment, say, while you're out for a run?"

"That's it!" she said. "Those bastards! I don't run with my phone and do leave it behind. So, while I was out for a run, they broke into my apartment, hacked into my phone and enabled the "Share My Location" feature. What do we do now?

Connor said, "There is lousy cell coverage under the streets of Virginia City in the mines, so I doubt they can track us there. Nevertheless, leave your phone with Brother Dillon behind the bar. He'll take care of it and any Russian Bastards who come looking for it, or its owner."

# CHAPTER THIRTY FOUR

Given his knowledge of the mines, Connor naturally took the lead as they entered the Ophir Mine. Affixing their Miner's Helmets and hefting their shovels, picks and other paraphernalia, off they went. As they proceeded a few hundred yards down the tunnel, it didn't take long to notice the tracks for mining carts. Connor mentioned that the Ophir Bonanza (one of six major bonanzas found in the first five years of the Comstock Lode) was located at about 500 feet below the surface. Quickly, they came upon a mine shaft elevator that would help lead them to the 1800 foot level where they thought Graham Stackhouse's strongbox was buried.

As they descended on the elevator they passed a timbering system called "square-set timbering. Square-set timbering was developed by a German engineer, explained Connor, and laid the foundation for mining so as to minimize the collapse of tunnel walls. Basically, it consisted of four squares of timber laid on the floor against each of four walls. Then additional timbers are added to each corner in upright fashion. Next ceiling timbers are added which connect to the prior layed timbers. Finally, cross timbers are placed at appropriate intervals to provide further bracing and thus creating a timber cube. Square-set timbering could be added to one another: side by side and on top of each other.

"It was very effective in preventing cave-ins," said Connor. "Before the adoption of square sets, there were nearly daily cave-ins and many injured or killed miners. Of course, the adoption of square-setting timbering created another problem," said Connor.

"What was that?" asked Coop.

"The miners and more appropriately, the mine owners, suddenly needed massive amounts of timber to construct the square-sets. This caused a significant deforestation of Tahoe forests, which, fortunately, 100 years later is not evident today," Connor explained. "There is evidence of remnants of the flumes which carried the timber logs by water sometimes many miles down the hill. Blocks of ice to help keep the miners reasonably cool also found their way down the flumes.

"I'm sure you're aware that the mines were very unpleasant places to work with temperatures well over 100 degrees and shifts lasting only 15 minutes or so. Also, the air was foul and the water was brackish," Connor added.

"Why was it so hot down here?" asked Jack.

"Mining and its exploration," explained Connor, "led to opening geothermal pockets and vast underground reservoirs which spewed scalding hot water into the mine shafts: hot enough to boil an egg, scald a man to death, or drown him. This necessitated the addition of blowers, giant fans and eventually the Sutro tunnel over eight years in the making and which helped drain away much of the hot geothermal water.

It drained up to four million gallons daily. The Sutro tunnel is an engineering marvel: it's nearly four miles long from near the top of Mount Davidson to its base and has two lateral drains: one nearly a mile long and the other a mile and a half in length. The tunnel also provided gravity assistance in removing ore from the mines."

"Connor, thanks for the mining context." Jack was aware of how the place and time made the briefing even more significant.

They exited the elevator at the 1800 foot level and noticed that the elevator immediately began to return to the surface.

"That's odd," observed Connor. "Could they have changed the timing on the return mechanism?"

The group proceeded to walk down a slope in the mine and noticed several branches off the main shaft.

Jack asked where the branches led and Connor explained some went to other mines and some to the Sutro Tunnel. Not only did the Sutro provide drainage out of the mines, it also provided ventilation for the miners.

"Remember the canary in the coal mine?" asked Connor.

"What about it?" asked Coop.

"In early days, miners would place a canary at the end of the mine and if the bird fell from its perch, miners would know tasteless and odorless gases were present and it was time to evacuate the mine. It was an early form of warning to the miners: and quite effective," Connor explained, "as long as someone kept their eye on the birdie."

Just then they heard the lift stop at their level, and someone shouted "fire in the hole!" Connor quickly herded the group into an adjacent arm of the mine, told them to place their hand over their ears and open their mouths. An ear deafening explosion rocked them off their feet. Rocks began to fall from the tunnel walls and a cave-in blocked their retreat back to the lift.

"What the heck was that?" yelled Jack. *Was this the act*

*of saboteurs wanting to cut off their exit from the mines,* Jack thought immediately.

Without answering, Connor quickly guided them along an adjacent tunnel which luckily had not been compromised, to the Sutro tunnel. They were able to walk quickly along the tunnel's downslope which would exit in about two miles at the base of Mount Davidson.

As they were jogging down the Sutro, they heard a rushing sound and noticed some water beginning to race under foot. What was initially an inch or so of water began to grow in depth and heat the water. When it covered their shoes, it made jogging difficult with a mile to go before exiting the Sutro.

Connor made an executive decision considering the distance yet to travel to safety, the growing level of the water and its heat. Instead of continuing down the Sutro, Connor directed the group to another tunnel which rose away from the Sutro.

He hustled the group up a steep incline until they reached a large underground cavern. Connor announced they should be "safe here." He looked over the group he was guiding.

"Someone doesn't like you and wants to prevent you from reaching that strongbox. They must have opened the Sutro tunnel floodgates. Do you understand what this means?"

"It's becoming obvious," commented Coop.

"Those goddamn Russian bastards," said Jack.

"How did they know we were headed down the Rabbit Hole?' asked Laura.

"I expect they spied us heading down," said Coop.

*Well it doesn't matter how, the question is what do we do now?* thought Jack.

"Seems to me you have two choices: either continue on, or get the heck out of here," said Connor.

"I'm in," said Jack.

"Others?" he asked.

Laura paused. Gave careful thought and declared that she was "in."

Coop thought about Veronica and if she would be safe despite what they were doing for her. He imagined the small of her back while holding her, her face turned up towards his. In a moment, all agreed to proceed: they had come too far to be deterred.

With that, Connor said he might know a way to circle back, crossing the Sutro "River" and move into the 1864 foot level of the Ophir mine.

"Before we proceed, I want to take a quick look ahead of where we're going."

Connor decided against saying he knew this was a huge risk and possibly a chance they would all die.

Coop said: "I have just the ticket" as he took his backpack off, and summoned his Tinker Bell drone.

Connor exclaimed, "What the heck?"

Coop explained, "I let her go and watch the phone as pictures emerge of the tunnel ahead."

Connor explained the tunnel led them back toward the Sutro Tunnel. As Tinker Bell approached the Tunnel, they saw with alarm it was now a river of scalding hot water headed swiftly downhill. It was moving too quickly and too hot to cross.

Nevertheless, the group followed Connor back toward the

Sutro Tunnel and stopped when they came upon the swiftly moving river of nearly boiling water. Connor looked up and down the river, then the ceiling of the tunnel.

"This should work," he said, taking out a gun resembling a flare gun from his knapsack and loading a line to a projectile, then fitting the projectile into the enlarged barrel of the pistol. He held the pistol with both hands and aimed it at the ceiling mid way between the banks of the river and shot the round.

"Success," he declared, as he pulled on the line to assure it would hold. "Be my guest," he offered the rope to Jack. Jack grabbed it, gave it a tug, and ran toward the river yelling "Geronimo!"

Jack swung over the Sutro River and landed on the other bank. After helping himself up and brushing himself off, he tied a rock to the end of the line and tossed it back across the river to Connor, who offered the line to Coop.

Coop then ran, jumped and swung across the river, declaring he was thrilled with the results. Back came the rope attached to a rock and Laura grabbed hold. She raced toward the river, took a big leap and did a mid-air flip, landing upright on her feet, holding the line, then bowing proudly to the group.

"Where did that come from?" asked Jack, incredulously.

"Well, I did take a semester of gymnastics," she laughed out loud.

"Cool," said Jack.

Connor tested the line to make sure it would support him, and he too, easily bridged the gap between the river banks and landed upright. He then secured the rock tied to the line to a large crack in the rock wall so no followers from the other side of the river could use it, but allowing for their escape back over the river, if necessary.

"Everyone ok?" asked Connor.

Looking at each other, Jack said, "Absolutely!"

"Then let's go this way," Connor directed with his hand. They proceeded about 100 yards, when Connor held up his hand signaling the group to stop. They'd come to a cross tunnel and had to decide which way to turn.

Jack wondered where in the heck they were: about 1800 feet underground, with some bad guys chasing them (and apparently attempting to kill or entomb them) and no precise location of the strongbox...

Just then, Jack heard a noise behind the group.

"Quiet, everyone," Jack whispered. Then he looked at Coop. "Coop, can you check out the noise?"

"On it," said Coop as he turned and headed in the opposite direction.

Jack then looked to Connor and signaled they should proceed: but which direction? Left or right? Connor's knowledge of the mines was invaluable. He turned right and the tunnel began to decline slightly. Had they turned left, Jack thought the tunnel would have risen. Since their goal was to reach 1864 feet, down hill seemed like the right call.

*Can't go too deep*, Jack thought, *or can you?*

After about another 50 yards down the right branch of the tunnel Jack quietly asked Connor how much farther he thought they had to proceed. Connor said he recalled a side chamber not too far ahead. Just then the group heard several loud bangs and flashes of light! Everyone hit the deck. Moments later Coop came running down the tunnel.

"What's up, Coop?" asked Jack.

"That noise was the goons following us," Coop responded.

"Did they get across the Sutro river?" Jack asked.

"Either they fished the line we used back across the river, or they followed a series of tunnels which connected them to the same side of the river as us," Coop speculated. "In either event, I caused them to rethink their plans with a couple of flashbangs."

"Nice work, partner."

The group leapt forward and began to jog down the tunnel sensing they were closing in on the long awaited treasure. And there it was; the side chamber Connor had mentioned a moment ago.

Jack surveyed the chamber which was thirty by thirty with a fifteen foot ceiling and asked Connor if he thought they had reached a depth of 1864 feet. Connor pointed to a timber on which was etched faintly the number, 1864.

"Eureka," exclaimed Jack, "we found it."

But where was "it"? Jack and the others began looking around the chamber searching for the strongbox that Graham Stackhouse no doubt had buried over 100 years ago after the San Francisco poker game and the box's lengthy travel to Virginia City. Where would I hide such a box, thought Jack: in, under, or on the floor, the ceiling, the walls? He closed his eyes and thought.

# CHAPTER THIRTY FIVE

Jack carefully examined the square-set timbering which supported the chamber and noticed that an extra timber with the year 1864 etched on it was leaning against one of the Chamber walls, connected to the floor and ceiling timbers.

"Come here and help me pull this timber out of the way," said Jack. "It does not appear to be a load bearing timber." Connor and Coop lent a hand.

They noticed the timber was not secured by nails and the three men began to rock the timber back and forth. It began to move. As it did, a small shaft in the side of the tunnel wall was uncovered. Jack asked Connor to shine his light in the shaft.

Lo and behold the light struck a silver box. "Help me get this out," instructed Jack. The three men pulled on the box and removed it from its hiding place. The side of the box was labeled "Niantic!"

"Ok gang," exclaimed Jack. "This is it. Now if only the key fits." Jack inserted the Niantic key in the strongbox lock. He paused, took a deep breath and then twisted it: *click*. The door to the box popped open even after all those years.

Jack smiled, feeling a real satisfaction in finding the strongbox at last. He mentally recounted his first meeting with Veronica Hill, the Niantic key, the Graham Stackhouse note ("This key unlocks a valuable treasure, keep it safe"), the hunt for the Niantic which led to the 1864 poker game, the trip up the American River to Sutter's Mill, the visit to Virginia City and exploration of the Mark Twain Museum complete with a review of the contents of the time capsule, then the Back of Bar map, the exploration of the mines and dodging the Russians!

This was a moment that was at once familiar but so different. Oftentimes, locating the prized item could turn into a moment of deflation or exhilaration. Sometimes both.

He dumped the contents on the tunnel floor. Out spilled socks filled with gold coins. "Wow," he said. "There must be dozens of gold coins in these socks."

"And gold is trading at nearly $1800 an ounce," said Coop.

"No doubt there's additional value in the fact that these are 1860 gold coins," he added

Jack noticed a paper wedged in the inside top of the strong box. He carefully pried the paper from the box and unfolded it. "Well, I'll be," said Jack.

"What is it?" asked Laura.

Pouring over it, Jack read the contents aloud. "A stock certificate executed by James Flood to the bearer of the certificate." The stock certificate represented thousands of shares of mines in the Comstock Lode. Additionally, Jack saw miscellaneous shares of the Central Pacific Railroad, the Virginia and Gold Hill Water Company, the Pacific Mill and Mining Company and the Pacific Wood, Lumber and Flume Company.

"What do you think these are worth?"

Laura said, "We will have to do a bit of research on that, Jack. Many of these businesses no longer exist and likely have little or no value, or in the case of the railroad, have been acquired by others. As for the large number of shares of Comstock mines, my instinct is this represents a very significant portion of the ownership of the mines. Mr. Flood must have lost his shirt in that poker game!"

Connor said that "Flood was an Irishman and with his pals, John McKay, James Fair and William S. O'Brien, they were the Bonanza Kings! They rivaled the Bank Crowd dominated by William Sharon, William Ralston and Charles Crocker of Bank of California and Crocker National Bank fame. The Irish Big Four controlled the Comstock Lode mines where the Big Bonanza was discovered. Thousands of shares is likely a big chunk of mine ownership."

Jack took the share certificates and carefully replaced them in the strongbox except for the Comstock Lode mines share certificate which he put in his back pocket. He then began picking up the gold coins which had spilled out of their socks onto the floor. As he was filling the last sock, an unknown voice said, "Finish filling the sock and give us the box, Mr. Armstrong."

Jack turned and saw four men holding 9mm Makarov (or PMM; Pistolet Makarava Modern) handguns. If Jack recalled correctly, the PPM Makarov is a Russian handgun and holds 12 rounds. That's 48 rounds staring them in the face, thought Jack. And Jack and his team were unarmed.

He quickly looked at Coop who shook his head signaling they should cooperate and not resist the attackers. Jack nodded, raising his hands.

"What do you want?"

"Mr. Armstrong, we appreciate your having led us to Mr. Stackhouse's strongbox and for that we have a simple question for you: your money, or your life?"

Jack answered, "That calls for a simple answer, here's the money," pushing the strongbox filled with gold coins and share certificates toward the armed men.

The leader spoke Russian to one of his followers and that individual then stepped forward and took the strongbox with the gold coins and stock certificates. Then the leader told another one of his followers to search the group. Each of Jack's group was patted down. Finding nothing from the strongbox, the Russian operative signaled the leader with a hands down indicating he had found nothing, and said:

"Uri, they are clean."

"Ok," uttered his comrade.

"Mr. Armstrong, please to step forward with your hands raised."

Jack did as requested and was hit on the side of the head with Uri's pistol. he slumped to the ground. Coop began to launch himself toward the attacker in defense of Jack, but stood down when three of the Russian gang pointed their guns at his head.

Uri reached down and withdrew the folded Flood stock certificate from Jack's back pocket.

He told Jack to stand up then added, "Don't make me lose my temper, Mr. Armstrong."

Pausing for several seconds, Uri told the group: "Now that I have your full attention, I want all of you to turn your backs to us, count backwards from 100 slowly and then you may try to leave."

Jack was wobbly but managed to stand. He joined the group and turned away as instructed. He wondered if they would be shot in the back. Then they heard receding footsteps at a jogging pace likely with two men carrying the heavy strongbox. He was thankful that the threat of assassination dissipated.

As his head cleared, Jack imagined Uri must have seen him slip the Comstock Lode stock certificate into his back pocket when the Russians entered the chamber behind them. *What did Uri mean when he said "then you may try to leave?"*

Laura had been counting softly and slowly backwards from 100: ... "Fire in the hole, Fire in the hole!" they heard.

*5,4,3,2,1,* Jack counted in his mind. Just then, he saw a blinding flash of light reflected off the chamber walls and a massive explosion, the blast from which propelled the group back several yards and slammed each of them to the ground on their backs.

What light there was went out and dust and debris began to fill the chamber which made breathing difficult and nearly impossible. Although Jack was able to roll over to protect himself, he felt several sharp rock chips find purchase in his back like little pins. Painful, but fortunately there were no large rocks on him and no cave-in of the tunnel chamber other than the entrance and, necessarily, the exit.

Still, being entombed 1800 feet under ground in total darkness despite severe injuries wasn't a gift at this point. Jack realized the events that had unfolded painted a bleak picture. Slowly, he began to gather himself and attempt to communicate with the others in spite of their hearing loss caused by the noise of the blast.

Connor, who was kneeling, switched on a flashlight he

had carried with him allowing Jack to begin to measure the conditions of his colleagues. First, seeing Laura prone on her back and not moving was his first point of reference. Next, seeing Coop, already standing and dusting himself off brought a smile to Jack's face. The most dependable guy ever, Jack thought.

Jack crawled over to Laura, seeing that she was slowly breathing he raised her head gently to give her a drink of water from the canteen on his belt. She accepted and began to open her eyes, recognizing Jack and breaking into a smile. Her unwavering positivity had always been there, even when they were young and at Berkeley. Jack brushed some debris from her.

"Does anything hurt? Can you move?"

Laura nodded but pointed to her ears. Jack understood. She couldn't hear due to the intensity of the blast. He helped her sit up. Shaking her head back and forth, she opened her mouth and made a small "ohhing" sound, as if to check to see if her voice still worked. She rubbed her ears and then smiled.

"I can hear you now."

Jack gave her a hug and helped her stand.

After several minutes, the group began to collect their thoughts and shake away their own wobbly headedness and hearing deterioration.

"They must have set a charge to close the mouth of the tunnel," said Connor. He had to repeat what he said several times to win nods of understanding from the group.

"Is anyone else hurt?" asked Jack.

Laura looked down over her torso and legs, ripped

jeans and scratched knees, bloodied from the impact in the mine. Her legs and arms moved haltingly but she nodded affirmatively. Each responded. Laura noticed that Jack had lacerations where he had been hit with Uri's gun. She reached out to touch and Jack pulled away.

"It's ok. I'm fine."

"Ok, so what do we do now?" mumbled Laura who became more lively after Jack had helped her up and given her water.

"We have two alternatives: Plan A or Plan B," said Connor.

"Which are?" asked Jack.

"Plan A is to see if we can clear a hole through the debris."

"With only a couple of shovels and picks and no means of communicating with anyone topside?" asked Jack.

"Primarily with our hands," responded Connor, "And we have limited water and air."

"And Plan B?" asked Coop.

"I'm working on it," answered Connor.

# CHAPTER THIRTY SIX

Rocks and debris covered the chamber entrance/exit from floor to ceiling but none of them said what was on their minds. Buried alive.

Connor said, "This is going to be quite a challenge."

Coop and Jack exchanged glances. Coop added, "You can say that again, Connor."

*Yes*, Jack thought, *the Russians were not satisfied with simply taking the strongbox under armed threat. They wanted to seal us in without the possibility of escape. Not a pleasant thought*, the optimistic Jack admitted inwardly. His thoughts began to scurry in different directions. They could have shot us rather than leave us to realize we were doomed. Which is worse, he didn't know.

*Whoa, buddy*, he quietly tugged at his interior self, the one he spoke to intently when things got bad. *You're beginning to go to the Dark Side, Armstrong. Don't give in, not now. Not with this group looking at you for something. But what?*

Jack knew from the many books he'd read when awake in the middle of the night, when confronted with a significant challenge it's human nature to adopt the worst scenario: the Dark Side of what is likely to happen. Presumably, that's a defense mechanism, a way to prepare one's mind and body for the worst in case it occurred when in fact the worst rarely occurred.

Typically, Jack blew off the Dark Side, believing it was a giant waste of time. Having to dispel Dark thoughts and convert his mental and physical energy into positive thinking wasn't going to be easy today. *But somehow… there was always a way out, he just needed to find it. Houdini found a way out of many impossible situations. Come on, man. Think, Jack, think!*

While Jack was thinking, Coop was doing. He began rolling rocks out of the way. Connor joined him, then even Laura did as well as she rolled up her sleeves and began to move debris. Jack joined but continued thinking.

Connor directed the group to focus on the top rocks:

"If we can create a hole at the top to wiggle though, we may be able to reach the other side."

After an hour of digging with their hands and using their shovels for debris removal, they had created a body sized hole near the top of the rock pile.

"The good news is that we have created a 10 foot mini path out of here," said Connor.

"What's the bad news?" asked Laura.

"We have no idea how far we have to go to reach the other side of the fallen rocks. It could be a couple more yards, or a hundred yards. It's tough to tell given the sizable charge that Russians set off and the existence of old mine timbers supporting the tunnel," Connor said. "Furthermore, the longer the escape tunnel we create, the more debris we have to remove from the hole we are creating."

This reminded Jack of the movie *The Great Escape* with Steve McQueen. The clever way the American POWs were able to remove tunnel dug dirt from their escape route without the Germans knowing. Quite an effort, which did not bode well for his group even without the need to hide the removed debris.

"And given the couple of water canteens we have, we will soon run out," said Coop.

Laura laughed in the way people laugh at a funeral. "For god's sake, it won't be lack of water that kills us. More likely the air will run out."

"Rather than dig in the dark of the escape tunnel, Connor placed the group's only flashlight at the head of their diggings. This helped immensely, but left the chamber in darkness as the miner's hat lights had been damaged in the explosion. Connor asked if someone would light a candle which they'd packed as a reserve source of light..

Laura did so and there was faint light which dimly illuminated the chamber.

"At least the air seems to be fine," commented Laura, as the candle flickered.

"What did you say, Laura?" asked Jack.

"I said, the air seems to be fine."

"Quiet everyone!" commanded Jack. He closed his eyes and listened.

After two long minutes of quiet,

Coop asked, "What do you hear?"

"It's not what I hear, it's what I feel, and what I see."

"Ok, what do you feel and see?" asked Connor.

"I feel a gentle, but steady stream of air coming from behind us," said Jack as he faced the debris blocking the tunnel entrance.

They all stopped digging and first watched the candle flame flicker in a direction away from the tunnel wall behind them, then they turned to face the wall in an effort to see where the air was emanating from.

"Rather than continuing to dig into the unknown, I suggest we locate and follow that airstream! It could lead us to an escape route."

"Good idea," Connor remarked. "If we find the source of the air, we could find an exit. That's our Plan B! Good thinking, Jack."

"But you said there are hundreds of mines and miles of tunnels under Virginia City, " said Laura.

"Yes, and I am an Irish Tunnel Rat a.k.a. A Friendly Son of St. Patrick who will find a tunnel exit and a path to those Russian bastards!"

"Here here!" said Coop. "I too have a score to settle with those low lifes and whoever put them up to murdering and stealing the Stackhouse strongbox."

"And I wouldn't mind figuring out how they followed and intercepted us: they knew of the treasure, even calling it Graham Stackhouse's treasure, if I recall correctly, and after all our hard work and sleuthing, had us lead them directly to it!" said Jack.

"For their convenience, " commented Coop.

"I'm glad you can joke." Connor said.

"One more mystery," posited Jack, "Was it really necessary to entomb us to retrieve the Stackhouse strongbox? Why not wait til we exited the mines and take the box from us then? Why attempt to kill us in Coloma while we investigated the tailrace for clues to the location of the strongbox?

"The questions and mystery can wait. Let's get to work and find our way out of here," said Connor. "Otherwise, we'll never see the light of day."

Jack responded, "We need to find the source of the air flow and hope it leads us to a tunnel that will help us escape! Feel for air flow: I know it's coming from somewhere in this chamber. Once we find it, we most likely find an exit from the chamber and hopefully an escape tunnel."

They all began to search. Laura took the candle and walked around the chamber near the walls. Then she held the flame toward the ceiling and even the floor. She saw nothing peculiar.

Connor divided up sectors of the chamber: ceiling, floor, and the walls on the left and right sides, and assigned each person one part. He encouraged them to close their eyes and try to feel from where the air might be flowing. He also required them to be silent in their hunt.

After a few minutes, Coop said: "I may have found something."

Touching the side of the wall at the furthest part of the tunnel away from the cave-in, he asked Connor to come over. Connor did and gently felt the wall and detected a slight draft of air. Connor then summoned Laura with the candle.

As the candle flame flickered, he turned and observed the location of the draft directly opposite the cave-in.

He concluded: "The blast must have damaged this wall" pointing to the area where he felt a draft which Coop had discovered.

"Our Russian friends may have done us a modest favor," commented Jack.

Connor took a pointed stone laying on the floor and used it to hammer the wall where the draft was felt most and the candle flickered greatly.

He chipped at the wall and slowly a hole in the wall began to emerge. Then the others found similar stones on the chamber floor and also began knocking around the hole that Connor had started. Coop used one of the two shovels to attack the wall. The hole grew in size and the flow of air increased.

"Just a minute," Coop said as he retrieved the flashlight which had been left at the entrance to the escape tunnel they'd been building. Pointing the light into the narrow hole in the wall showed another tunnel only a few yards away. It was solid rock that they had to breach to reach it. It would take hours of chipping away to make a hole large enough for them to pass.

Coop had an idea: "Just a minute," he said as he reached into his knapsack and took out a flash bang. Let's use this to advance our effort. He placed the small explosive into the hole in the wall that had been created and told everyone to retreat to the furthest end of the chamber, turn their heads away, close their eyes, open their mouths and cup their hand over their ears. They did as instructed. Coop set the charge and ran away from it.

The flash bang blew and created a blinding surge of light, a loud bang, and when the dust settled there was a hole the size of a small person.

Coop quipped: "I guess we can call ourselves The Hole in the Wall Gang!"

Jack rolled his eyes at Coop's attempt at humor. It was never his strong suit.

Connor looked through the hole and saw another tunnel. He scratched his head and took out his pocket map of the Consolidated Virginia Mine. After twisting the map a couple of times, he declared:

"By the Luck of the Irish, I think we are about to enter the Yellow Jacket Mine."

"The Yellow Jacket Mine?" asked Jack.

"It was the site of the largest and deadliest mine fire in Nevada mining history," commented Connor. On the morning of April 7, 1869, a fire spread at the 1800 foot level in the Yellow Jacket Mine. Firefighters entered the mine to fight it and were unsuccessful. The poisonous gases from the mine pushed them back and the fire spread into the Kentucky and Crown Point mines. The fires persisted and burned for months and were hot for years. The mines were sealed and 35 lives were lost.

"If I am correct and this is the Yellow Jacket, we may see some bodies on our way out," warned Connor.

"Well let's not join them," said Jack who headed to the hole in the wall and began to wiggle through. He was followed by Connor, then Laura and Coop brought up the rear. Once in Yellow Jacket, Connor again checked his map with his flashlight and pointed out their direction of travel.

They continued for what seemed to be a mile, before coming to a boarded up mine exit and entrance. Fortunately, they had passed no bodies on the way.

"These must be the remnants of the Yellow Jacket Mine Fire seals," said Connor. "Let's see if we can break through them."

As with most construction, it's often easier to break out than to break in. With some diligent effort, they were able to remove the aged timbers and create a mini exit from the mine shaft. Their first sighting of the sun and smell of fresh air was welcome and exhilarating. They breathed deeply and rested for a few minutes. Then Connor pointed them in the direction of his brother's bar to which they went with renewed vigor.

# CHAPTER THIRTY SEVEN

Jack and his colleagues reached the Union Brewery a few minutes later. Connor immediately approached his brother, Dillon, gave him a big Irish brotherly hug and ordered beers for each of them. The beers were gladly accepted and Coop and Jack chugged theirs.

Then, Connor explained to Dillon what had happened. Dillon was slack-jawed. "I had no idea," he said. "Wow, I could have lost you, bro!"

"Yes you almost did, my Irish brother, but for the luck of the Irish," Connor replied. " It will take more than a gang of Russians and a collapsed tunnel to trap this Son of Saint Patrick!" he declared. "Bye the bye, did you happen to see our fine furry friends skulking around town asking questions?"

Dillon replied, "I may have seen a few odd characters a bit earlier."

"Do you happen to know where they went?" asked Connor.

"I heard one say the Opera House."

"Piper's Opera House?" repeated Connor.

"I believe so."

"That's odd," said Connor. "The Opera House isn't hosting any events today."

"Maybe they simply wanted an out-of-the-way place to meet," said Dillon.

Laura turned to Jack and Coop and mentioned that Piper's Opera House was an historic performing arts venue in Virginia City. It opened in 1863 at about the same time as the San

Francisco poker game in which Mark Twain participated. It burned to the ground in the Virginia City fire of 1875 and was rebuilt in 1878. Then the rebuilt Opera House burned again in 1883 and was again rebuilt in 1885. It was used for musical performances and even as a training facility for Gentleman Jim Corbett to prepare for his bout with Bob Fitzsimmons. It was also the stage for Hal Holbrook's one man play entitled "Mark Twain Tonight!"

"You are a friggin' encyclopedia, Laura," said Jack.

"Well, you knew that, Jack. Isn't that why you asked me to join you and be part of your team?"

"You got that right," he said, "And you have been incredibly helpful as well as darned good company!"

Laura blushed. "Guys, has anyone heard from Veronica? We have been so out of touch. I do hope all is well."

Coop said he would give her a call later that evening and added, "Besides the fact I do like opera, shouldn't we head over to the Opera House and see if we can find some Russians to dine on?"

Jack smiled, then turned to Laura. "Perhaps you wouldn't mind sitting the next scene out, kiddo, as I expect that things may get dicey and move in a direction a bit beyond your area of professorial and historical expertise. "And Laura?"

"Yes, Jack."

"Could you give some thought as to why the treasure was so important to them? Or, was it the location of the treasure in which they were so interested?"

Laura nodded, and Jack asked Dillon and Connor if they would like to join Coop and him on a little foray to the Opera House. Both men readily agreed.

Jack suggested they stop by Coop's BMW and retrieve some armament, "just in case."

Coop had an assortment of weapons under the modified floorboard of his BMW. There were handguns, long guns, flash bang grenades like the ones used in the mines, knives of various lengths, scopes, night vision goggles, tactical radios and bullet proof vests. Coop asked Connor if he had ever used a handgun.

"Our dad was a cop in NYC for 25 years. He made sure that Dillon and I were proficient marksmen with various weapons."

With that, Coop handed a bullet proof vest to each person, a tack radio with an ear piece and invited them to choose the weapon of their liking.

"Remember fellas, we have the element of surprise on our Russian friends. They think we're dead. Boy will they be surprised to see us!"

"We have a serious score to settle," offered Coop.

"And I wouldn't mind retrieving the loot they took," said Jack. With that, they started heading to Piper's Opera House just a couple of blocks away to hear a Russian opera.

"Ok, partner, what's our plan?" Jack asked Coop, explaining Coop's background in law enforcement and Navy Seal training to Dillon and Connor.

"Let's try to figure their point of entry and whether they left any watchers." replied Coop. "I have my Tinker Bell which can help with an overview of the premises."

With that, Coop reached into his backpack, pulled and primed his drone. Off it went, 40 feet into the air and down the street toward the Opera House. Once there, Coop maneuvered it over the top of the building and slowly around the outside. They watched the video on Coop's iPhone and saw no one on the rooftop or around the edge of the building.

Coop directed the drone down the back of the Opera House and caused it to hover next to each of the building's back windows allowing them to view inside. Coop noticed some movement out one window and hovered there. He saw one of the Russians peering out the window and up and down the back alley. From that movement, he concluded they were being careful about intruders.

"One located," he said.

He then directed the drone to the left side of the building and performed the same check. Again, he found one of the Russian's looking out the window. Similarly, he noted a third peering out the right side of the building. That one to cover the front, he thought.

Just then he noticed a black car pull up in front of the Opera House and a man got out and entered.

"See what I see?" asked Jack of Coop.

"Yep: it's Max Hill," Coop said.

"Cool," responded Jack. "I wonder what he wants."

"The contents of the strongbox, no doubt," commented Coop.

"But why couldn't his henchmen bring the Mountain to Mohammed? They could have brought the loot to him."

"Unless there is something more valuable than gold coins in play here," speculated Coop.

"Or he does not trust even his own men," commented Connor.

"I bet the Comstock share certificates have something to do with it," said Jack. "Perhaps we can ask a few questions when we join their party."

Max entered Piper's Opera House and gathered his men in the manager's office. Then he received a call from Adamoff.

With a curt voice Adamoff said, "Did you take care of Armstrong as you were instructed Mr. Hill?

"Yes, they're buried 1800 feet below ground in one of the Comstock mines," Max responded.

"And what is in the strongbox, Mr. Hill?"

"I have just opened it and see bags of coins and share certificates."

"I don't give a shit about the gold, Mr. Hill. What interests me are the shares certificates. What do they represent?"

"There's a water company, a lumber company, a transcontinental railroad…."

Before he could finish, Adamoff cut him off and demanded to know if the certificates represented "The mining interests, you fool!"

"And shares in the Comstock mines," responded Max.

"Good, don't let those out of your possession!"

Max couldn't understand why Adamoff didn't care about the gold and interests in business other than the Comstock mines. So he posed the simple question,

"Why are you not interested in anything other than the mining interests?"

"That's for me to know Mr. Hill. There is no need for you to know. Let's just say my interest is a mystery mineral and access thereto is the same," explained Adamoff as he closed the call.

"Listen up," said Coop firmly. "We attack from the rear. There's a better chance not being seen coming from the rear. Besides, the Russians will be preoccupied with Max inside up front. Let's hit it."

Down the side of a nearby building they proceeded to the alley which would lead to the rear of the Opera House. Quietly and carefully they used the alley to the target building. Fortunately, the Opera House was flush with the back of the other buildings and did not give a sight advantage to someone looking out the back window.

Jack enjoyed watching his friend and partner's skillful direction, keeping them all the while behind various walls, overhangs, and alleys and away from the sightline of the Russians.

One building from the Opera House, Coop held up his hand directing them to stop. The group were in sync and didn't question him. Coop keyed his mic and whispered for the group to stay put while he took care of some business and disappeared.

About 10 minutes later he returned and motioned the group slowly forward. Entering the alley between the Opera House and the building they stood behind Coop while he directed Tinker Bell to scout the back windows of the Opera House. He then directed her to investigate the windows facing the alley between the buildings. Seeing no one watching out of windows he assumed those inside were focused on Max Hill toward the front of the building.

He glanced toward the entrance and motioned the group

to proceed across the alley to the back of the Opera House. Once there, he found the rear to the building and tried the door knob. It was locked, but not secured by a sophisticated lock.

Coop took out a fiber optic camera attached to a wire and slipped it under the door. He attached it to his iPhone and saw a picture of the inside of the back of the Opera House. He did not see anyone and reached inside his pocket for a lock pick. Within 30 seconds he had unlocked the door.

Quietly and slowly he listened for any movement. Since it was an old building, he felt secure there was a lack of alarms. Once open, the group quietly entered. Coop motioned for Connor and Dillon to move left and Jack and Coop right.

They found themselves in a room at the back of the Opera House stage. Coop slipped his fiber optic camera under the cyclorama and searched for Russians. Seeing none, he motioned the two groups to advance along the sides of the stage behind the curtains. Then he held his fist in the air in a hold motion and after checking his watch, showed five fingers, four, three, two, one: and suddenly there was an explosion in front of the Opera House. Coop motioned the men to move forward across the stage and up the aisles toward the front of the building.

The explosion had drawn Max Hill and his Russian operatives from the Manager's Office where they'd been meeting to the entrance of the building in an attempt to determine what had happened.

Coop had anticipated the same and took advantage of the confusion. Jack looked at Coop and gave him a thumbs up sign.

As Coop's cohorts opened the aisle doors leading to the entrance, one of the Russians turned with a gun in hand and opened fire, missing Coop's head by an inch.

Coop immediately responded and shot him between the eyes.

*One down*, Coop counted to himself.

Another turned and fired as well. This time, Connor downed him with a shot to the heart.

*Two down*, thought Coop.

Two Russians ran up the stairs leading to the Opera House balcony. Coop and Jack chased them up the stairs, Coop up the right stairway and Jack up the left stairway while Connor and Dillon checked those who'd been shot to assure they were no longer a threat.

Shots zipped from the upstairs balcony. Coop and Jack dropped on the stairway and took cover from the railing. Coop signaled Jack and silently communicated his next move, to which Jack nodded his understanding.

Coop lobbed one of his fabled flash bangs over the stairway rail and up to the balcony landing. After the explosion, he and Jack scurried up the stairs to the balcony and told the Russians to drop their weapons and raise their hands.

"Against the wall and hands up," shouted Coop. The disoriented Russians did as directed.

Jack, approaching from the opposite stairway, moved forward and searched each of them while Coop covered them, one of whom was Uri, the gang's leader.

"It's nice to see you again Uri. This time under slightly different circumstances. As we like to say in America, 'Turnabout is fair play.'"

"How did you escape the tunnel Mr. Armstrong?" Uri asked in disbelief.

"With the help of an Irish Leprechaun…. Nah, you wouldn't understand," Jack answered.

"Two of your men are dead, and we now have you and your colleague. Where's Max?"

"I'm pleased to say that Max has escaped," Uri said.

"Escaped?" Jack exclaimed.

"Yes, when the explosion occurred in front of the Opera House, Max finished a telephone call, grabbed some of the treasure from the strongbox and told us to go inside and hold off the attackers while he hopped in his car," Uri explained.

Jack thought, *Luck of the Irish, we had him and he slipped away. Darn!*

"Let's see what he may have left behind," Jack said to Coop.

They tied Uri's hands and those of his partner behind their backs with flex cuffs, then motioned to Uri and his partner to move to the stairs and head down to the lobby. Once there, Jack and Coop asked Connor and Dillon to side bar with them out of earshot of the two Russians.

"So we have two dead and two in custody," said Jack. "Was the strong box left behind?"

"It may be in the Manager's office," said Connor.

"Coop and I will take a look. You and Dillon keep an eye on our friends."

Coop and Jack entered the manager's office and saw the strongbox on the desk. It was open. The two peered in and saw socks filled with gold coins. They did not see the Comstock Lode mine share certificates.

208

"It looks like we have half a loaf," said Coop.

"Or less," said Jack, "Depending on the value of what the share certificates represent."

"What's next?" asked Coop.

"I need to brief Veronica about what happened and the results of our efforts. She should be pleased with our recovery of what is likely to be worth well over a million dollars in gold, but disappointed in the evaporation of the share certificates for the Comstock and the disappearance of the mastermind: one Mr. Max Hill."

"So back to The City! " summarized Coop.

"You got it, partner, but first we have to quiz Uri and his pal and see if there is anything to be gained from them."

# CHAPTER THIRTY EIGHT

Connor and Dillon marched Uri and his pals to the back of the Union Brewery bar and sat them in a secure store room. Jack and Coop joined them.

"Fellas, you're in deep doo-doo!" Jack announced. "That's an American legal term for 'shit' if you were wondering. We can file charges of attempted murder by causing an explosion that entombed us, grand theft of Veronica's strongbox and its contents, and aggravated assault with deadly weapons against the four of us which resulted in killing two of your colleagues in our defense for which you will be found responsible under California's felony murder rule.

"With a little more effort, I am confident we can develop charges against you involving the other shooters in Coloma, the reckless endangerment caused by the motorcyclist in Sacramento, and possibly running me off the road on my bicycle in the San Francisco Presidio. All told, I expect you'll never see another day without prison bars staring you in the face. And I need not add that American prisons are not accommodating to Russians. So it would be in your best interest to come clean now."

Uri said, "I hope you appreciate I did not have my men shoot you and your friends when we had the easy opportunity in the mine." He smiled smugly and continued, "That has to count for something, Mr. Armstrong, otherwise we would not be in your hands now and you'd not be here. What is it you wish to know?"

210

"For starters, where is Max Hill?"

"He headed out of town, but I do not know where he was going," said Uri.

"Did he have the share certificates from the strongbox with him?" asked Jack.

"I believe he did if they were not left in the strongbox. As you know, we don't have them," Uri replied.

"Why would he take the shares with him and not the gold?"

"I'm wondering why you ask these questions. Are you in this business or what? The gold is heavy and difficult to move quickly. As you know, things happened in a big way after the front door blast."

"Perhaps so, but Max's dogged pursuit of us and the strongbox leads us to believe there's more value in the shares than the gold he left behind."

Uri thought for a minute. His ego got the best of him. "You are a fool Mr. Armstrong to be fighting with Mother Russia, a fight you can never win!"

Jack looked at Coop as he saw Coop step forward. Don't, he thought. Don't do anything stupid!

Coop grabbed one of the Russians by the collar and threw him to the ground. He stepped on his neck while taking a small angled and sharp object out of his pocket and tossing it toward the neck of his comrade. The silver piece lodged in the man's neck, just to the side of his Adam's Apple.

The man was in excruciating pain, moaning and screaming. Uri realized they were serious and blurted: "Max was acting on orders from someone high up in the Russian government who thought it was in Mother Russia's best interest to keep you and your team away from Virginia City and its mines."

"Ok, why?"

"I'm not sure," Uri said. "Clearly they thought there was something of value to Russia or the United States other than the Stackhouse strongbox which they either wanted to own or wanted to prevent the U.S. from owning."

"What could that be?" asked Jack. "These are abandoned mines. There are no more significant silver or gold deposits. Miners and mining companies have been all over these mines for decades. I can't believe they left any significant amount of silver or gold behind."

"This is true, Mr. Armstrong."

"So what do the Russians see that we don't see?"

"I'm not sure even Max knows what mystery the Comstock Lode mines hold," speculated Uri.

"Nevertheless, he is a good place to start," said Jack. "So we need to know where Max is, Uri. Where is he likely to go? San Francisco or the Peninsula where his house is located? Another city? Russia?"

"I would start with San Francisco and the Russian Consulate."

"Why do you say that?"

"He has the share certificates representing a significant portion of the ownership in the Comstock mines and that seems to be the target of the Russian interest," offered Uri.

Jack looked to Connor and Dillon and asked if they would keep their guests secure while he headed to San Francisco.

"Of course, we will," said Connor. "It would be our privilege to have such guests of Virginia City while you do what is necessary. We'll alert my cousin, Matt Corroon, Virginia City

Sheriff, to keep them safely in our fabulous jail which was originally built in 1870 and little improved. In the meantime, we will make life slightly more comfortable for Uri's colleague and remove the scalpel you impaled in his neck."

"Thanks, fellas." Then Jack whispered to Coop: "It's the Corroon Family Enterprise. The three Corroon brothers basically own Virginia City."

And to Connor he expressed, "Our deepest gratitude."

"I'm not sure *own* is the proper word," said Connor. "How about 'serve' or 'control'?"

As they walked to Coop's car they discussed next steps.

"Coop, if you agree, I would like you to join me on a trip back to San Francisco and see if we can find Max. In the meantime, we can ask Laura to continue investigating the unknown value of the Comstock Lode stock. There has to be something big we are missing and she's the best person to figure that out."

"Got it."

# CHAPTER THIRTY NINE

Coop and Jack headed to Coop's car, lugging with them the strongbox containing gold from Graham Stackhouse's poker winnings. They started driving toward San Francisco.

This time they were chasing someone, not the other way round. Although the goal was yet illusive, catching up with Max and the Comstock Lode share certificates was the next order of business. And what they had achieved to date felt good. They had managed to break the mystery of the key and the note and stay alive under some pretty harrowing conditions.

Still, there was work to be done. Jack and Coop were determined not to let Max escape with any portion of the treasure let alone possibly the more valuable piece. Jack owed that to his client, Veronica.

It was as if Coop was reading his mind. "Jack, I had said earlier I should check in with Veronica unless you think otherwise."

"Why don't you do that? She would appreciate hearing from the team."

Coop grabbed his phone and dialed her number. Jack tried not to appear too attentive.

"Veronica? It's Coop. How are you doing?" He listened for a bit and then responded, "Ok, I understand. I want you to know things are going well. Max? No, we just missed him in Virginia city."

A moment later he said, "Well, be careful. And I know Jack would agree, please do not leak any of this to your friend or anyone else. Things are at a critical stage."

A moment later he whispered, "Me too. Speak later."

Jack knew at that point that something was happening and if this thing worked out, he would love to see Coop and her get together. Coop deserved it—Veronica seemed like a good gal. And if she doesn't carry too much baggage, she could be good for him.

Jack asked Coop, "So she is with Sidney at Stinson?"

"Yes, she needed some answers directly from Sidney about her relation with Max."

Without asking, Coop also volunteered, "She knows to keep her mouth shut about important matters."

Jack nodded.

Later, along the way, Jack asked Coop what he knew about the Russian Consulate in San Francisco. "Not much. I've never been in it. I do know it's located in lower Pacific Heights and has about 50 antennas on the roof."

"I had heard some in the neighborhood around the Consulate complained about interference with TV, cell phone and WiFi caused by the Russian rooftop broadcasts," commented Jack.

On further reflections, Jack thought aloud "Maybe we don't have to head there. Besides, it won't be open by the time we, or Max, can get there, if that is where he's heading according to Uri."

"What do you have in mind?"

"I think there's a good chance Max is headed to Sidney's house in Stinson Beach. He'll likely spend the night, then make his Russian connection and deliver the share certificates tomorrow. I doubt he thinks we'll look for him at his girlfriend's house."

"You could be right, Jack. Since Veronica's there, we should hustle. She could be in danger with Max knowing she's hired us. Let's head him off at the pass."

"My thoughts exactly," Jack replied. "And, perhaps we can add a bit of drama. I will give Veronica a call at Sidney's so the two of them can welcome Max and create further confusion and even a distraction so we can arrive unnoticed. He will never expect to see Veronica there."

They left Interstate 80 in Vallejo and took the Richmond San Rafael Bridge across the Northern end of San Francisco Bay toward San Rafael. From there they began heading South past San Quentin, and Jack fantasized Max and his goons would wind up there. Taking Highway 101 South, they passed Corte Madera, and left Highway 101 at Mill Valley proceeding West around Mount Tamalpais and Muir Woods toward the Pacific Ocean.

"Obviously you know Stinson Beach a bit," Coop mentioned.

"Visited many times. My grandmother lived in Mill Valley along Stinson Beach road and my brother and I used to visit her as kids with our folks. Stinson is a small town with a population of about 600. It is frequented by wealthy San Franciscans because of the mild temperatures and gorgeous views of the Pacific Ocean and the Bolinas Lagoon which helps frame the beach. There's also another inner Lagoon framed by Seadrift Road on the Ocean side and Dipsea Road on the Bolinas Lagoon side."

Coop enjoyed hearing Jack's musings about the area.

Jack continued. "After the San Francisco Great Fire and

Earthquake of 1906, some San Franciscans migrated to Stinson Beach and used it as a refuge. Little did they know they were moving closer to the epicenter of the earthquake, near Olema in Point Reyes, about 14 miles away."

Jack enjoyed regaling Coop with his local California roots. "Also unique to Stinson Beach is its attraction of great white sharks. It is part of the Northern California version of the Bermuda triangle. One of the highest shark attack rates in the United States occurs off the sandy beaches called Stinson. Something to be mindful of."

"Isn't Stinson the destination for one of the longest running cross country foot races in the United States, The Dipsea?"

"Yep," confirmed Jack. "It started in 1905, the year before the Great Fire and Earthquake, covers 7.5 miles and begins in Mill Valley. Many say the start is the most challenging part of the race: it begins with runners climbing 700 stairs. Some die-hards do what's called a Double Dipsea: from Mill Valley to Stinson Beach and back, and for the truly abnormal, there's the Quad Dipsea!

"Stinson's a great calling card for musicians as well, : Steve Miller and Jerry Garcia. Janis Joplin's cremated ashes were scattered along the beach. As a film setting, *Play it Again, Sam* and *Basic Instinct* have scenes filmed there."

"So it's a bit artsy and craftsy in style," said Coop. *That fits with Sidney's lifestyle as a painter,* he thought.

"What's the game plan?" he asked.

"Let's make sure Max is there. Then we can figure out how we're going to approach him. I doubt he has had time to organize a defense with some of his other Russian goons, but we should be careful nevertheless."

"We still should have the secret of surprise. He doesn't know we know Sidney is his girlfriend? " Coop added.

"Correct."

"Let's drive by her residence on Seadrift Road and see if Max's car is parked there." They did as Jack suggested and cruised slowly by Sidney's house. They did not see Max's car. They did see Veronica's car.

"It's possible Max's car is in her garage," said Coop. "We need to have some eyes on the house."

"Let's drive around the block on Dipsea Road and try to take a peak from across the Lagoon," suggested Jack.

Coop proceeded as described and stopped where he thought they were opposite Sidney's house. He got out of the car and opened the cargo area. Under the covered floor board he located his binos. He pulled out a pair of Steiner 15 X 80 binoculars. The multi-coated optics deliver incredible brightness, which Coop would need in the dimming light. He also attached an ear bud and offered one to Jack to facilitate some communication between them.

Coop looked at Jack and nodded indicating he was headed alongside the house in front of which they'd parked in an effort to reach the edge of the Lagoon. Fortunately, the house was empty and there was no fence, or dogs, with which to contend.

Coop slid silently along the side of the house to the back of it. The back had a nice view of the Lagoon and the distant ocean beyond. He trained his glasses on what appeared to be Sidney's house. He confirmed it was when he saw Veronica speaking to Sidney in the kitchen. Max was not visible, however.

"We may have struck out, partner. No Max."

Coop continued to search the house with his glasses. To the left he saw what appeared to be the master bedroom which had a view of the Lagoon facing his way. Next to the right was the kitchen, in the center of the house. To the right of the kitchen was the Great room with a view of the Lagoon as well. All three rooms were facing Coop with a view of the Lagoon. Presumably a second and possibly third bedroom was located behind the Master bedroom together with baths. Behind the Great room would be the garage. The home's entryway was in the middle of the house leading into the great room and facing a stunning view of the Lagoon and mountains behind Coop.

In back of Sidney's house was a 20 foot dock with a small boat and paddle boards. There was also a seating area around a fire pit. Small hedges acted like fences on each side of the backyard.

Coop continued to survey Sidney's house, and in walked Max. He had either been in the bath or one of the back bedrooms.

"Touchdown," said Coop indicating he saw Max.

Max looked somewhat agitated as he confronted Veronica. No doubt he was questioning why she was there and she, in turn, questioning why he was there, Coop described in ad lib fashion to Jack over a two way radio:

"Confusion and mystery; just what the doctor ordered," said Coop.

"Let's move on them," said Jack. "Coop, I'm thinking a sneak attack from the back of the house. Can you swim the Lagoon and approach from the rear?"

"Does a goose do what, where?" asked Coop comically. "Of

course I can. Just give me a few minutes to get outfitted in my wetsuit and ready up some waterproof weapons."

"Ok," said Jack. "I will drive around the block and approach from the front. I think I will simply knock on the front door while the confusion and finger pointing continues. My presence should add another element to the mix."

"Let's hope Max isn't armed and doesn't attempt to take one of the women hostage," said Coop.

"Let's hope so," agreed Jack.

"Once we gain entry and control the situation we need to relieve Max of the share certificates," reminded Jack.

"I should be in position at the back door within 15 minutes," estimated Coop.

"I will drive around the Lagoon now and begin knocking in 15. See you soon, partner."

Off Jack drove along Dipsea Road around the Lagoon to Seadrift. He set his watch to time his knock with Coop's arrival at the back door. As he approached Sidney's house, he turned his car lights off quietly and came to a stop on the street a couple of houses away. He turned the dome light off before opening the door and exited the car and did not set the alarm as he wanted to avoid the chirping sound that the alarm had been set.

Meanwhile Coop swam quietly across the quarter mile wide Lagoon in his wetsuit with his Glock 19 Mariner and a waterproof bag of extra equipment. The Glock Mariner was one of Coop's favorites because it has maritime spring cups, an internal part that captures the striker spring in the slide. As advertised, "it allows water, oil, and debris to exit the firing pin channel. This enables the pistol to be fired after it's been submerged in water and in extreme hostile environments without field stripping the slide assembly."

So into the water, Glock and all, Coop began to quietly breast stroke across the Lagoon with his swim mask, snorkel and flippers.

The swim was easy as pie, he thought. A moon lit night with no bad guys shooting at you on a lake as flat as a mirror. What could be more relaxing, he thought. As he approached the dock leading from Sidney's house, he kept low in the water so as not to be accidentally seen from her house, or even a nearby home. The last thing he and Jack needed was police interceding in their operation without being briefed.

He took cover under the dock upon reaching it. He slid along its edge toward the house and finding purchase with the ground beneath his feet, he slowly walked along the dock toward the lagoon front. He checked his watch and noted Jack would knock in four minutes.

Slowly he removed his gear, walked out of the water, careful not to make any noise or show signs of surreptitious.

Jack, meanwhile, walked quietly along the street to Sidney's house, turned up the entry path and headed to the front door. There were side windows along the front which did not provide clear views of the street or guests approaching the house. He checked his watch: two minutes to go.

Coop carefully walked on the grass, keeping low and aligning with a wall or beam from which he would not be noticed. As he crept closer, he heard the heated voices of Veronica.

"How can you do this to me Max? Messing around with my best friend, Sidney? And how can you, Sidney, my best friend, carry on with Max behind my back?"

"You don't understand," said Sidney. "It's not what it appears"

"Well it appears to be despicable to me!" exclaimed Veronica.

"And what do you have to say, Max, you low life?"

"It's over between us, Veronica. Get over it! I've bigger and better things to do now!"

Just then, Coop heard a knock on the front door and the three occupants looked at each other.

"Who the heck is that? asked Max.

"I have no idea," offered Sidney.

"Veronica, did you tell anyone you were going to be here?" Max asked.

Before she could answer, another louder knock occurred.

"Sid, you go to the door and check it out."

As she did, Max moved closer to Veronica.

Opening the front door, Sidney said, "What are you doing here?"

"I'm looking for Veronica, is she here?" Jack asked.

"It's Veronica's attorney," Sidney shouted to be heard by Max. "He's looking for Veronica."

"No he isn't," shouted Max. "He's looking for me." As he said that, he grabbed Veronica, held her with his left hand around her waist and grabbed a gun which had been in the back of his pants under his loose shirt. He pointed it at Veronica's head.

Max said to Sidney, "Let him in."

Sidney looked imploringly at Max and then to Veronica. She would have to go along for the time being. Max turned out to be a mess of a guy. But for now, she obeyed instructions.

Jack walked into the Great room and sized up the situation.

"Hi Max, long time no see! Now, is that any way to treat your wife?"

"Ok, wiseguy, who's going to have the last laugh now," said Max who began to point his gun at Jack.

Jack walked toward him but stopped opposite him so Max was holding Veronica and facing the front of the house.

Just then Coop quietly slid the back door open and stepped inside. With everyone except Jack facing the front of the house, they did not notice Coop quietly step behind Max, held his gun to Max's head.

"We will! It's not nice to point a gun at my partner. Drop your gun now or I'll drop it for you with a bullet to your head : 5,4,3,2…" before Coop reached one, Max dropped his gun.

Coop wrapped his left arm around Max's neck and yanked him away from Veronica with the gun still pointed to his head. Jack immediately jumped forward and picked up Max's gun.

Coop told Jack to retrieve some flex cuffs from the bag tied to his waist and adorn Max with them. Jack did so with relish.

Coop slammed Max into a nearby chair. The ladies stood nearby.

"We have a little unfinished business," Jack said as he stood over him. "Let's have a little chat. Specifically, we have a couple of questions: we want the share certificates that you took from the strongbox. Where are they?"

"They're mine," Max asserted.

"I doubt that Max. They're your wife's."

"Community Property," Max asserted.

"Not quite," answered Jack. "It was derived by your wife from her inheritance and has not been commingled with the community estate," Jack said, remembering his law school property professor Rabin instructing him to 'Say it in a clear, concise and lawyer-like manner.'"

"Nice lawyering, Jack!" exclaimed Coop.

"Not so quick, Mr. Armstrong. Where I come from: possession's nine tenths of the law. Or, finders keepers, losers weepers. So all you need do is find where I hid them. Armstrong, unless you want to make a deal."

"What did you have in mind, Max?"

"I can show you where the share certificates have been hidden and you can let me go," Max offered.

"I still don't know why anyone would want shares in a depleted and abandoned silver mine?" questioned Jack

"Well, I can't give away all my secrets, Armstrong. Suffice it to say, we've been very watchful of you ever since you agreed to represent my wife and with her inheritance."

"And who is 'we'," asked Jack.

"Let's just say me and my friends."

Sidney and Veronica had stepped back and were standing near a large abstract painting behind the sofa. Veronica did her best to avoid connecting eyes with Coop's. It was clear she had feelings for him. She was so proud of him right now.

Jack thought Max Hill was not telling the whole truth: there must be some hidden value attached to the mine, and there was a bigger "we" than Max was leading Jack to believe.

Jack took Coop aside while keeping a gun trained upon Max.

"Max Hill went to too much trouble to simply steal some gold coins, as valuable as they may appear, and there must be some value attached to the ownership of the silver mine."

"Agreed," said Coop.

"What do you think it is?" asked Jack.

"Gold's trading at nearly $1800 per ounce today. There are probably over 50 pounds of gold in the strong box, so, we are talking $1.5 Million, ball park. And there will be value to the historic coins themselves. In 1860's mindset, that's a chunk of money for one poker game," offered Coop.

Jack let out a low whistle.

"Still, there has got to be more to it than that. Max still has thousands of shares of the Comstock Lode mines," added Jack, "which he's reluctant to part with and which suggests a value unbeknownst to us."

"Max, to be clear, you will give us the location of the shares in exchange for your release" Jack announced while standing over Max.

Max was quiet. Jack prodded him.

"Sir, you are in a world of trouble: I'm sure we can see you do lengthy time in prison for conspiracy to commit murder, attempted murder, extortion, and murder by virtue of California's felony murder rule. In case you're unfamiliar with that law, when you participate in a felony like grand theft of a strongbox and its contents and someone's killed, anyone killed, you are held responsible. Murder and all the other charges are going to land you in prison for a very long time.

As I explained to your compatriot, Uri, American prisons are not kind to Russians. So it would be in your best interest to come clean with us.

"I'll have to think about it," said Max.

"Don't think too long as we'll be calling the police in a few minutes. Once they become involved we have to inform them of the attempted murder in the mine and your involvement in the Opera House shoot out."

"You said you had a couple of questions. What else?" asked Max.

"Not to get too far ahead of ourselves, Max, but we also would like to know why you and presumably the Russians have interest in ownership of the Comstock Lode mines. As you know, they've been depleted of silver and gold for many years and stand abandoned."

"What if I told you the location of the shares but said I do not know what interest Russians have in the mine? asked Max. "All I know is that they may lead to a mystery mineral."

Jack thought for a moment. To him and his client, the shares were the most important part of the puzzle. If they had the shares, they may be able to reverse engineer Russian interest in the residual value of the mines and the so-called mystery mineral. Even if they knew what the Russians were up to, without the evidence of ownership, it would be a moot point. If law enforcement became involved, who knows how long it would take to sort out the ownership and possession of gold and shares from the strongbox. Further, guys like Max always end up being caught.

As Jack was pausing to think, so was Max. He could always

tell Adamoff and his Russian colleagues that Armstrong and Cooper got the drop on him and made him give up the Comstock shares. What would be more difficult to explain, even if he knew, is why the Russians had interest in owning the abandoned mine and how they became aware of its value. That could raise international and national interests, he thought.

Max needed to steer clear of volunteering information. Let them try to figure it out by themselves. Currently, all they had were suspicions of a greater value: something, somewhere.

Furthermore, there may be other ways to acquire ownership of the mines. Max had asked several of his men to visit Virginia City and see if they could acquire shares in mines related to the Comstock Lode, which they were doing. He suspected Veronica owned through the San Francisco Gold Rush poker game and her inheritance, a significant portion of the mines, but not all of them as the majority interest had been owned by the Bonanza Kings: Flood, Fair, MacKay, and O'Brien. Even if she possessed all of Flood's interest there had to be more shares still to be gained. And of course, it may be possible to engineer the return of the Comstock shares if he had a chance and was not arrested.

"So, Armstrong, if I turn over the shares, what'll you tell the authorities?"

"We will give you a head start. Then, we'll tell them some Russian operatives attempted to kill us in the Comstock by causing a cave-in. After we escaped, we found and confronted them at the old Opera House while they were dividing the loot from the strongbox we'd been hunting. There followed a shoot out where two of them died while we defended ourselves.

Three are in our custody and one got away. We don't know where the escapee is headed," Jack summarized.

"Will you disclose my name if asked?"

"I will not volunteer it, but will disclose it if asked. This is the best deal you could have under the circumstances, Maxie. Take it or leave it. I need to know in 30 seconds, or I'll call the cops."

"I'll take it," commented Max. "But how do I know if you're a man of your word."

"You don't, but there are three witnesses who should support my offer, for what that's worth."

Max looked at each of those in the room.

"The share certificates are in the glove box of my car parked in Sidney's garage.

Coop headed to the garage, retrieved the shares and produced them for the group. Jack then cut the flex cuffs off of Max's hands and told him to get lost. He warned, "If we ever meet again, Max, it will be your last time!"

Max hurried from the room toward the garage. In a few minutes they heard the garage door open and a car engine start. Soon after, Max was gone with the wind.

Jack inspected the share certificates and deemed they appeared to be the real deal. He told Veronica he would keep them safe for her and obtain a valuation of the gold they'd recovered from the strongbox.

"I just want to thank you both, and Laura, for your persistent professionalism and help in solving the mystery of the key and the note of Great Great Grandfather Stackhouse. I can't believe you did it!" Veronica said.

Jack thanked her for her faith in him and his team. Then he added there was an unfinished piece of business.

"What is that?" asked Veronica.

"We still don't know why the Russians are so motivated to have ownership of an old abandoned silver mine, or what the mystery mineral is. If you don't mind, we'll continue our adventure in an effort to find the truth to this seemingly never ending puzzle. Besides, if we find the mine is worth more than it appears, it will benefit you and your ownership interest therein."

"I don't mind, but do be careful, Mr. Armstrong!" Veronica said as she stepped forward and gave him a kiss on the cheek.

"Wow, how nice!" said Jack, as Coop looked on with a smile. "Let's saddle up Coop and head to your folks place in Sonoma. Veronica, why don't you ride with Coop, and I'll take your car. As for you, Sidney, we hope you sell a lot of your paintings because there will be no pot of gold at the end of this rainbow, or any windfall from Max."

Sidney watched as Veronica, Coop, and Jack left her house. She closed her eyes for a moment then turned and walked to her bar. With shaking hands, Sidney made herself a vodka on the rocks. Three gulps later she put the empty glass down, turned and headed to the bedroom. Getting on her knees she looked under the bed and pulled out a suitcase. Her hands were now steady as she packed for a very long trip.

# CHAPTER FORTY

Sara's phone rang. She seemed to sense it would be him and had to stop herself from answering before the first ring was finished. Hearing his voice, she smiled.

"Well, hello stranger. I've been wondering about you. It seems quite a long time since I've seen you." The sound of her voice gave him a peaceful and contented feeling, something sorely missing over the last week.

"Yes, it's been a while and I'm sorry about that. It's been a heck of a week and an even longer story. Suffice it to say, we were successful and found the treasure, the answer to the key and the note."

"That's fantastic, Jack! I had faith you could do it, and you did!"

"Not without great effort, some luck and the help of others, particularly Coop, Laura and a couple of guys called The Corroon Brothers. Let's smuggle a bottle of wine to the top of Russian Hill and have a glass or two while I tell you about it. I need a full dose of beauty right now, and I don't mean the Bay."

Sara blushed. "Terrific idea, Jack. Let me pack a small picnic basket with a few bites to go along with the wine."

They met outside Sara's apartment. She placed the basket on the floor and put her arms around Jack's neck. They melted together as if no time had gone by. Hand in hand they began walking toward Russian Hill and one of Jack's favorite views. From the top of the hill was a small park where he could see a 180 degree view of the City and particularly the Bay. Skies

230

were crystal clear and the water in the near distance a brilliant blue.

After a glass or two of wine and some deep breaths, Jack began to relax and tell Sara the story. It seemed to go on forever, and Jack worried he was boring her. Sara sensed he didn't want to barrage her with too much information but she was mesmerized by what Jack told her. He realized she never interrupted once except to seek clarification.

After he finished, she leaned over and kissed him long and hard. "Job well done, Mr. Armstrong."

"Not quite," said Jack. "There are a few loose ends that need to be tied up."

"Such as?" asked Sara.

"Such as: *what's the value of the gold we retrieved?*"

"That shouldn't be too difficult to assess," said Sara.

"Agreed," said Jack. "Then there's the question of the value of the share certificates, particularly those related to the Comstock Lode mines. What's *their* value?

"Those men, the ones who tried to hurt you and steal the strongbox, wouldn't it be a simple matter of Max trying to outwit his wife and steal her inheritance?"

"Perhaps you're right. But they have alluded to a mystery mineral in the mine that could lead to great value. We just want to tie up these loose ends which shouldn't take too long." Jack decided to move beyond the discussion of the Russians.

"Sara, after I take care of a few things, I'm thinking of driving the Z-8 up the coast and spending a night or two in Mendocino. I'd love for you to join me."

"What a sweet idea," Sara leaned into Jack's arm which had moved around her shoulders.

"How's tomorrow morning, say 9am. I thought we could cruise the Russian River, stop in Jenner by the Sea for lunch, tour Fort Ross and a winery I know located just before the Fort, then be in Mendocino by late afternoon. What do you think?"

"I love it. I'll be ready to roll at 9am. Anything you'd like me to bring?"

"Just your pretty self. What will you do with Miss Charlotte?"

"She loves the kennel."

Thereafter, they walked back down Russian Hill to their apartments and parted while Jack took care of some business. He called Coop and told him he and Sara would be out of town for a few days while he traveled to Mendocino. Coop alerted him to be careful with Max on the loose.

"You just never know what that guy is likely to do."

"You're right, Coop. Gone, but not forgotten. I'll keep my eyes open for signs of trouble. I think Mr. Hill has probably gone underground for a while, given our discussion back at Stinson Beach. I also intend to contact Laura, bring her up to date on what transpired there, and ask her to continue some sleuthing in regards the interest of the Russians in the Comstock Lode mines.. I'll keep in touch by text and cell."

"Roger that," responded Coop. "I spent the night at my folks home with Veronica in the cottage and will head back to Virginia City in a day or two to help Laura and the Corroon boys."

"Good idea," said Jack.

Then he gave Laura a call and brought her up to date on the Stinson Beach developments: the release of Max in exchange for the share certificates, Veronica's confrontation with Sidney; and the need to find out what was driving the Russians.

In the latter regard, Jack asked Laura if she could hang around Virginia City for a few days and help with the investigation. He said he would "make it worth her while and that Coop would soon join her." She agreed and said she would notify the University she was taking a short leave of absence.

Jack suggested she check into one of the nearby Reno hotels and do some shopping for clothes and other essentials. He'd reimburse her. He then told her he was taking a couple of days off, but could be reached by cell phone or text.

Laura acquiesced and before hanging up said, "Jack, this area hasn't seen the kind of trouble we have just witnessed for a long time. I have an idea or two I'd like to follow up on before sharing with you. If nothing pans out, I'll head back to Berkeley."

"Thanks, Lovely Lady. You're the best. There's no one better at figuring out complex problems than you."

"Flattery will get you everywhere," joked Laura.

After the call with Laura, Jack began packing a few things for his road trip with Sara.

The next morning, Jack and Sara left San Francisco in Jack's Z-8: top down and a little Bob Marley music playing. The weather was terrific: blue skies, 70 degrees and slight wind. They crossed the Golden Gate Bridge looking at the water 270 feet below, Alcatraz on the right, the Farallons on the left and the Marin headlands before them. Whenever he crossed the bridge he was proud to be a native San Franciscan. Jack was also aware of a car that seemed to be following them, or was it his imagination?

They drove for an hour and a half past Santa Rosa and turned off Highway 101, the Old Redwoods Highway, onto River Road, the strange car still behind them.

As they slowed their rate of travel, Jack noticed the low water level in the Russian River near Odd Fellows Park, where his brother owned a second home and past Korbel winery. Apparently, the drought had begun to wreak havoc on the vineyards, the residents, the fish and wildlife as well as the watershed.

"What we take for granted," remarked Jack as he surveyed the surrounding brown hills and uncovered river banks. He also commented that the drought enhances the opportunity for wildfires which are very difficult to contain and often consume hundreds of thousands of acres. In one recent wildfire, Jack noted one million acres had been burned in Northern California.

Sara sighed. "So sad!"

At the mouth of the Russian River, they arrived at Jenner By the Sea, a small town of fewer than 150 people. Of course, they chose the River's End Restaurant and Inn for lunch. Jack took a look around as they entered the restaurant and did not see the car that had been following them.

"Jack, why is it named the Russian River?" asked Sara.

Wishing to distract Sara from any thought of danger, Jack responded, "I think it was named by a Russian explorer from the Russian-American Company, who navigated the river in the early 19th century and helped establish Fort Ross, which we'll see this afternoon."

Jack began to think it might have been a little risky to bring

Sara on this trip. He sure seemed to be up to his ears in all things Russian. Their intense interest in the Comstock Lode mines, Max, the goons, multiple escapes from them and now driving along the Russian River toward a Russian Fort Ross.

*Pretty strange to be in California and have so much Russian presence. And I can't be sure that Max will not reappear,* he thought. If he so much as sees one of the thugs, they will throw their bags back in the car and hightail it out of there. Sara didn't deserve any trouble.

After lunch they headed North along Highway 1. The car handled like it was made for the road. Very tight suspension married to an all aluminum body and being propelled by 400 horsepower. And, perhaps best of all, the top was down.

Normally, Jack would be grinning ear to ear as nothing made him happier than to drive the winding roads with a breathtaking ocean to one side and a car that could handle the windy road with ease. The beautiful woman was the cherry on top. But today he kept an eye in the rear view mirror and his mouth shut. Let's just get there, he thought.

Not far from Jenner, Jack took a quick turn off of the Coast Highway for the Meyers Grade in the hope of ditching whoever may have been following them. The Meyers Grade rose hundreds of feet above the Pacific Ocean and the Coast Highway below. He stopped the car and invited Sara to get out and enjoy the view for a moment.

It was a quintessential view of the California coast. He couldn't help but pull her close with a quick kiss on her neck as she continued to absorb the non-stop 360 degree view of the ocean as the mountains disappeared into the sea below.

"Jack, this is fantastic. How did you find it?"

"I've taken a few trips up the coast when I needed to clear my head. On my last trip, I discovered the Meyers Grade turn-off and the view." Jack enjoyed hearing her appreciation.

She turned and kissed him on the mouth. She really was a fabulous woman.

"Come on, I have more to show you."

They hopped into the car and took off along the Meyers Grade until they reached the Fort Ross Vineyard Tasting Room. There they had a glass of wine on the back deck which featured another breathtaking view of the Pacific hundreds of feet below. Sipping the wine with its deep sultry and silky texture, ripe berry flavor and earthy nuances, Jack began to relax, seeing no sign of anything untoward on the road to which they had a perfect view.

After they finished their wine tasting, Jack bought a bottle for later and they trundled down the hill to Fort Ross, a mile from the winery. As they entered the Fort, Jack commented, "I think of this as California's Constantinople: where East meets West."

"How so?" asked Sara.

"Modern day Istanbul (the former Constantinople) is divided by the Bosporus Sea. That strait is recognized as dividing or some may say joining the East with the West Continents. Similarly, we know that the Spanish presence in California began with Columbus in 1492, traveling from the East (Spain) to the West (the Western Hemisphere). The Russian expansion moved across Siberia and the Northern Pacific from the West to the East. The two forces met in California and Fort Ross symbolized that meeting and possible confrontation.

"Indeed, the Governor of Alta, California was so concerned about the Russian encroachment upon their territory he commanded General Vallejo of Sonoma to establish a presidio in Sonoma to combat the Russians if they moved further South from the Fort, which was only 60 miles north."

"Jack, your knowledge of history is impeccable. How did you ever learn all of it?"

"Before I became a lawyer, I dabbled at being a college history professor and wrote several essays which I'm proud to say were published. The pay was definitely not what I needed to build a life from so off to law school I went.

"Jack, was there ever a real threat of Russian possession of California?"

"Let's take a look," Jack said as he turned to a historical sign located near the entry to the Fort. It said,

In 1808 two Russian ships on an expedition to establish Russian settlements for the Russian-American Company had instructions to bury secret signs (possession plaques) with appropriate ceremonies in Bodega Bay and on the shore north of San Francisco, indicating Russian claims to the land. After exploration and following instructions from their homeland, the Russian explorers established Fortress Ross 15 miles north of Bodega Bay.

Fort Ross was established as an agricultural base from which the northern Russian settlements could be supplied with food and carry on trade with Alta, California. Fort Ross was the site of California's first windmills and ship building. Also, European glass windows were introduced to Alta, California by the Russians.

The Fort was sold to Sutter for $30,000 and some Russian historians assert that the sum was never paid therefore alleging that legal title to the settlement was never transferred to Sutter and still belongs to the Russian people. Recent historical accounts assert that an agent of Sutter paid an agent of the Russian-American Company $19,788 in 1849, thereby settling the debt for the sale of Fort Ross and Bodega.

"Why don't we wander around, and not try to referee the ownership of Fort Ross" suggested Jack. As they did, Jack got a sense they were being watched and tightened his sense of security and defensiveness. The last thing he wanted was someone taking pot shots at him and Sara like the goons did in Coloma.

After an hour of exploring the Fort, Jack motioned to the car and said, "The late afternoon is approaching, we should continue to Mendocino if we intend to make it by nightfall."

"It's been a long day already, Jack, I'm ready to move on."

"Mendocino's about 75 miles up the road, and we should be there in less than two hours," Jack estimated. They traveled North along the Pacific Coast Highway.

"What a great road, " Jack commented. "The PCH, Highway 1, travels the length of California from North to South and hugs the coast like a fine fitting glove. I love driving this road. There's nothing like it in the U.S."

"Can we turn on a little music?" asked Sara.

"Sure, what would you like?"

"I have a great playlist I think you might like." She reached over and turned the dial.

The smooth sounds of Ella Fitzgerald and Louie Armstrong filled the car. The two sat quietly, enjoying music and the sounds of the Z8 roaring over the road. Suddenly Jack noticed a car fast approaching from behind. He began to press the pedal to the metal and the Z-8 leapt forward.

"I feel the need for speed," Jack said, channeling one of his favorite characters from Top Gun.

Even with 400 HP, his car was not outrunning the oncoming car. As it got closer, he recognized the make: a Tesla Model S. Just then, the Model S moved to the left to pass them and blew by them leaving them in its wake.

"Well, what do you know! "I think that was a Tesla Model S Plaid! If so, it's the fastest production car made. It does zero to 60 in under 2 seconds and can reach 200 mph. It's an amazing car and for its relatively cheap price in the mid one hundreds, it makes other exotic cars laughable. Heck my baby only does zero to 60 in 4.4 seconds, and it cost me about the same as the Plaid."

# CHAPTER FORTY ONE

They entered the quaint town of Mendocino, with a population of fewer than 1,000. It sat high on a bluff that jutted out into the Pacific Ocean. Essentially a one or two street town, it possessed interesting shops and restaurants together with B & B's and a couple of small hotels with art shops sprinkled throughout the town.

The draw was the nearby ocean and Mediterranean climate. Although it was best not to visit during parts of the late summer as the heat from California's Central Valley acted to draw the fog in from the coast. Still, it was a fitting end to a nice day trip from San Francisco, thought Jack as he checked them into a beautiful little inn with a magnificent view of the ocean and a garden populated with vibrant native plants. Sara was impressed as Jack thought she would be.

"This is wonderful! After that long and winding drive, I could use a quick rest. Hope you don't mind."

"Not at all. I'll take a quick walk around town and see if I can find a couple of things to go with our bottle of wine. I'll be back in 45 minutes, if that's ok with you."

"Perfect."

Jack had calls to make and didn't want to disturb Sara. While he walked into town, he called Coop and briefed him on the tail he thought might be following them.

"Coop, I'm beginning to think I'm being a bit paranoid."

"Better to be paranoid than dead," Coop responded.

"I guess you're right. Still, I can't figure why these guys

continue to follow us. It seems to be more like surveillance than deterrence or harm. I wonder if they simply wish to know where we're going,"

"Or where you're not going, like the Comstock Lode," said Coop.

"You could be right. I'll conference Laura into our call and see if she has discovered anything," Jack said.

Back at the Union Brewery, Laura was seated at a table with her laptop open when Jack called.

"Laura, Coop and I figure we have over $1 Million in gold coins from the strongbox which could be worth twice as much given the historic nature of the coins, and the shares of Comstock Lode mining stock together with the miscellaneous shares of the other 1860's companies. The value of the gold is relatively easy to estimate: what's the value of the mining stock and other stock? Is it worthless as a depleted silver mine, or is there some residual value?"

Laura smiled as she answered. "I've been giving it some thought and computer research. Let's focus on the mining stock and the Russian interest. You're correct, the mine's depleted. Production from Comstock mines from 1859 through the 1870s was about $320 million with a value of $500 billion in today's dollars. The bonanza period ended by 1880. Deep underground mining and exploration continued sporadically until 1918, when the last of the pumps was shut off, allowing the mines to flood to the Sutro Tunnel Level (approximately 1640 feet beneath Virginia City). All mining from 1920 to the present has taken place above the Sutro Tunnel level."

"Meanwhile," she continued, "through the early years of

the 20th century, the ownership of mineral rights along the length of the Comstock Lode was consolidated primarily into a handful of companies, most of them privately held. This structure was a departure from that of the 1800s, when as many as 400 mining companies operated on the Comstock, with at least 150 of them publicly traded."

"So where does that lead us?" asked Jack.

"If the shares in the Comstock Lode Veronica inherited, was part of the mining share consolidation which resulted in them being privately held, it's possible Veronica owns a significant portion of 400 mines, not just one "

Coop offered, "Nothing plus nothing is still nothing. These are depleted and abandoned mines, Laura."

"Yes," said Laura, "that's where the second part of our analysis comes in: late stage mining has been above the Sutro Tunnel level because of the water level. Remember when mining occurred before the Sutro Tunnel was finished, water and geothermal heat created furnace-like work conditions. Men in the mines could only work 15 minute shifts and had to be frequently iced down! The working conditions were miserable. I've been thinking those same conditions could be perfect for creating minerals other than silver ore. Those other minerals may have some intrinsic value, Jack."

"Whoa, Laura, you might be onto something. The Russian's kept referring to some mystery mineral. What if it turns out we discover minerals other than silver and gold in the abandoned mines and Veronica is the owner of a significant portion of them?"

"And the Russian involvement?" asked Coop.

Both Laura and Jack began taking over each other with the same conclusion: if the minerals were of sufficient value, the Russians would want a piece of the action, if they could get their hands on it. Russia, as the natural commercial competitor of the United States, would want to control any mineral that could inhibit the commercial growth of the United States.

"What if the Russians had a little assistance from our government?" asked Coop.

"Now that's pure speculation, Coop. Are you inventing conspiracy theories?"

"Maybe so," said Coop, "but there've been some crazy things going on between Putin and our government lately and I wouldn't put anything past them."

"Are you suggesting our government has knowledge of some valuable minerals it might share with Russia?" asked Laura.

"You bet," said Coop. "Stuff has been going on between these countries, or at least certain individuals in these countries, that may not be up to snuff."

"Let's decide if there's a there there before we try to pin the tail on the donkey. What do we have to do next to locate the there there?"

"I think we should consult our Irish Tunnel Brothers, Connor and Dillon," said Coop. "They should know how we assess whether minerals other than silver may exist and where to find them."

"Good idea," said Jack. "Laura, can you check with them discreetly? I should be able to join you in a day and a half.

"Sounds good," Laura said.

"I'll meet the two of you in Virginia City the day after tomorrow," said Coop.

Jack raced back to the B & B where he knew Sara would be waking. That night they had a lovely dinner at a local restaurant and returned to their room for that bottle of wine purchased at the Fort Ross Vineyard.

They sat on a couple of Adirondack chairs on a deck off their room looking at the ocean, stars, moon, talking about their lives. Jack was a hardcore romantic and lived for just those types of moments. They both slept snuggly in each other's arms.

The next morning, Jack mentioned although he wanted to extend their stay he had some stuff he had to take care of.

"What kind of stuff?" Sara asked, trying hard not to sound disappointed.

"Unfortunately, I have to head back to Virginia City and tie up some loose ends."

She was not happy about cutting their trip short, but understood the situation and the need for Jack to follow his instincts.

"Ok, Jack, what a fun trip this has been. Let's return here when time permits."

# CHAPTER FORTY TWO

As Coop was looking for Dillon and Connor, Laura took a moment to talk with Jack about her research. "What minerals, other than silver ore, do you think are likely to be found in the mines, Laura?"

"I'm intrigued by the Sutro Tunnel and why it was created, Jack. It became a big multi-mile drainage tunnel for immense quantities of water filling the mines, and it dissipated great heat created by geothermal activity in the mines. I would like to see what elements this combination of water and geothermal heat produces. Perhaps the Corroon Boys can help with that," she added. Just then, Coop appeared with the brothers Dillon and Connor.

"Fellas, we could once again use your counsel," said Jack. "Laura 's been doing some poking around and has a few questions for you."

"Dillon and Connor, given your knowledge of the tunnels and mining history of Virginia City, besides silver, do you know what other mineral elements may exist in the mines? I know there's geothermal activity which caused great amounts of heated water to enter the mines, caused the miners great grief and was the basis for the creation of the Sutro Tunnel. Usually, that combination creates opportunities for other minerals to exist. Do you happen to know if that is the case below?"

Dillon looked at Connor and Connor returned the look. They shrugged their shoulders and then Connor said, "go ahead."

Dillon proceeded, "A few days ago a guy who said he was from the US Environmental Protections Agency was here and did some investigations about water leaching from the Comstock Lode into the groundwater and fouling the same. Something about cobalt and zinc mixed into watery brine that geothermal activity in the mines produces."

"Didn't he also say he'd found traces of arsenic, lead and barium?" asked Connor.

"That he did," confirmed Dillon. "This cocktail of toxic chemicals he said was leaching into the groundwater and could contaminate drinking water in Virginia City and surrounding areas."

"Cobalt and zinc mixed in watery brine with traces of arsenic, lead and barium?" asked Laura thoughtfully. "I'm no geologist, rock hound or chemist," she added. "I think we need some input from someone more knowledgeable than us, unless the EPA guy told you more."

"Nope, he was a secretive lad, I remember thinking at the time," said Connor.

"Yes, you're right brother. Didn't he keep asking about ownership of the mines?"

Jack perked up. "Did he? What did you tell him?"

"What *could* I tell him? Dillon retorted. "These mines had been conglomerated by venture capitalists and the mines for the most part are now in private hands. We, of course, had no knowledge of the ownership interest associated with Graham Stackhouse's buried treasure."

"How did he gain his samples?"

"He paid us $100 a piece and asked us to lead him to some

spots in the Comstock which were below the water level of the mine," said Connor. "Then he asked us to take him to the downside end of the Sutro Tunnel so he could take samples there. He also drilled some holes and took more samples."

The Tunnel drains into an open plain that used to be an ancient volcanic lake," offered Dillon.

"Did he say what the EPA would do if he was correct in his analysis and the drinking water'd been contaminated?" asked Coop.

"He said the mines and Sutro Tunnel would have to be closed except for EPA approved and badged workers. Furthermore, residents of the city would have to drink water trucked in, or, they would have to move out of the city. Signs would be erected deterring people from drinking contaminated water and tourists would be 'encouraged' not to visit Virginia City."

"Whoa," said Jack, "That's what we call a 'magilla'. Effectively closing the city to tourists and even residents. Pretty soon this would be a ghost town except for EPA workers. Why didn't you guys give us a heads up?"

"Heads up? You wanted immediate help in finding the buried Stackhouse treasure. We didn't think you were interested in Virginia City water problems and EPA samples." said Connor. "You were intent on finding the treasure. Then, of course, you nearly got blown up and when Connor helped you escape, you chased the bad guys to Piper's Opera House for a shoot out and Stinson Beach for a home invasion. Don't give me any crap about why we gave you no heads up, Jack."

"Sorry, Connor and Dillon," Jack sheepishly said. "This now seems important. Thanks for setting us straight."

"Did this EPA guy give you his name?" asked Coop.

"He gave me his card," Connor said. "Let me find it for you." Connor then searched his pockets and located the EPA card in his wallet, which he gave to Coop. It read "Steven Morrison, Environmental Protection Agency Scientist."

"I thought at the time it was an odd name for a guy with a Russian accent."

They all looked at Connor. "What did you say?'

"It was an odd name for a guy with a Russian accent."

"What did this guy look like?" Jack asked.

He had a strange haircut. Buzzed on the sides and a bit high on top. What was really weird was the tattoo on the back of his neck. I remember wondering what 'BB" meant."

Coop blurted out, "Boris Bettinoff?

"Or Brighton Beach," said Jack.

"Isn't that the guy we busted in Berkeley as he peered into Laura's apartment?" Coop pulled out his phone and opened it to the photos where he had saved a picture of Boris in case it might be needed. He showed it to Connor.

Connor's eyes widened. "Geez, that's the guy."

"EPA Scientist my ass! This creates a whole new enchilada." As he faced Dillon and Connor he explained. "Fellas, we can be relatively sure that this guy is no EPA Scientist. He's a Russian thug who works for Max Hill. What he told you is probably all BS. There is no problem with Virginia City's drinking water caused by leaching contaminants from the Comstock. Instead, Max and his boys are after something of value about which we know nothing. They needed to clear the town so they could complete their investigative work and lay claim to what mineral they found. They were fearful that Veronica's treasure hunt might lead them to Virginia City given the nature of the winnings in the 1860s poker game by Graham Stackhouse and they wanted us to keep out. Thank God we were able to get Veronica's shares to the Comstock mines back from Max."

"Everyone listen up," Jack said demonstrably. "We have to split into three focus groups to solve this riddle and determine if there is a 'there there'. Laura, do you have a contact who is knowledgeable about geothermal geology, chemistry and minerals?"

"Let me think," she said. Then she replied, "Yes, I do!" Laura mentioned she had a friend, Lisa, who worked as a scientist at the Lawrence Berkeley National Laboratory. Lisa had expertise in geology, chemistry, minerals and riparian characteristics.

"Great," Jack said. "Can you invite her up here to investigate and take some samples for analysis?"

"I'll try," said Laura. "She's a very good friend, and I think she will cooperate, if she can get the time off from work."

"Thank you," said Jack. "Next, Connor and Dillon, I would like you to investigate the ownership of the mines in and around the Comstock Lode. My suspicion is there is a new Mother Lode there, and I want to know who owns it. Can you guys work on that?" He paused for a moment. "I know this is way beyond the original scope of work. I can guarantee you we will compensate very fairly."

Connor nodded and said, "Dillon, can you put a call in to cousin Jerry? He runs the Nevada Bureau of Land Management in Reno."

"Sure, if I happen to have a bottle of Jameson's with me at the time of the chat," said Dillon.

"Perfect!" said Jack.

"What *don't* the Corroon's run around here: the mines, the sheriff, the Nevada Bureau of Land Management?"

"That leaves us, Coop. Let's do some sniffing around and see if your conspiracy theory about the Russians and our White House holds water."

# CHAPTER FORTY THREE

Laura called Lisa and asked if she would be available to discuss a confidential matter. The two had been friends since childhood.

The Lawrence Berkeley National Laboratory, a United States laboratory, conducted scientific research on behalf of the Department of Energy. Over the years, thirteen research associates won Nobel Prizes and 23 Berkeley Lab employees shared the 2007 Nobel Peace Prize with former Vice President Al Gore. The Lab where Lisa worked overlooked the UC Berkeley campus.

Laura and Lisa frequently met for lunchtime picnics on Strawberry Hill near Memorial Stadium with a view of the Bay.

"Hi, Lisa! How you doing?" Laura quickly greeted her good friend by phone.

Lisa was happy to hear from her friend and to take a quick break from a long afternoon examining slides for a new project.

"Lisa, do you remember my former boyfriend, Jack Armstrong?"

"Of course, he was a very nice guy and quite handsome," Lisa said.

"I'm working with him and his long time friend, Gary Cooper on a discreet project, and I need your assistance."

"I remember Gary too. How can I help?"

"Let me explain," offered Laura. "We're trying to determine whether there might be valuable minerals at a location that offers geothermal activity together with cobalt, zinc, and a watery brine mixed with traces of arsenic, lead and barium. We think the combination could lead to an unexpected find of significant value. Jack represents the owner of the location."

"That's quite a geological cocktail. Where might this be located?"

"In a mine in Virginia City, Nevada," answered Laura. "Any chance you might be able to get a little time off and come visit Virginia City with me?"

"Let me see." Lisa checked her online calendar and saw there was nothing pressing for the next week. Perfect timing. I have a few days open if I can move something. Yes, I can. Where and when should we meet?"

"If you can leave tomorrow morning, meet me at the Union Brewery on "C" Street in Virginia City. The Brewery is our makeshift office while we're in town. It's owned by a couple of Irish guys who share the last name Corroon."

"Ok, look forward to seeing you then," Lisa said.

Laura called Jack on his cell and reported Lisa would be in Virginia City tomorrow afternoon. Jack expressed his pleasure and gratitude for her quick action. "Have you heard from the Corroons about their meeting with the Bureau of Land Management?" he asked.

"No Jack, but it's early," Laura said.

"I think I will give Connor a call," said Jack, picking up his phone. "Connor, it's Jack. Any luck connecting with your relative at the Bureau of Land Management?"

"Bull's eye," responded Connor. We're on for dinner tonight at a Basque restaurant in Reno. Do you want to join us? "

"If you don't mind, I think I will. Do you mind if Coop tags along?" asked Jack.

"Not at all, Dillon will be with me too. We'll have some fun," responded Connor.

At 7 pm in Reno, Jack and Coop met Connor, Dillon and their cousin Jerry at a Basque Restaurant called the Basque Corner. After a round of introductions, Jerry suggested they take a large round table in the back of the restaurant. He then introduced them to the owner and his wife and gave a bit of history about the restaurant.

"They started the restaurant years ago as a testament to their Basque heritage. They are emigrants from the Pyrenees, France. They thrive on family style cuisines, simple but expertly prepared for which the Basques are famous."

"We Irish," explained Connor, "love Basque food." He explained that the Basques have been living in Northern Nevada since the Gold Rush days. They have been known for their sheep herding expertise and their related family style cooking, which the Corroons thought was "excellent." He particularly enjoyed sharing a restaurant table with other groups. All there for good food and a good time, Jerry thought.

As they gathered around the table, Connor presented a bottle of Jameson to help mesh the Irish with the Basques.

"Now we can properly get things started," he said.

"As a Son of St. Patrick, I will not refuse to share a wee bit of a prelude to tomorrow's Irish Flu," said cousin Jerry. Down went his first shot, with no doubt many to follow that night.

"Before we get too far along in toasting the Irish and swapping one too many untrue stories," Dillon said, ``We have a wee bit of business to discuss with you, Jerry."

"Don't you always have a wee bit of business to discuss, cousin?" responded Jerry.

"Our friends here, Jack and Coop, have had a run in with the Russians at the Comstock up the hill in Virginia City. The Russians tried to blow them apart 1800 feet down under in one of the mines as they were searching for treasure buried more than 100 years ago. Fortunately, Coop helped save them and Connor led them out of the collapsed mine to safety. They caught up with five of the culprits, but one escaped. The escapee, the leader of the group, a guy by the name of Max Hill was apprehended by Jack and Coop at his girlfriend's house in Stinson Beach. In exchange for his release, he turned over what he'd stolen, shares in the Comstock Lode mines."

"Those are worthless," said Jerry. "Everyone knows that."

"Not necessarily so," said Jack. "We have reason to believe there may be residual value to the mine and its contents."

"What 'residual' value?" asked Jerry. "If you're thinking there is more silver or gold buried there, think again. Hundreds of miners have been over nearly every inch of the mines and withdrew all the gold and silver they could find. Sure, there may be minor traces of those minerals, but it would take many millions of dollars to extract and purify the traces to make it profitable for trading purposes. There simply are no more significant veins. So save your time and money and wishful thinking."

"We're not talking about gold or silver," said Jack.

"That's the only stuff of any value," countered Jerry.

"Hold on," said Jack, holding up his hand in a halt sign. "We don't know precisely what minerals exist other than silver or gold. However, we are aware there has been interest expressed by the Russians in buying mines and property in

Virginia City. We wanted to know from you if you have seen an uptick in mine or claim sales or recordations in and around the Comstock."

"We have over a million records of mining claims on public land managed by the Nevada Bureau of Land Management. Of these, there are nearly a quarter million records of active mining claims and over one million records of closed mining claims. Most of these records relate to gold, or silver.

"I haven't seen increased transactions by individuals. But there has been some activity by the Feds," Jerry said.

"The Fed's?" asked Jack.

"Yep," Jerry then explained, "A federal mining claim, or a patented mining claim is one for which the Federal Government has passed its title to the claimant, giving him or her exclusive title to the locatable minerals and, in most cases, the surface and all resources. However, effective October 1, 1994, Congress imposed a moratorium on spending appropriated funds for the acceptance or processing of mineral patent applications that had not yet reached a defined point in the patent review process before a certain cut-off-date."

"So there are no federal mining claims being processed," said Coop.

"Not exactly," said Jerry. "Recently, the President signed an executive order which allowed certain federal mining claims to be processed. One of those claims included some land adjacent to the Comstock Lode."

That stunned the group.

"You have got to be kidding," said Jack.

"I told you the White House was up to no good," said Coop.

"Can you tell who benefits from the Federal claim to be processed?" asked Jack.

"It's the Brighton Beach Mining Company," said Jerry.

"That has got to be a cover for Max Hill and his gang and a front for the Russians," said Coop.

"We will do a corporate search and see what it yields. But, Coop is likely correct," said Jack.

"Time out," said Connor. "Let me get this straight. You are saying the President of the United States has signed an Executive Order allowing ownership of a portion of Virginia City property to vest in a Russian owned enterprise?"

"That's exactly what I'm saying, thanks to Coop's conspiracy instincts," said Jack.

"Why would the White House do that?" asked Jerry.

"Yet to be determined," replied Jack.

The group was silent and thinking about the implications of what was just discussed. The bottle of Jameson was passed around the table. It seemed everyone took a couple of shots. A waiter appeared and a robust order of lamb chops with grilled and seasoned veggies was ordered. As the meal was devoured by all, the bottle kept circling the table.

After the third passing of the bottle, Jack said, "I have an idea. We need to keep it a secret. Talk about this to others, and we're doomed. But keep it between all of us and if I'm correct, we stand to be very wealthy men."

"What do you have in mind?" asked Coop.

They all leaned in Jack's direction and listened to him explain. Thereafter, they thought quietly for a moment, then nodded heads in agreement.

"I think it can work," Jerry said.

"OK," said Jack, "Coop and I will reach out to some friends about some funding. Connor, Dillon, and Jerry, check the recorded ownership of mines and property in and around the Comstock Lode. Let's reconvene here in two days."

All agreed.

## CHAPTER FORTY FOUR

"Hi Lisa, welcome to Virginia City. Thank you for coming," Laura gave her a big hug. Spreading her arms, she announced.

"This is our makeshift office."

Lisa took a look around and said, "Looks like a bar to me."

"It is a bar, silly. In fact, it used to be Mark Twain's favorite. Have a seat."

"Nice to be here, I think. On my way I realized your friends Jack and Coop tend to get themselves into some sticky situations. What's all of this about?"

"Before we get started, let's have a bite to eat and a drink," said Laura. "How about a burger and a beer?"

"Perfect," said Lisa.

They placed their orders and sat back to relax and enjoy each other's company. A few moments later the beer arrived and they toasted each other.

"I'm ready to get to work," said Lisa. "Can you brief me a bit more on the situation."

Laura provided background and swore Lisa to secrecy.

"The important thing is to determine if after removing the strongbox, there wasn't a bigger treasure left behind. You can help us determine that, Lisa. We suspect there are some valuable minerals we may have overlooked."

"Where do we start?" asked Lisa.

"Just a minute," Laura said as she checked with Dillon behind the bar as to whether he or Connor could take them down the mine. Dillon told her that Connor would be by in a few minutes and could lead them "under."

Shortly thereafter, Connor appeared, walked directly across the bar and greeted the ladies. Laura explained Lisa was an expert in geology, minerals and chemistry from the Berkeley Laboratory and was there to help them discover whether there was a there there. Connor extended his hand to Lisa's.

Lisa looked warmly into Connor's eyes, appreciating his size and visible strength. Connor held her gaze and admired her beauty. Laura smiled at her two attractive friends.

"Would you like me to show you both below?" Connor asked.

Without waiting for an answer, he pointed to the back door of the Brewery and led them out the bar and down the alley to the mouth of the Comstock.

"What part of the mine would you like to see?" he asked.

"What interests me most is the area where the Russian took samples. Starting below the water line in the Sutro Tunnel," said Laura. "Let's head there."

Off they went into the Comstock then into the elevator. When they reached the 1800 foot level, the elevator leveled off and they exited. Laura began to have some apprehension as this was near where the Russians attempted to seal them in with explosives. She got closer to Connor and kept looking around. Connor noticed her fear.

"You'll be fine, Laura, I'm with you." That gentle reassurance calmed her. They continued about a quarter mile to the Sutro Tunnel and the spot where Connor said the Russian had taken the samples.

Lisa unpacked her backpack and took out some sample tubes. She noticed the tunnel was quite hot and she dipped her tubes into some briny water pooling in the Tunnel. She asked Connor if the briny water collected in an appreciable amount. He said that it did and told the ladies to follow him further.

About another quarter mile down the Tunnel, he led them to a lateral drain from the Tunnel. The lateral drain led to a large underground reservoir of the "stuff" as he referred to it. He said it had appeared to pool here after the Sutro Tunnel was built and then closed off.

"So the stuff couldn't drain out and if it did drain out, more of it would seep up from below and maintain a proper level," Connor explained.

Apparently, the brine was created from remnants of an ancient sea occupying much of the area around the end of the Sutro Tunnel, many years ago.

"I wonder if more is located beneath this cavern," said Lisa.

"I wouldn't be surprised if there was more," said Connor, "Given the geothermal nature of Mount Davidson and the need for the Sutro Tunnel to drain about 4 million gallons of scalding briny water a day from the mines, it's inevitable there would be a huge body of the stuff."

"When was the last time the pumps operated to help drain water through the Sutro Tunnel?" asked Laura.

"All of the mines stopped pumping water by about 1880 and water was allowed to rise to the level of the tunnel," said Connor.

"So, by the mid 1880s, no scalding water was being pumped out of the mines through the Tunnel," observed Lisa.

"Geologically speaking, there has to be a large underground reservoir beneath these mines and Mount Davidson."

"Connor," Laura asked, "What do you think is the very best access point to the underground reservoir?"

"The Sutro Tunnel through the Comstock Lode" remarked Connor. "Remember, the Tunnel's about four miles long and has two lateral tunnels: the North one is 4400 feet in length and the South one's nearly 8500 feet long. The Comstock is also thousands of feet deep. If one wanted access to any underground reservoir, the Sutro Tunnel is where I would concentrate my efforts."

"And is the Sutro Tunnel within the Comstock Lode, Connor?" asked Lisa.

"Much of it is; however, ownership of the Tunnel itself is vested in the Sutro Tunnel Company, which sold stock to raise funds for the construction of the Tunnel in the 1800's."

"So, he who owns the Comstock mines and the Sutro Tunnel, owns access to the hot briny water below," concluded Laura.

"You got it," said Connor.

"Who owns shares in the Sutro Tunnel Company?" asked Laura.

"We would have to check with cousin Jerry at the Bureau of Land Management."

"Let's head back up and do that," suggested Laura. She also asked Lisa how long it would take to process the samples.

"I should know in a day or two what the results are," said Lisa. "Rather than travel back to Berkeley, I'll go to the Nevada Bureau of Mines and Geology at the University of Nevada in

Reno and run tests. The equipment there should be fine for analyzing the samples, and I know the Director, with whom I have worked on several projects."

"Can he or she keep a secret, Lisa?"

"I would trust her implicitly."

# CHAPTER FORTY FIVE

They next met at their Union Brewery office. Mark Twain would be proud of them, thought Jack. Following in his footsteps (with a beer in hand).

"What did you and Lisa discover?" asked Jack.

"Nothing definite. Yet. The samples are being run at the University of Nevada, Reno through the Director who is a personal friend of Lisa's. Still, Lisa thinks the samples she took are promising and could lead to a mineral or commodity deposit of which we were unaware. Connor helped us assess the best access point for the deposit. It's through the Comstock mines and the Sutro Tunnel."

"Good work," said Jack. "Who owns the Sutro Tunnel?" he asked.

An entity called the Sutro Tunnel Company which was formed in the 1860s by Adolph Sutro to fund construction of the tunnel."

"Dillon or Connor, can one of you check with cousin Jerry about the current ownership of the Sutro Tunnel Company?" asked Jack.

"Sure, we'll ask him today," responded Dillon.

"Did you boys also get a handle on the ownership of the claims and property surrounding the Comstock Lode mines?"

"We did," said Dillon. "We found 63 properties and 48 claims in and around the Comstock Lode mines.

"And you have the names of the owners?" asked Jack.

"We do," answered Dillon, "including the Brighton Beach

Mining Company's ownership of the Federal land adjacent to the Comstock.

"Ok here is what I would like you fellas to do," said Jack suddenly. "First, do you have a large room where we can do some office work and strategy?"

"Sure, you can use our banquet room over there," Dillon said, pointing to french doors opening into a large room.

"Perfect," said Jack. "On one wall, let's construct a large white board with a map showing Virginia City, the mining claims, the property and each owner connected to it. I've got a call to make. Let's meet back here tonight."

# CHAPTER FORTY SIX

Max called Boris, "What have you found in the mine?"
"I took samples like you told me to. I told the locals I was from the EPA," Boris said.

"Did they buy it?"

"Buy what?

"Did they believe you?"

"Of course, I had on a pair of scientific looking overalls, rubber gloves, a fishing tackle box with test tubes and an EPA business card announcing I was an 'Environmental Protection Agency Scientist.' What's not to buy, as you say?"

"Good. Did you send the test samples you took to the Russian Consulate in San Francisco?

"Yes, I told them to deliver the results to you and no one else, as you instructed," said Boris.

"Perfect. How long before we hear of the results?"

"In about a week."

Although Max had a gut feeling he already knew what the test result would yield, he was determined to find out what Adamoff's mystery mineral was, and to gain ownership of mines containing the same, if the mineral was as he suspected. Just maybe he could win back his good stead with Adamoff and the higher ups in the Russian government as well as the Brighton Beach crowd. So what if he did not deter or eliminate Armstrong and failed to retain Veronica's shares as instructed. He would achieve a higher goal that would be even more beneficial to Mother Russia if his plan worked. Further, he had a plan to win back the Comstock shares.

It was Russia's good fortune, he thought, that the Big Boss put in a good word with the White House to arrange for purchase of the Federal property in Virginia City before others knew about the value locked up in the Comstock Lode mines. Max wondered what motivated the White House to accede to the Kremlin's request. And what motivated the Kremlin to make the request in the first place!

As for the Americans, maybe it was the pledge to allow the building of that luxury condo project near the Kremlin.

"Was it as simple as that?" Max smiled, thinking it was reassuring how stupid the Americans were.

As for the Kremlin's request for the property in the first place, he had experience with Russian mining ventures in South America (Chile, Argentina, Bolivia) and Australia which had provided fodder for his instincts and perhaps others in his government as well. Someone, probably Adamoff, as Minister of Mining and Energy, had concluded that what was found in those other countries could be found here. Again, as simple as that, he thought.

He had better alert the Brighton Beach crowd that if his instincts were correct, land values (really mining values) would skyrocket once his discovery was announced. It would be in their best interests to buy property and mines now before the announcement when prices were low.

The Stackhouse treasure was enticing, but the real treasure was what he suspected was undiscovered minerals in the earth. *It's also a bit of good luck Jack Armstrong had no idea we are after bigger fish than the Stackhouse strongbox. If I'm correct, the truly valuable minerals are located throughout*

*Mount Davidson and not confined to the Comstock mines owned by Veronica.* Nevertheless, it would be convenient to have Veronica's Comstock mining shares as well to perfect his plot.

Uri had been turned over to the police but Max wasn't concerned. Uri and Boris were ignorant regarding The Brighton Beach Plan as it had become known to those few who needed to know. All they knew was the strongbox was an object of great interest to me and perhaps some others. But he had to thank Boris for bringing back the samples that got Max excited. Those samples would even excite Moscow for their international implications.

If Russia could corner, or at least possess a significant portion of the market for the mineral for which Max was testing and confirming, then they would be off to the races and the US would be at a further disadvantage. There was only so much of this stuff worldwide and the demand was increasing exponentially!

Max's big concern now was that somehow Jack Armstrong and his rookie gang would stumble across the real value contained in the mine Max thought was likely to exist. This he had to prevent, or at least deter and delay Jack and his gang until Brighton Beach could confirm discovery of the mystery mineral, lay claim to it and monetize the value of the land.

The results from the test samples would be announced in a week. In the meantime, he would proceed to acquire as much property and mines as possible.

"Boris, I would like you to take several of your people and head to Virginia City. Acquire as much of the Comstock Lode as you can. We're likely to have a showdown with Armstrong and his group. I want you to take care of them."

"Sure, Boss."

Max said to himself: "Now for Veronica and some unfinished business, the retrieval of the Comstock share certificates."

## CHAPTER FORTY SEVEN

Jack called Veronica and told her his instincts suggested her ownership interest in the Comstock mines would yield significant value if he was correct in assessing the residual mineral value contained in the mines. Also, her interests could be increased substantially if she were willing to invest more in the adjacent mines and Sutro Tunnel.

"But Jack, as you recall, I have no money. That's why I couldn't pay you. Instead we agreed you would receive a 25% interest in what was found."

"And we found 1860 gold coins together with shares of stock in various companies. The bulk value of the gold alone is likely to be worth millions.. And some gold coins of that vintage are worth thousands of dollars each. We recovered dozens of them. So, you are in the money, Veronica."

"Wow, I never thought of that, Jack," said Veronica, as she sat silently and absorbed the news. Then, she suddenly saw a text come across her phone from an unknown sender:

"Ms Hill, we are watching you. Tell Robin Hood and his Merry Men to stand down. Your health is at stake."

After she pondered the message, she read it to Jack.

"I can't tell you there isn't risk to you or your inheritance, Veronica. Perhaps you should just take the treasure we've discovered and not pursue what might be considered a half-baked scheme. My thought is whatever is invested is likely to result in a return many times the investment. Specifically, I suggest we co-invest our new found assets in the acquisition of the Sutro Tunnel and adjacent mining interests."

"What are the risks, Jack?" she asked.

"We could lose everything. Your inheritance and my share could evaporate. And, of course, we need to be careful as people are watching us."

"You've been on the money so far, Jack. I would be no worse off than I am today. So I'm in." Quietly recalling the note she just received, she said, "If anything happens to me personally, please notify my family."

Jack realized the text had frightened her.

"Coop will be there soon to pick you up. Pack a bag for a week. Stay calm. This will work I assure you. And we all will be taking a well deserved vacation soon."

Veronica felt reassured when she learned Coop was on his way.

Jack closed his phone. He sighed. What was he doing asking this woman who had gone through so much to trust him now? Jack Armstrong, strung out lawyer turned PI? He began to wonder if he should tell everyone to go home and let Veronica have her inheritance. Jack rarely questioned himself, and felt deflated on his walk to the meeting.

When he arrived at the Union Brewery, Jack took Coop aside and explained he had a telephone conversation with Veronica about investing her inheritance and the text she received indicated she might be in trouble.

"Coop, I think you should go to her at your folk's home in Sonoma and make sure that she is alright. I have a feeling she may need your help. She is anxious with Max on the run."

"I'll take care of her, Jack. You know I will."

"And I'll wrap things up here in Virginia City," confirmed Jack.

Laura and Connor noticed a significant change in Jack's energy when they saw him and began to anticipate some bad news. As he called the meeting to order and a round of beers and pizza arrived, Jack sat forward and announced Coop had left to pick up Veronica. Before he could continue, Laura decided to interrupt and capture the moment.

"Jack, the results are in and you were correct! The minerals proved to be of a compound which is very much in demand worldwide. *It's Lithium!* And Lisa will brief us on the significance of the discovery."

"Yes, Lithium's found in a brine-like substance created by geothermal heat and activity like that in The Sutro Tunnel. That's the good news," stated Lisa.

"What's the bad news?" asked Laura.

"We've found no significant deposits or production of Lithium in the United States. There are two types of Lithium harvesting that take place in the world today: open pit mines, found in Australia, and evaporation ponds in the Lithium Triangle—Chile, Argentina and Bolivia. China also produces Lithium. In countries where Lithium *is* mined, the process uses a lot of water, and contaminates waterways with acid and other hazardous materials. In the geothermal process, hazardous minerals, such as arsenic, lead and barium exist."

"If a sizable deposit were found in Virginia City, what would that mean?" asked Coop.

"Well, it would assist greatly with the United States effort to achieve energy independence from fossil fuels (primarily coal, oil and natural gas). Natural gas has often been thought of as the bridge between fossil fuels and alternative energy (wind mills, solar, hydroelectric and geothermal). Natural gas produces one tenth of the particulate matter that coal produces and 50 percent of the greenhouse gas emissions. Nevertheless, it's still a fossil fuel and does create greenhouse gases which lead to global warming and climate change. And, natural gas is a source of Methane which destroys our atmosphere."

"And how would Lithium lead us away from greenhouse gases?" asked Laura.

"Utilization of Lithium batteries, would greatly reduce our dependence on fossil fuels, and allow us to store energy in power walls or large power battery plants. This storage ability would aid in supplementing the production of alternative energy. For example, when it's a cloudy day and the sun isn't shining. Or, when the wind doesn't blow and energy continues to be needed. Of course, it also has been proven to provide energy for cars, trucks, tools and anything else that is battery powered."

"So discovery of a sizable Lithium deposit could be quite valuable," concluded Laura.

"You bet. Every country is looking to discover or enhance production of Lithium. There's simply not enough to satisfy the future demand. And demand will increase. Heck, Tesla's producing hundreds of thousands of cars each year which require Lithium car batteries, and California recently stated new gas powered cars will be prohibited beginning in 2035. Japan jumped on board with the same edict. GM says it will convert its entire car lineup to electric vehicles by 2035 and Ford's investing billions of dollars to do the same, beginning in Europe. Speaking of Europe, VW announced it will only produce EVs beginning in 2035"

"And this is all related to climate change?" asked Jack.

"Yes," responded Lisa. "The world needs to figure out how to remove 51 billion tons of greenhouse gases from the atmosphere annually or temperature will continue to rise leading to rising sea levels, mass migration of people and animals, and related events like wildfires and droughts."

"I knew it! We *are* onto something, and the Russians want a part of it!" Jack let out.

"You bet your sweet Rubles the Russians want this little prize," said Connor. "This could help them control a significant portion of the energy market, depending upon the size of our discovery."

Lisa added, "The Russians have no Lithium deposits of their own. So acquiring, or controlling the deposits of other nations, especially any in the U.S. is a top priority for them."

"And that's why they were so interested in Virginia City," speculated Jack. "They've been sniffing around the U.S. testing for Lithium and thought that conditions in Virginia City were similar to those they encountered in South America. Then they arranged for the Kremlin's Big Guy to work a deal with the White House to grant the Federal land near the Comstock Lode to the Brighton Beach Mining Company, which is controlled by the Russian Mafia and no doubt connected to higher ups in the Kremlin."

"Only they're holding an empty Lithium bag," said Lisa. "There's no evidence of Lithium in the property they own or have been acquiring. The Comstock Lithium is concentrated in Veronica's ownership interest and the Sutro Tunnel."

# CHAPTER FORTY EIGHT

Jack began to feel his spirits revive as he cleared his throat. He announced he had secured cash financing for the purchase of Sutro Tunnel stock and any adjacent mining stock. He said the group needed to keep the find a secret for his plan to work. Then he described in detail what he was trying to accomplish.

"You have got to be kidding," said Connor. "If your plan works, it would be beautiful."

Jack then announced he considered the group "his partners" and "each of you will share equally in the 25% interest Veronica had agreed at the outset of her engagement of Jack's Solutions."

Laura, Lisa, the Corroon brothers all hoisted their beer mugs.

"Here's to Jack," Connor sang out.

The group concurred. "To Jack!"

Jack smiled and realized he hadn't been far off on his suspicions about the mine. "I've explained to Veronica what we are attempting to accomplish and she is in. As Jack remembered his first meeting with Veronica, thinking, "In for a dime, in for a dollar."

"So let's get to work, We need to lock up the ownership of the Sutro Tunnel Company first," said Jack. "Corroons, have you secured the ownership info via Jerry?"

"We have," said Connor.

"Is there a way to approach the owner and make him or her an offer that would be tough to turn down?" asked Jack.

"Of course," said Connor. "The owners view the company

as worthless and a liability if anyone is hurt. Nothing has been mined there for nearly 100 years."

"Good," said Jack. "Go lock up the Sutro and make sure it's registered with the Bureau of Land Management asap."

"Next," Jack instructed, "let's also lock up the remaining shares of the Comstock Lode mines adjacent to the Sutro Tunnel and as much of the land and mines available, with the exception of the Federal land granted to the Brighton Beach Mining Company. Use the same 'pitch': 'we're here to take a possible liability off your hands of a worthless silver mine.' Be discreet. We don't want our Russian friends to know what we're up to, so let's hustle and meet back here tomorrow morning."

The next morning, Jack asked how they made out with the Tunnel purchase.

Connor responded, "Done deal, piece of cake. The current owners saw no value, only liability in the tunnel. Indeed, they had been defending several lawsuits against them originated by the parents of kids who'd been injured playing in the Tunnel. I told them we would pay handsomely so they would have enough to settle the lawsuit and then some. They were relieved and agreed to the sale. And, I had another relative who is a lawyer in town prepare the paperwork, finalize the sale and make the filing with cousin Jerry."

"I guess it pays to have a big family, Connor," said Jack. "How about The Comstock mines and property adjacent to it?"

"Dillon and I have been successful in reaching a sales agreement," reported Laura. "Seems like everyone's ready to cash out, especially to locals like the Corroon brothers."

Jack sat back in his seat. After a minute he looked up. The group saw Jack's face and said simultaneously.

"He's GOT AN IDEA."

Bursting into laughter, Jack smiled and motioned Connor to walk back to his hotel with him.

# CHAPTER FORTY NINE

Dillon was behind his bar. He studied the crowd and found the spot where Archie Latham normally sat near the end of the bar. The bartender regularly kept Archie's seat open till he arrived. Archie Latham was the best storyteller in town and if he was at the bar, tips would be great that night.

Archie arrived as predicted and headed straight for the open seat at the bar. Dillon polished his glassware and nodded toward Archie.

"Have a seat, Arch. The usual?"

Archie hadn't been home to change out of his bus driver's outfit. After 30 years of driving a bus around Virginia City, he wasn't tired of the job, it gave him a purpose after the wife passed away and seemed he never got tired of telling those on his bus the latest gossip. He picked up the drink Dillon set before him and smiled.

Not by coincidence, Connor occupied the seat next to Archie. He nodded to Dillon and Dillon leaned over the bar, his head resting on his hands.

"What's up?"

Connor spoke quietly but forcefully to his brother behind the bar.

"I have to tell you something and you gotta keep it quiet."

As expected, Connor noticed a slight turn of Archie's nearby head.

"You know it sounds crazy but they've found a new mineral in the Comstock mines. Pretty soon this town's going to be alive again."

Dillon nodded.

"Oh yeah? What could be such a big deal? They've been digging there forever. Mostly it's just been a trap for innocent people who let their curiosity get the best of them."

Connor lowered his voice and leaned in again.

"Have you heard of Lithium?" He held his finger up to his lips signaling secrecy.

He looked up and saw Archie with his head cocked and looking up at them in the mirror behind the bar. He wasn't missing any of the action, especially the excitement on their faces and Connor placing his finger to his lips.

Archie then did what Jack knew he would do. He quietly excused himself from the bar and went outside. He walked down the street and met with his friend Harry. Harry nodded and, naturally, walked away until he met his buddy Chris. By the end of the night, all three bars in town were talking about the new discovery in the mines.

The following day, Archie was driving his Number 17 bus. And if it wasn't once, it was a dozen times, people taking the bus told each other and their friends

"Did you hear the latest? Lithium's been discovered in the mines!!"

Retired school teacher George Wilson grumbled, "What in the hell is Lithium?"

Another person said, "Hell if I know."

Mildred, a widowed woman who primarily rode the bus so she could be around people said, "I think it's used by dentists to put people out before dental surgery."

Sue Wilkes, new to town, laughed and said "Don't be silly. Lithium's used to inflate balloons."

Later that afternoon before Archie's shift was over he heard another passenger say Lithium was like sodium pentothal which is used to get POWS to tell the truth.

As word spread about the discovery of Lithium, there was mass confusion on the streets of Virginia City. There was excitement in the air. Whatever Lithium was, it had to be good, because it was a "secret," and if it was a new discovery in the mines it was good for Virginia City, which was barely more than a ghost town.

The biggest current attractions in town were tunnel tours starting at the back of the Bucket of Blood saloon, Piper's Opera House, the Mark Twain Museum and, of course, local bars where old stories were told. Suddenly, there was hope in the air! A new beginning which spread like a tunnel fire. And the sale and value of the mines would explode, just like the old days! Now, if only the townspeople could agree upon whatever the heck Lithium was!

Jack was observing all that was happening. He was amused by Connor's acting with Archie and setting the stage with his overheard whisper to Dillon, as Jack had rehearsed with them.

Connor's antics also reminded Jack of the Samuel Brannan stories where he raced on foot through the streets of San Francisco yelling "Gold, Gold has been discovered," while holding aloft a vial of gold dust, all in an attempt to sell overpriced mining equipment which would soon make him rich.

*Well*, thought Jack, *if it worked for Brannan over 150 years ago, maybe it will work for us. People don't change, only circumstances do.* It was only a matter of time that word of the Lithium discovery would reach the Russians.

How sweet and tidy is that?" concluded Connor. "I knew those a-holes had something up their sleeves. And now, Jack, we've started a new "Silver Rush," or should I say "Lithium Rush," with my whisper to my brother. You might call it the 'Whisper Heard Round the World'! Kinda like Bobby Thompson's 'Shot Heard Round the World'! So, what's next in store to nail those Bastards?"

# CHAPTER FIFTY

"He said what?" asked Max excitedly of Boris. "Connor Corroon was overheard telling his brother, Dillon, they've discovered Lithium."

"Crap," Max said. "This will undermine our effort to buy land cheap to capture the US Lithium market."

"What do we do now, Boss?" asked Boris.

Max thoughtfully explained his plan.

"Well, we have the Federal land which was acquired next to nothing from the generosity of the White House. We also know there's Lithium under Virginia City in its mines and tunnels because of your exploratory efforts, Boris. So, with the resources of the Brighton Beach Mining Company behind us, let's continue to buy all the land and mines we can acquire! Go to it, Boris. And report back as to your progress. We need to act quickly before too many know the significance of the find and the property prices rise through the roof."

"Will do, Boss," said Boris as he quickly exited Max's office.

Max said rhetorically, "I have some business to complete to get even with Jack Armstrong and retrieve those share certificates."

Jack was studying the Wall Map in the Union Brewery Office.

"I see we've acquired the outstanding shares of the Comstock mines adjacent to the Sutro Tunnel. Additionally, we have acquired the shares of the Sutro Tunnel Company which owns the Sutro Tunnel.

"Laura, did you confirm with Lisa and Connor that access to any meaningful Lithium deposits are only through the Sutro Tunnel and the Comstock Lode?"

"Yes, I did, Jack. She's certain of that."

"With the Sutro Tunnel and adjacent Comstock mines locked up, we're in great shape!" Jack punched his fist in the air.

"The Russians will be squeezed out," said Laura with emphasis.

"Now for the *coup de grace*," said Jack. "Connor, have you confirmed the Russians have been buying property at inflated prices given your Lithium discovery pronouncements?"

"Yes, I checked with cousin Jerry, and they've been filing claims willy nilly at exorbitant prices!"

"Good," said Jack. "Laura, have you met with the Editor of the new Territorial Enterprise?"

"Yes, I have."

"And he'll run the story?"

"It will appear one week from today."

"Perfect," Jack saluted her. "That will give our Russian friends time to buy even more worthless mines at inflated prices."

# CHAPTER FIFTY ONE

Coop drove his Beemer down the Hill at a frightening pace. He had one thing in mind: to save Veronica from whatever was threatening her. He tried calling her and there was no answer. He also tried calling his father to ask if everything was alright at their house with Veronica. Again, no answer. He began to be concerned.

As he approached his parent's Sonoma property, he noticed two things out of the ordinary: the lights were out in the main house even though it was before his parent's bedtime, and he saw their car in the driveway.

He also noticed a strange car parked on the road a block away from the entrance to their home on what was usually a vacant street. Given the conditions, Coop decided to approach the house with his lights off and park down the street.

He exited his car and picked a few self defense items from under the floorboard in the back of his car. He noticed some lights in the cottage in which Veronica was staying and decided to approach the cottage surreptitiously. As he neared the cottage, he heard some conversation but could not make out what was being said. He crept closer and quietly took the three steps to the deck surrounding the cottage. He was careful to step on the outside of the steps so as to avoid making any unnecessary noise. He crept close to the front door knowing it would block the view of him as he approached the house.

He listened carefully for the voice to resume and estimated its location toward the back of the cottage in or near the kitchen. Carefully, he circumnavigated the cottage near the source of the voice. As he passed a window, he peeked in and saw his parents, each tied to a chair and with duct tape sealing their mouths. He noticed a welt on his father's forehead, a torn shirt and bruises on his left arm and some blood dripping from his lip.

His father was conscious and alert. Coop knew his father to be a tough old bird, so his injuries were not too concerning. His mother too had some bruises around her cheek and mouth. He had more concern for her, and he was determined to find out who had abused his parents and get even!

Coop moved closer to the voice and recognized it as Max's.

*I should have known*, he thought. *Once a bad guy, always a bad guy.*

He attached a listening device to the window nearest Max so he could hear what was going on. Max was speaking on a phone to someone. He was making demands for Veronica's mining shares, and as Coop peeked through the lower corner of the window, he saw Veronica also tied to a chair with her mouth sealed. She too had bruised cheeks and blood dripping from her lip. The front of her blouse was torn open revealing part of her breast. Now Coop was enraged.

*Max, you have met your match*, he thought. *This time there will be no catch and release.*

He listened carefully and understood Max was negotiating presumably with Jack, the release of his captives in exchange for shares of the Comstock mines and Sutro Tunnel. Max held a 9mm Makarov and was waving it around.

*This must be very important to him and those who he*

*represented,* thought Coop. To rough up three innocent people and hold them captive in exchange for some mining rights, was unthinkable in Coop's book. *Now to get even.*

Coop texted Jack and confirmed that he, Jack, was on the phone with Max. Coop related where he was and told him to keep the negotiations going while he hatched a plan. Once he formulated what he was going to do, he texted Jack and said he needed 10 more minutes to execute his plan.

"Can you hold him for 10 more minutes?" Coop asked Jack by text.

"I'll do my best," was Jack's response.

Both Jack and Coop were concerned for the safety of Max's captives if the negotiations broke down.

If Jack did not hear back in 10 minutes from Coop, Jack was to call law enforcement and explain the situation. Besides fearing for the safety of his parents and Veronica, Coop did not want the police interfering with him and what he intended to do.

Off the porch he quietly jumped and did a tuck and roll when he hit the ground. He quickly crawled under the porch and turned on his high intensity flashlight searching for a cut out he remembered when the cottage was being built. He found it and pulled the loose board covering the under floor entry through which he crawled.

"Three minutes down, seven to go'" he counted.

He crawled toward the center of the house and saw a cord hanging from a floor joist marking the spot where the floorboard entry to the house was located. As quietly as possible, Coop raised the floorboard slightly and inserted a fiber optic camera through the gap he'd created between the floor and the hatch. He saw no danger through the camera and slid the hatch to one side knowing he would now be able to enter the kitchen pantry, the door to which was closed.

He pulled himself into the kitchen pantry and heard Max's voice on the phone with Jack. Max was beginning to be anxious and was starting to shout into the phone.

*Six minutes down, four to go,* thought Coop.

He quickly deployed Tinker Bell from the pouch he carried as a belt and opened the door to the pantry to launch her in search of Max and his captives. Tinker Bell quietly rose to ceiling height and surveyed the kitchen from a distant corner.

Coop was able to see Max in the kitchen with his back to the pantry and his captives tied to chairs in the nearby dining room. Max's cell phone was in one hand and a Russian pistol in the other. With two minutes left, Coop slid out of the pantry and moved toward Max from behind. The eyes of his mother, father and Veronica became enlarged recognizing he was there. Then he softly whistled. Max sensed something was wrong and began to turn around.

As he turned, Coop unfurled a heavy duty metal extension baton and brought it down forcefully on the wrist of Max's right gun hand. His wrist broke and he immediately dropped the gun.

Next, Coop whipped the military grade extension baton against Max's left knee, crushing it. His knee immediately collapsed, and he began falling to the ground with the cell phone flying and him screaming at the top of his lungs.

Coop reached down and picked up the fallen gun and used

it to hit Max solidly on the side of the head causing him to immediately lose consciousness. He then picked up Max's cell phone and said to Jack:

"Everything's under control, partner. No need to call the cavalry."

Coop untied his mother, father and Veronica and removed the tape from their mouths.

"Fancy meeting you guys here," he said. "How about a drink?"

All three of them gave him a group hug.

"Dad, why don't you do the honors and wrap this piece of garbage up," pointing to an unconscious Max.

"My pleasure, son," said Jake as he took some flex cuffs from Coop and secured Max's hands and feet.

"Perhaps you can give your old BPD friends a call and have someone arrange to come and pick up this load of sh-t."

There was no doubt Max was going away for a very long time and the way American prisoners did not like Russians, his stay was not going to be comfortable.

# CHAPTER FIFTY TWO

A week later, the Territorial Enterprise published an article entitled:

Who Owns the Lithium?
Virginia City's new Silver Rush
Who is the winner of the Lithium sweepstakes? Well it is those who own the land and mines and tunnels in which the Lithium deposits have been discovered and who have direct ownership interest. They're the recently divorced, Veronica Hill and her group of investors led by Jack Armstrong of Jack's Solutions, Laura Lovewell, a UC Berkeley Professor of History, and the Corroon Brothers, Connor and Dillon. It appears they own title to the only meaningful Lithium deposits and access thereto as confirmed by Lisa Mitchell of the Berkeley National Laboratory.

Those deposits are considered to be the largest in the United States.

So the true winners of the deposits are not only those aforementioned, but include the good people of this fine town: the citizens of Virginia City. Happy Days are here again! Jobs for miners, infrastructure, tax assessments on the lucrative operations, will all be a *sine qua non* for our Fair City!

And one might ask who the losers are: well, it can be none other than the Brighton Beach Mining Company who bet big on the investment in Virginia City's abandoned mines and land. They paid the high price for what will be a worthless investment: the abandoned mines and tunnels under our Fair City which offer little more than exposure to liability. Little did they know that unlike silver and gold, it is the nature of Lithium to concentrate in one place and not be sprinkled here and there. The brine is key here and is only located and accessible through the Sutro Tunnel and its adjacent Comstock mines. No Brine, No Lithium!

And this treasure hunt raises another question for our dear readers and Americans everywhere who love this Great Country: What in the Heck was the White House doing granting a Federal Land Grant by Executive Order, to the Brighton Beach Mining Company? Perhaps it would be in our country's best interest for Congress to investigate the same. In the famed words of Mark Twain, *To Be Continued!*

Jack finished reading the article and smiled ear to ear. Jack's Solutions had managed to unwind the "unsolvable'" mystery of Graham Stackhouse's Niantic key and note, dodged Russian attacks, start a Lithium Rush in Virginia City and make a few bucks for his client, himself and his friends. He now could "pay the rent."

As he sipped a beer he also took satisfaction in knowing the Brighton Beach Mining Company would be bankrupt from investing millions in defunct mines which were worthless except for their exposure to liability.

No doubt the already severely injured Max Hill and the Brighton Beach Mining Company will suffer consequences from a very upset Kremlin, which will not end nicely for Max as he recovers.

As for the White House, Congressional investigations promise to be eye opening and consequential.

Jack gathered the group which now included Veronica. He praised their perspicacity, tenaciousness, and success. Then raised his glass and toasted a remembrance from Nelson Mandela: "*It always seems impossible until it is done.* Here's to the Impossible!" shouted Jack.

"Now for that well deserved vacation," he added.

A LIST OF MATERIALS CONSULTED

*The Bonanza King* by Gregory Crouch
*How to Avoid a Climate Disaster* by Bill Gates
*The Age of Gold* by H.W. Brands
*Men to Match My Mountains* by Irving Stone
*Leland Stanford* by Charles River Editors
*Roughing It* by Mark Twain
*Comstock Lode* by Louis L'Amour
*Jack London State Historical Park Brochure*
San Francisco Maritime National Historical Park website
*SF Gate*: "The San Francisco Cable Car Museum"
Nevada Bureau of Land Management: *Mining Statistics*
*Sonoma Magazine*: "Wine Country Black Winemakers"
CLTA *History of Title Insurance*
*Virginia City Mines & Mining History*
Inspiring Quotes
*The Eureka Museum Comstock Mines & Sutro Tunnel Maps*
*National Geographic* :
 "New Map Reveals Ships Buried Below San Francisco"
*Wikipedia:*
 Russian Mafia
 Lithium
 Comstock Lode
 Virginia City, Nevada
 Sutro Tunnel
 Piper's Opera House
 Mark Twain
 Big Four (Central Pacific Railroad)
 San Francisco
 San Francisco Maritime Historical Park
 California Gold Rush
 Fort Ross, California

Sonoma, California
Samuel Brannan
Bonanza Kings
George S. Patton (Attorney)
Henry E. Huntington
Central Pacific Railroad
Niantic (Whaling Ship)
*When the Water Comes Up to Montgomery Street* by Charles Fracchia
*Codebreaker* by Walter Isaacson
*Silver Kings* by Oscar Lewis
*Grant* by Ron Chernow
*In the Heart of the Sea*, Nathaniel Philbrick
*The Virginia City Trail* by Ralph Compton
*The Transcontinental Railroad* by Charles River Editors
*Nothing Like It in the World* by Stephen E. Ambrose
*Gold* by Fred Rosen
*California* by Kevin Starr
*The Compton Cowboys* by Walter Thompson-Hernandez
*The Pioneers* by David McCullough
*The Call of the Wild* by Jack London
*Valley of the Moon* by Jack London
*White Fang* by Jack London
*And There Was Light* by Jon Meacham

## ACKNOWLEDGEMENTS

After playing golf with Kip Altman on a sunny July day, I asked him 'If you had it to do over again, what would you do?' Kip responded that he would probably have been a professor. Then he turned the tables and asked me the same question. I thought for a moment, then replied, I would like to be a writer, but it is rather late in my career to do that. To which Kip immediately responded 'It is never too late to write.'

The next day, I drove over 400 miles from our home in Sonoma to our apartment in Santa Monica. During the drive, I mentally outlined what we now refer to as *The Caper* complete with story and characters, and upon arrival in Santa Monica, I began writing. Two years later here we are with a finished product. Thank you Kip for inspiring me to follow my dream!

Of course, *The Caper* would have never been completed without the help of my wife, Valerie, who read many drafts, suggested word changes, edited, counseled and provided great encouragement for me. Her attention to detail and a woman's perspective were particularly helpful. Valerie, you're the Best, and I love you dearly!

A writer always worries about publishing his or her finished work. Moon Mountain Publications, named after a mountain in Sonoma, was invaluable in making the transition from manuscript to book. Besides easing the publication worry, my daughter, Heather, provided invaluable guidance and editorial insight given her expansive publication experience. And, it was a life fulfilling pleasure working with her. Thank you Heather, I love you!

Finally, I would like to thank my good friends David and Ginny Freeman who have brought World Class authors to Sonoma through their creation of the Sonoma Author's Festival. Where would The Valley of the Moon be culturally without the contribution of David and Ginny and their Author's Festival? Jack London would be proud!

Made in the USA
Middletown, DE
24 February 2023